After Her

by

Mario Almonte

Mario Almonte

Published by New Meadows Press
New York, New York

ISBN: 9798685052377

Printed in the United States of America.

Contact the author at almonte22@yahoo.com. All comments, critiques, advice, and suggestions are welcomed and appreciated.

1

Every man meets a woman who will scar him for life. She'll contaminate everything he's ever done and everything he'll ever do. He will credit her for his success and curse her for his failure. But he will not have lived without her. And he will not have been a man without her.

I had followed her down to Bermuda to the White Horse Tavern, a popular restaurant by the water in St. George's Parish, close to where the cruise ships docked. She had apparently taken up singing and liked to display her talent there. It was getting close to her set, and I sat in the darkest corner of the dining room, my back against the wall, to minimize the chances of her seeing me first. An old piano occupied the bare stage across the room, a solitary microphone on a stand nearby awaiting its first performer.

Then I saw her. She was dressed in a beige sweater and dark blue jeans, with straight blond hair streaming down practically to her ass. Two long earrings framed her face, which was punctuated by glistening red lips and brilliant white teeth. It was a little-girl's face, with big blue eyes and a straight, chiseled nose that any plastic surgeon would have given a year's wages to take credit for, and maybe some had. Her normally pale skin was tanned to almost a bronze: unusual, because Kerry never liked to expose her body. At least not in public. And then that impossibly slim body, with an ass that stuck out in a lewd sort of way. In the right clothing – or rather, the wrong clothing – she could have been a porn star. Yet, I still couldn't be sure about her breasts. She told me one time that a boyfriend had paid fifteen thousand dollars to a Hollywood plastic surgeon to enhance them. She had the receipt to prove it, but I could never actually confirm that she was telling the truth. They felt exceedingly real. She fancied herself a comedienne, sometimes.

Now as I watched her, I wondered if maybe the breasts were real after all. They had just the right bounce to them as she paraded herself across the floor. They served her like a magician's sleight-of-hand trick: They kept one's eyes away from her calculating mind. You didn't see all the mental gears in motion, getting your number, figuring you out. If a man ever took the time to pull his gaze away from that chest, he might be frightened by what he'd see in her eyes. Hers was a cold, callous mind that had no goal but its own gratification; a mind that had no consideration for others or any desire to improve anyone else's lot but its own. She was a gold digger for the new millennium. A pussy with an attitude.

Goddamn it, I thought to myself. I've been using violent, sexist words since she left me. She was evil incarnate. Pure, unrelenting, unsympathetic. She was a bitch and a half.

Kerry consulted her watch as the emcee leaped onto the stage and announced the official start of her set. "Tonight," said the emcee, "we have a special treat for you. Bermuda's most famous celebrity: the Temptress of Treasury Bonds, the Fugitive from Finance, Kerry Daniels."

I watched as she retreated from view. It took all of my strength not to jump up and chase after her – I was afraid she would give me the slip again. She reappeared soon enough, however, with a young man in tow. He clutched an acoustic guitar as they ascended the stage to deafening applause. Kerry had the kind of walk that always seemed to take her through a sea of deafening applause.

She wasted no time plunging into her song, "Vincent," by Don MacLean, cooing the opening lyrics in a soft, but clear voice. "Starry, starry night, paint your palette blue and grey."

I didn't even know she could sing, and she was actually pretty good. But that's how she surprised me. She dragged me to opening night art exhibitions at MOMA and classical concerts at the Met, when you'd expect her to be spoiled and to fawn instead over the latest collections from Gucci and Prada. She scanned through *The New Yorker* for film festivals of Norwegian actress Liv Ullmann, when other women her age couldn't get enough of Julia Roberts and Renée Zellweger. At the same time, she could run through a spread sheet with a hundred calculations, work out the trajectory of thirty stocks on the New York Stock Exchange and tell you which ones were good investments, and she was usually right.

Her sweater was showing just a little cleavage tonight, but it was enough to suggest ample and well-formed breasts, and it was tight enough to frame a neat little stomach. She shook back her long blond hair. My God, she was so beautiful. I was ready to forgive her all her treachery. In fact, I was ready to let her keep all my money – well, at least share it with only minor conditions – just so that she would smile at me one more time, just me and not the entire Goddamn world.

The crowd ate it up. Rather, they ate her up. They applauded continuously, called out, "Kerry. Kerry." Maybe I was mistaken. Maybe they were simply chanting, "Starry, starry night…" along with her. In any event, she held out her hands, waved them at the crowd. I thought at first that she was shyly begging them not to adore her so much, but I realized that she was simply digging deeper into the song, waving her hands emotionally.

In the next instant, I found myself weaving through the tables, bumping into people who were passing through the aisles, and heading straight for her. I pushed a waitress aside too roughly and she let out a small scream. Several patrons turned toward the sound. Kerry kept on singing, but her eyes wandered lazily toward the disturbance too, and she watched dispassionately as a shadowy, familiar figure made its way to her.

Someone called out, "Hey, it's him!" and now people began to notice. Heads turned in my direction and then quickly rotated toward the stage, then back to me again, as if they were watching a tennis match. I was ten feet from the stage and she had not yet moved. I could smell her perfume – or at least I thought I could. She kept on singing, but she was staring straight at me now. Maybe she was frozen with fear, or maybe she was simply blinded by the bright lights, figuratively and literally, and couldn't tell who I was.

Suddenly, she grabbed the young guitarist and shoved him roughly off the stage. I should have simply stepped aside; instead, I instinctively reached out to catch him. We fell in a heap on the floor, the guitar making a loud, sickening sound as the wood cracked and the strings snapped off. The startled young man scrambled to his feet and, in the process, knocked me back to the ground. I quickly recovered and jumped onto the stage, but by then she was gone.

The audience stared at me, bewildered, expectantly. A small laugh emanated from the crowd. It grew louder, joined by a few "Ooh's." Then the entire room was laughing. I slunk off the stage, crimson with embarrassment. The crowd began to chant "Kerry! Kerry!" again.

Throwing pride to the cool Bermuda wind, I circled the building several times, searching for her. Finally, realizing that my actions were ridiculous and nonsensical, I yielded to the sickening reality that she had gotten away from me – again. There was no point in asking anyone if they knew where she had gone. They would say they didn't know, and they wouldn't necessarily be lying.

I pulled out my phone to call a cab, but as I did so, I noticed that the driver who had originally brought me here was standing nearby, apparently waiting for a fare. Had he also enjoyed tonight's entertainment? It did not matter. I needed to put distance between me and my latest social gaffe.

"Hey, it's my friend!" exclaimed the driver, catching sight of my skulking figure.

"Take me back," I said, jumping into the back seat.

We cruised down North Shore Road toward Paget Parish, swerving through the narrow roads of the island, navigating a gentle terrain that plunged into dark patches of woods one moment and then suddenly broke free into views of a shimmering ocean. The windows of the taxi were shut tight, the heater holding back the cool night air. Even so, it could not shut out completely the brisk, salty smell of the tropical sea.

After a while, my heartbeat began returning to normal. The driver had tuned the radio to a mellow Jazz station. The music blended perfectly with the night – the starry, starry night! I could not help being impressed by the explosion of stars in the black Bermuda sky. It was a perfect place for Kerry, I grudgingly admitted.

I asked the driver the obvious question.

"Kerry Daniels?" he replied. "She's a beautiful girl, isn't she?"

"Do you know where I can find her?"

"Do you know where the wind begins? Because if you do, that's where you'll find her."

"Seems like she turns everyone she meets into a poet."

"She has that effect on people, doesn't she? But why are you looking for her? Did she break your heart, too?"

"No, not my heart. Just my pride."

"Ah, you got let off easy. You could have been that Cain Kahn guy back in the States. He was taken for eight million dollars, eh? That was a piece of art."

"That was a masterpiece. But the figure was closer to $8.3 million."

The driver regarded me in the rear-view mirror with renewed interest. "All that noise at the White Horse Tavern – were you the one running around the building that everyone was laughing at?"

"Yes," I said, and felt my cheeks burning hot.

He turned around for a moment and stared at me. "Missed her again, didn't you?"

"Watch the road."

"You keep escaping with your life, man," he said. "Count your blessings and move on."

"What do you mean?"

"You're still young, right? There are plenty of other fish in the sea. What more do you need out of life?"

My money. I suddenly realized that I had forgotten my jacket back at the restaurant and it contained my wallet. I was about to ask him to take me back, but didn't see the point in subjecting myself to further humiliation. I had not left much cash behind and just some miscellaneous credit cards. No big loss. All my cards were maxed out anyway.

"Life's a beach, eh?" he said.

"And then you freaking die," I responded.

"No, no," he corrected me, "Life's a <u>beach</u>. You know, sand, surf…"

"Well, then you fucking drown."

We arrived at the parking lot of the Elbow Beach resort, where he made a point of coming out and holding the door open for me. To get a better look at the legendary Victim. He was dark-skinned and in his mid-forties, with a muscular bulk filling out a floral print shirt.

A thick growth of gray-streaked beard framed his wide, smiling mouth. He easily dwarfed those around him, but at six-foot-two, I managed to hold my own next to him, in length and bulk. Lately, I had been taking out my anger in the gym.

He clamped onto my hand and shook it firmly. I gave him a $100 bill on a $40 fare and told him to keep the change. I wasn't feeling generous. I simply had no other denomination. I was in a hurry to hide away and die in some little dark hole away from prying eyes. "By the way, what's your name?" I asked him.

"Troy. Troy Wesley."

"Yeah, Troy Wesley, can you pick me up early tomorrow? Say, six in the morning? I'm catching the first flight off this island."

"That's more like it. Let her go."

"No, I'm not going to let her go. I'm going to get her."

"Bitterness is a poison, my friend."

"It's my fucking money," I said. "The whole frigging world seems to think this is all a joke. But I worked hard for that money."

"So, make yourself some more. It's replaceable."

"You know what? Your car's replaceable, too. Why don't I push it off a cliff and then you go and buy yourself another one?"

"Well, now, that's different. This car's my baby. She's been with me a long time. She's not replaceable."

"Yeah, yeah. It's all very funny."

I walked into the hotel and, after several wrong turns, I found my room. I tried to slam the door shut, but the hard springs prevented me from doing so. Irritably, pushing as hard as I could, I finally shut away the world.

A wild and disoriented face stared back at me in the bathroom mirror. My blond hair was spiky with sweat. Traces of a five-o'clock shadow stained my tightly clenched jaw, giving my otherwise smooth face a haggard, homeless look. Angry crimson veins ringed my eyes. My God! Tears! No wonder the driver had been amused. There was no bigger joke in the world than a man leaking tears over a woman.

I threw myself under the hot shower, letting it boil my skin to a bright pink. I welcomed the pain. It was the only way I could convince myself that I was still alive. It was the only way I could burn away the continuing stench of humiliation that welled up in my throat like vomit.

Presently, I padded out to the porch, a towel around my waist. My room was ground level to the beach. A few more steps took me to the cool Bermuda sand. The sky was encrusted with thousands of glittering stars, the ocean dark and featureless, marked off from the beach by the white, foamy waves that tumbled upon the shore. I was looking out at a little cove, where it was said that pirates used to hide from the law. I thought of walking out for a swim. How could one come to Bermuda and not go for a swim? But I decided against it. It was foolish to swim at night. Hidden undertows were always ready to suck you away. I was crazy mad with anger over what Kerry had done to me. But I was not foolishly mad. Not yet, anyway.

I didn't believe in dreams, but tonight I wanted desperately to dream about her. I wanted desperately to hold her tightly against me to feel her warmth – or was it to squeeze the life out of her? And finally, I let myself cry again. I could do it safely here, away from prying eyes.

2

I landed in New York at ten-thirty the next morning. That was the nice thing about Bermuda. You could be home in two hours, door-to-door, New York traffic permitting. The problem was, New York traffic rarely permitted. In rush hour, the JFK-to-Manhattan leg of the trip took longer than the actual flight itself. Today, traffic was especially slow and I didn't reach my office at Capital Partners until eleven-thirty.

Jake Crowley emerged from the kitchen with a bag of miniature donuts from the junk food vending machines. Every office has someone who prides himself on being the bearer of bad news. At Capital Partners, it was Crowley. His oily, thinning dark hair and pencil-thin mustache didn't do much to soften the image. He looked like a slimy, used-car salesman.

"You're early today," he remarked, catching me at the door. "Donut?"

"No thanks."

"John Denver's here. Not the musician. He's dead. The hardware tycoon."

"Thanks for clearing that up. How long?"

"Over two hours. Your meeting was for ten o'clock, good buddy. This is the third time you screwed up this month, not that anyone's keeping score."

"Are you just wasting my time or is there a reason as to why you're pestering me?"

"The Boss Man wants to see you right away. My job's to get you to him pronto."

"Let me check my emails first."

"Partner, 'pronto' only has one speed: immediately. The boss hasn't taken too kindly to your latest adventure."

"Do you always talk in code because you lack proper communication skills or are you just incapable of coherent speech?"

"Sticks and stones, my friend. *I'm* not the one in hot water."

I made my way to Dan Cameron's office. Cameron, founder and CEO of Capital Partners, was arguing passionately on the phone, trying to get someone to perform some kind of service for him.

"Goddamn it, is it too much trouble to squeeze me in?" he asked. The answer he got didn't seem to meet his approval. "You expect me to wait a week for a frigging haircut? It's not like I want someone to stick their finger up my ass and check for cancer!" He slammed the phone down without waiting for a response.

"Unfucking believable!" he exclaimed. "I just wasted fifteen minutes of my life arguing with a receptionist. She couldn't have been more than sixteen years old, by the sound of her."

Dan combed back his gray-streaked blond hair and regarded me from behind deep, wary eyes. At 55, he was still a handsome man, with the big head, smoldering blue eyes and prominent, square jaw that were standard-issued attributes of the male model. On the wall behind him was a plaque of himself on the cover of GQ magazine from his younger days. Back then, he was one of the most sought-after models in the industry, but a mysterious scandal got him blacklisted from every major agency in town. His income stream dried up quickly, and with few options in sight, he was forced to take a real job in the corporate world.

It turned out that he was a financial genius. He put his nest egg into technology companies when the Internet was just coming to the attention of Wall Street and watched it grow considerably. Today his net worth was well over $50 million. Meanwhile, all of his friends from the modeling days now worked in the men's department of Macy's and Lord & Taylor. Every now and then, I considered asking him about that scandal.

Dan pushed aside a crumbled bag of McDonald's and motioned me in. The office was redolent with the smell of greasy fried sausages.

"You know the tech stocks got battered again yesterday," he said.

"Yeah. I heard rumors."

"Down two hundred frigging points. You've heard today's news? Down another hundred points at the opening bell."

"Don't be a worrywart."

"Just wanted you to know that. I know you've been gallivanting about Bermuda again, skipping gaily in the moonlight like you're in the frigging Garden of Eden. You're like fucking Nero fiddling while Rome burns."

"Thank you for the vote of confidence."

"Ah, you know I fucking love you, Cain. It's just that I'm worried. We've got a couple of big clients lined up at the trough, waiting for us to get them funding."

"I'm not cut off from the world, you know. These days, finding investors is like matchmaking. There's always someone out there that's your perfect mate, no matter how unattractive you are. Someone always wants to give away his money and someone always wants to take it. I bring the two together and they live happily ever after, or a reasonable facsimile."

"Thanks for the fucking fairy tale lesson, Mr. Matchmaker. Now, how about making me a match with Denver? If you pull this off, I'll put a solid gold name plate on your door."

"Your generosity humbles me."

"Okay, just wanted to make sure we're on the same page. This sickening plunge in the NASDAQ is burning a hole in my stomach."

"Are you sure it's not those Big Breakfast specials you scarf down every morning? The grease they soak those sausages in has been known to kill laboratory rats."

"Thank God I'm not a laboratory rat."

We filed out of the office, Dan leading the way, escorting me into the conference room like I was the next King of Prussia. Crowley had the common sense to hang back. He quickly slapped his hands against his pants, knocking off the white donut confection that clung to his fingers, before shaking Denver's hands.

Denver was a plump little guy, with enough fat on his pasty cheeks and arms to make him a credible stand-in for the Pillsbury Doughboy. He wore thick, steel-rimmed glasses, behind which peered back a flushed, anxious face. He had the look of someone clinging to the slimmest branch at the edge of a cliff. I liked them desperate. It made my success appear that much more impressive.

Denver had worked as CEO for Ace Hardware and quit to start his own business. He mortgaged himself up to his ass to develop an Internet-based company called PipeStation, a cyberspace version of Home Depot. But he had jumped on the tech stock bandwagon too late. The Internet was losing its luster. Everyone knew the technology was great; they just didn't know what to do with it.

Denver wanted $25 million for an aggressive national launch. Not much in the scheme of things. But in today's paranoia-fueled trading landscape, he had a better chance of finding that kind of money under his grandmother's mattress.

I had studied the company's prospectus and thought the projected two years to profitability overly optimistic, but I suspected Denver's endgame was to prove the stability of his inventory system; get himself noticed by the big boys – maybe Home Depot or Lowe's – then sell out to them. That was fair enough. PipeStation could be considered advance field-testing, and a $25 million investment wasn't too unrealistic. Once Denver proved its fundamental value as an e-commerce platform and worked out the bugs, the big boys could step in and incorporate the technology into their systems, having taken little or no risk in testing it out themselves. At that point, everybody would win.

I dialed the conference phone and got Brill Lambert, president and CEO of Lambert, Bernstein & Novak, on the line. Brill was a robust, hearty fellow who thought everything funny. Yeah, life was a beach when your liquid assets alone topped a billion dollars. Yes, he had five million to burn. "Let me check my pockets for small change. Ha, ha." It was a similar story with five other investors. They all liked me. I had a knack for picking winners. I also made for a good topic of conversation at dinner parties. "Hey, guess who just hit me up for five million? Yeah, *that* Cain Kahn!" By late afternoon, I had lined up $27 million to buy into PipeStation.

"Goddamn it, does this man have big balls or what?" said Cameron, holding out his cupped hands to illustrate their size and weight. Denver heartedly agreed.

By the end of the day, contracts had been sketched out, dates set for closings, and my work was done. I followed Dan and several other coworkers to a bar at the South Street Seaport, where I guzzled down a couple of Daiquiris before deciding to head back to my little hole in the ground off Avenue D. After Kerry, little holes in the ground seemed to be my only habitats. Places that any skulking rat would be happy to call home.

Before I could leave, however, someone recognized me at the bar and felt compelled to share his story with the audience. He had just come back from Bermuda, where he'd read in the *Bermuda Sun* about my humiliating performance at the White Horse Tavern. I muttered "asshole" under my breath and he took offence. Moments later, excited patrons were separating us, but not before I had bloodied his nose. I staggered out into the warm Manhattan night, or perhaps I was pushed out, and continued home.

Kerry's exploits as a wanted fugitive and my efforts to catch her continued to make news, though not with the same intensity as those first heady months after she stole my money. I devoured every piece of information on her and studied her travel patterns in an effort to anticipate her next move. I chased her through every state in the country, determined to catch her myself, since the authorities couldn't seem to get the job done. I'd often get close, but she'd somehow elude me. The story of my failed effort would then quickly find its way to the front pages of every major newspaper, supermarket tabloid and gossip blog, further eroding my credibility.

How often did I check my bank balance? Some twenty times a day? Just to confirm the money was gone, thinking each time that I would wake up from my nightmare and find it all there again. She was either brilliant in her method or ruthless in her execution. Some said she was brilliant in her ruthlessness. She had installed a keystroke capture program on my home computer to obtain my passwords; then, in a single day, she cashed in my stocks and IRA's, emptied out my bank accounts, and transferred all my money – $8.3 million – to off-shore accounts, which were nearly impossible to trace. Finally, she triggered my overdraft protection by $9.27, and no more, though she could have easily pushed it to its full $200,000 credit limit. And that odd little sum of $9.27 proved to be the final twist of the knife in an already gaping wound. It gave her the upper hand in public opinion.

That $9.27 was the exact cost of our first night out, when I bought her a hamburger and Coke at Wendy's. She made that fact abundantly clear in all her interviews with the press, suggesting that she was driven to take revenge on me because, in addition to cheating on her, I had been a cheapskate from the start. While my affair with her boss was the last straw that drove her over the edge, she said, it was practically anticlimactic. It was another act of humiliation that revealed my utter lack of respect for her.

But Wendy's had been her choice. She had told me that she was bored with the pretentious bullshit of Nobu. Of course, that was redundant, "pretentious bullshit," and it should have given me a clue as to what was to come. Then again, I was so hot for her that she could have easily dropped ten-ton weights of clues on my head and I would simply have looked up and searched the sky for rain, thinking I had felt a couple of drops.

When the *New York Post* first caught the story, the overdraft generated a small, humorous item on Page Six. It would have died there, but *The New York Times* followed suit in an editorial, injecting Kerry's actions with mythical symbolism. They called it another chapter in the eternal battle of the sexes in the world of finance, where women still encountered the glass ceiling. Regis took a stab at it on his show with Kathie Lee.; then those chatty women on *The View* followed suit. They celebrated it as a victory for the Sisterhood and a warning to any man who should think of betraying his lover's trust.

Talk show hosts, Jay Leno and David Letterman picked up on it in their monologues, dedicating an entire month to my plight. The number of times Letterman mentioned my name set a new record on the show, edging out the one for Buttofucco, the Long Island mechanic whose teenage girlfriend shot his wife out of jealousy. Radio "shock jock" Howard Stern invited me to participate in an on-air fund drive to pay off my $9.27 overdraft. He mercilessly crushed my final ounce of self-respect by airing audio clips of me running away from one of his on-the-street reporters, who chased me into the subway with ludicrous questions about my ability to urinate standing up, now that I was emasculated.

The $8.3 million stolen was a crime of passion. The $9.27 overdraft was a joke. And the utter humiliation she brought me, brilliant in the totality of its destruction, made our affair a global sensation. It cost me my seven-figure job as the head of the hottest mutual fund at Merrill Lynch and my standing appointment for a bi-monthly haircut at *Frederic's*. She truly had emasculated me, completely and utterly. She was the Lorena Bobbitt of Wall Street.

About a year into the drama, she finally escaped to Bermuda and fell off the grid. An extradition request proved futile. The locals formed a protective shield of silence around her that hid her movements. And when she proved a boon to tourism, the Bermuda government lost any incentive to find her. Visitors from all over the world were flocking to the island, filling up the hotels, patronizing the restaurants and tourist attractions, eager to catch a glimpse of the elusive fugitive.

I hadn't minded the publicity at first. It was kind of flattering to be the talk of the town, even if the context was not the most positive. I was confident the truth would eventually win out; that people would come to recognize her action for what it was: a brazen criminal act. The police would catch her, the courts would indict her, and I would recover my money.

But when the detectives stopped taking my calls at the precinct, I felt that sinking feeling in the pit of my stomach, as if I had eaten something questionable at an ethnic street fair. When photographers stopped staking out my apartment and stalking me through the streets, my worst fears were confirmed. The fickle public had moved on to the next celebrity scandal.

I soon became another poor soul on the sidewalks of New York who railed against the injustices of the System. Poor in every way. I was forced to surrender my luxury condo on Park Avenue to lick my wounds in a five-floor walk-up on the fringes of Alphabet City. I began tapping into my credit cards as I dragged my sorry ass through countless interviews on Wall Street, trying to get back into the Game. No one wanted to take a chance on me, fearing the media circus that I attracted. At the point when even a job at McDonald's was starting to look good (Wendy's was out of the question), I got a call from Capital Partners. Dan thought my notoriety would be good for business. The job paid significantly less than what I was accustomed to, but it would keep my mounting debts at bay.

It turned out that I was pretty good at attracting venture capital. I had first-hand experience at giving away money – my money – and convincing others to do the same came surprisingly easy.

And the Big Boys from every filthy rich investment firm in the city loved me. It was worth their money to talk about me. They bought me drinks at the South Street Seaport. They pumped my hand proudly, slapped me on the back like I was the cowboy who rode the bull to the bell. Sure, Kerry had knocked me to the ground and crushed my manhood in the process, but no one else had ever ridden her that far before and gotten back on his feet, even if just barely.

Now that it was all over, everyone had an ominous story to tell me about Kerry's former lovers. Where were these stories when I was dating her? There was the one about a wealthy bonds trader who was found with his nose pressed against the window of the Federal Reserve Bank on Liberty Street, dressed only in his silk tie. Another unlucky suitor was discovered inside the ATM vestibule of the Chase Manhattan Bank, banging away at the machines with a bat and yelling at the screen at three o'clock in the morning. A third was found sleeping naked in the reception area of his office, mumbling incoherently about losing his shirt.

Stories subsequently emerged of their involvement in nefarious businesses that bankrupted them. They vehemently denied their veracity, insisting instead that someone had somehow hacked every single one of their accounts, even the off-shore ones, to alter bill of sales, titles, contracts and similar documents, and drain the funds. That seemed highly unlikely. People with their wealth had extraordinary layers of safeguards against such a calamity. It would have taken enormous resources, technological expertise, and possibly many months of meticulous planning to pull it off. The actions, therefore, could not have been done overnight, as they claimed.

When they sought solace in Kerry's arms, she shut the door on them and refused to ever see them again. They shouldn't have been surprised. They knew the kind of person she was when they started dating her. She readily admitted her interest in only men who could be an asset to her career. They had made the unforgiveable mistake of becoming poor and, worse, losing their valuable connections.

"The incidents also signaled the start of a downward spiral for them that eventually caused them their jobs, their families and friends and, finally, their reputations. They became poison on the street. No one would hire them, fearing their connection to some secret scandals. Shunned by everyone, they disappeared in shame into the murky swamps of anonymity, never to be heard from again on Wall Street. Their defeat was that complete.

Some did speculate about Kerry's part in the drama. It seemed too much of a coincidence that every man she became involved with would meet the same ignominious end. If anyone was in a position to find their passwords and hack their accounts, it was her. But in every instance, she readily opened her financial records to investigators to confirm they were clean. Moreover, she never displayed any behavior to suggest she had come into sudden wealth and, in fact, appeared to go through a respectable period of mourning before landing the next unfortunate soul.

In the aftermath, the utter disgrace and downfall of men who had dated her – some who were among the most powerful on Wall Street – made her flame burn that much brighter. It added to her mystique. She was that wild, dangerous stallion whom every man wanted to ride for the instant notoriety it brought them – but at the risk of losing it all, even, maybe, their lives.

But Kerry got careless or too blind with rage in my case. She hacked my accounts herself and the police traced the IP address back to her own computer. By the time the authorities came to execute the warrant for her arrest, however, she had moved all the money to untraceable accounts and disappeared. In the following weeks, she'd frequently pop up in interviews with reporters to express her outrage over my betrayal and to break down in tears. The public ate it all up and, as time went by and she eluded capture, she won their admiration. She was beauty to my beast, the ultimate tragic heroine.

And so began my relentless journey to catch her myself, since the law seemed incapable of doing it any time soon – or unwilling to try. I finally swallowed my pride and actually began to enjoy my dubious fame. My masculinity trickled back into my soul until I could walk with my chest out, my shoulders back, and I could think of women again without the blood rushing out of my manhood and leaving behind that limp noodle of pride that she had so masterfully tenderized with a single blow.

As I rode the subway home – I was too broke to take a cab – I started to think. I was going about this the wrong way. Chasing after Kerry like a whiny little boy was getting me nowhere. She had an uncanny knack for generating publicity in her favor, winning the public's sympathy, discouraging the police from bringing her to justice. I needed the help of a higher power.

Emerging from the subway, I saw that Alphabet City had no starry nights. Just a lot of traffic, a lot of strange, lurking figures in the streets: an eclectic mix of prostitutes, junkies, drug dealers, homeless people, starving young actors, and scruffy immigrants from every corner of the world. Latin Salsa and Hip Hop poured out of open windows, mingling with the seductive whispers of the streetwalkers on the corners. Was there a point when these skinny, crack-addicted whores simply packed up their traveling bags of humiliation and went back home? Or would they just continue to drag their sorry asses through the streets like I did every night, refusing to accept that their best days were behind them? One day, I was afraid, I might invite one of them back to my little hole in the ground.

I jiggled the key in the front door and finally forced it open, pushing aside a bulging trash bag that someone had thought best to leave in the way. The narrow hallway smelled vaguely of vomit. The banister felt stickier than usual. Reaching my fourth-floor walk-up, I quickly rushed inside, grateful for the familiar smells of my own apartment.

I threw my jacket on the white leather sofa, the only luxury item I had managed to hold onto from my previous life. A roach protested at the sudden interruption of its nap and angrily scurried away to a less disruptive part of the neighborhood, somewhere under the cushions. Normally I did not appreciate sharing my sofa with anyone, but tonight any company was welcomed. I picked up a box of half-eaten Chinese food, which I had unfortunately forgotten to refrigerate, and discovered that several other roaches were already enjoying it. "Bon appetite," I mumbled, throwing the box into the garbage.

The answering machine registered twenty-two messages, typical after her. I fast forwarded through them. Some were from former colleagues trying out a new variation of the old John Wayne Bobbitt joke. Others were from dubious promoters with get-rich quick schemes to cash in on my notoriety, usually involving porno films or lending my name to questionable enterprises. One female voice caught my attention, my therapist, Bambi Blue. She reminded me that I had missed our session yesterday.

Therapy had been my one safe haven during the early days, because Bambi was the only person who took my whining seriously. She was getting paid good money to do so. My one *unsafe* haven had been drinking, but I finally cut it out altogether. I didn't want to forget what was driving me to drink. That, and the fact that I was waking up every morning feeling like my head was under the wheels of a truck.

I showered and scrubbed myself extra hard. The sweaty bastard at the South Street Seaport had attempted to shake my hand after insulting me, to show me there were no hard feelings. I slept with the round-trip tickets in my hand.

The next day I was on the plane again, and 90 minutes later I saw the familiar sprinkling of white roofs across the splash of green that was Bermuda. For an island paradise, the airport was startling unglamorous, barely giving a hint of the lazy beauty of the island beyond. Troy was waiting by the taxi stand, smiling his usual smile. I had called him from the States. I figured that if I was going to humiliate myself again, I might as well do so in front of someone who already knew me. Why bring more people into the equation?

The big man grabbed the carry-on and swung it into the back of the van. "My wife's invited you to dinner tonight," he said. "She's making Bermuda fish chowder and Wahoo in your honor."

"I won't be here that long. Thanks anyway."

"We'll drink some dark and stormies until we fall flat on our faces."

"I've already been there. It's not pleasant."

I started for the back seat but he held me back. "Up front," he commanded. "I want to keep my eyes on you."

"Are you afraid I'll slit my throat in your cab?"

"Do what you want with your life. I just want a chance to stop you before you stain my upholstery."

"I'm beyond that."

"You could have fooled me."

"Do all Bermudian cabbies fancy themselves stand-up comics?"

"Do you think people come here from all over the world for our tropical weather and pink, sandy beaches?"

"I would answer yes, but I'm sure you'd tell me I'm wrong."

"You would be. I'll tell you why they come here: for our friendly disposition and sense of humor. What do they remember of their visits? The luxury hotels? The beautiful beaches? The great food? Yeah, they're all nice, but it's the friendly cab drivers that make them return. Friendly cab drivers, man, that's the secret to a successful tourism campaign."

"How do you explain the 50 million visitors to New York City every year? Our cabbies are surly, even hostile. They don't crack jokes. They complain about the traffic and the rotten world we live in – at least those who can actually speak English. The others just rip off unsuspecting tourists. Yet they keep coming back."

"I won't deny that those things happen, but there's a misconception about tourists using cabs in Manhattan. For the most part, except for the trip to and from the airport, most tourists take the bus and trains. Mass transit might seem filthy and antiquated to the locals, but tourists think it all quaint, part of the New York City experience. Cab drivers hardly figure into the equation for most visitors."

"Is that so?"

"Yes. Think about it: Why would tourists need cabs? They're not rushing to important meetings or trying to get anywhere as fast as they can. The whole point of their visits is to explore the city, shop the big stores like Macy's and Lord & Taylor, walk the busy streets that are packed with people from all walks of life and from all over the world. Only in New York can you come across 100 different nationalities in the course of a single day's tour. Getting from point A to point B as quickly as possible would defeat the purpose. Only the locals are in a hurry. They don't have a choice but to put up with surly drivers."

"Really? You seem to know a lot about New York."

"I got my business degree from Baruch. I also interned for a year at the New York Visitors and Convention Bureau. Being a taxi driver in the Big Apple paid my way through college."

"After going through all that trouble for a degree in the States, how did you end up driving a cab here?"

"I was planning to join our tourism department. Then I realized I could actually accomplish a lot more by driving a cab. People on vacation are the nicest people in the world. Their whole reason for being here is to have a good time. This island has a way of stripping all your worries from you like an eager lover tearing off your clothes."

"Do you ever just speak in plain English?"

"Do you ever just take the bug out of your ass?"

He glanced at me and broke out into a wide grin, punching me on the shoulder.

"Just messing with you, man," he said. "Relax. Enjoy the view."

"I'm not letting her get away with this, you know?"

"You've got to catch her first."

"No one seems to know where she lives. Or no one's willing to tell me."

"Probably the latter. Or even the first. People see her all the time around here, but they don't ask her where she's going and she doesn't tell them. In fact, I've seen her a couple of times myself, when she's taken my cab."

"You must know where to find her, then?"

"I've never driven her home, at least, as far as I know. I told you, man, she's like the wind. Try to hold it in a box. Or see where it goes…"

"I can see exactly where she's going. To jail. We'll see how well that will hold her."

We turned into a narrow, winding road that was enclosed by limestone walls covered with white and red oleanders. Small, pink cottages dotted a meticulously manicured hill populated with cedars, palmettos and Australian pine trees. Dominating the hilltop was the peach-colored Elbow Beach resort, a graceful arc embracing an outdoor pool whose outline was traced in multicolored national flags.

Reaching the parking lot, I grabbed my bag from the van and threw my fare on the front seat, refusing Troy's help. As I crossed the lobby, the Bell Captain slapped me on the back, exclaiming, "Welcome back, my friend!"

A passing bellboy shouted, "Hey, there! Welcome back!"

The assistant hotel manager, emerging from behind the reception desk, shook my hand vigorously. "A pleasure to see you again, Sir," he said. You'd think I was a returning rock star.

To the right of reception was a lounge, its patrons silhouetted against a floor-to-ceiling window that ran half the length of the hotel. Every dusk, the window treated guests to the spectacle of exploding colors that was the slowly setting sun in Bermuda.

At the front desk, the young female receptionist stared at me. I braced for an insult to my manhood that typically followed such a look. Most women did not take kindly to what they believed I had done to Kerry.

The girl said, "I've got something for you." She disappeared momentarily into the back office and returned with a small package. I opened it skeptically and found my jacket inside, the one I had left behind at the White Horse Tavern. My wallet was on top, my credit cards and all my cash intact. I wasn't surprised. Bermudians were known for their honesty. But there was something else: A note.

"Three o'clock at the lighthouse today," said the note. It was signed with a large and rather ostentatious "K," much like The Artist Formerly Known as Prince would have signed.

I took a deep breath. That didn't do any good. It was still hard to breathe. I thanked the receptionist in a hoarse voice and clutched my room key, waving away the eager bellboy who tried to grab my bag. I didn't want a witness to another public meltdown.

Safely reaching my room, I threw myself on the bed. Kerry meant Gibbs Hill Lighthouse, about fifteen minutes away. That gave me plenty of time to brace for the meeting and map out my strategy. I took a shower and shaved – the second time that day – and tried to follow the news on Wall Street. My mind, however, kept racing ahead, considering every possibility but fearing only one: She might give me the slip again.

I decided to start for the lighthouse immediately. Getting there in advance was probably the better course of action. In war, one always reconnoitered the field of battle before engaging the enemy.

I looked out of the large windows of my room, at the green eucalyptus and casuarina trees framing the terrace. They offered a perfect contrast to the deep blue of the ocean and bright haze of the sky. Every color before me was meticulously painted to evoke the image of paradise. A breeze infused the air with the light, cool fragrance of the tropical sea. I shut the window and drew the blinds. It wouldn't do to go crazy about the island. I wasn't here on vacation.

Troy was in the lobby, chatting with the Bell Captain, an equally tall and robust Bermudian. The two men suddenly fell into a fit of laughter, throwing their heads back and letting out deep, hearty bellows of noise, shoving each other roughly, amicably. Troy straightened out upon seeing me, patted the Bell Captain's shoulder and came over.

"Ready to go? I'll get my cab."

"I'd rather have someone else drive me, thanks."

"It's a short trip, right? On me. A goodwill gesture."

I eyed him suspiciously. "Why would you assume I'm only going for a short trip?"

"Everywhere on this island is a short trip."

I didn't have the energy to refuse him. In any event, the whole point of my contacting him had been to limit the circle of people who knew what I was up to. It definitely would minimize my potential embarrassment. Or maybe not. I was too familiar a figure to get away with much around here. Still, it did help to have a friendly person to talk to.

"Our second date was to the Empire State Building," I said. "She made me stay on the observation deck for more than an hour, in the middle of January. I froze my nuts off."

"Yeah, but she warmed you right back up that night, didn't she?"

"Yes," I admitted, thoughtfully, climbing into the van.

"That wasn't nice of you, throwing your money into my car," he said, pulling away.

"I'm sorry about that."

"There's a point when you just move on, you know?"

"I guess I've yet to reach that point."

I watched the scenery float by. The ragged edges of the white shoreline, the hazy shimmering of the water along the coast, the deep blue of the ocean in the distance; the silky sheen of the scattered clouds that hung like strips of cotton over the land – all seemed perfectly synchronized to create an ideal balance of nature. A perfect contrast to the black chaos in me.

I rolled down the window as the radio played, "I Think I Love You," by the Partridge Family, a song straight out of the 70's. Pop music was so innocent back then: dramatic ballads of love; mournful pleads for the satisfaction of a feeling so powerful that it dwarfed all other emotions. But Keith Partridge got it wrong. Life wasn't made for love. It was made for lust. Not sexual lust, but a lust that gnawed at every organ of your body like a malignant tumor. A lust that did not wane until it consumed every morsel of your lover: her arms, her legs, her whole body. What impressed me about Kerry were her droopy eyelids after we'd make love, and then she would cry "Ahh" as if it contained all the secrets of the universe, all its promises, all its riches, all its dangers. Yes, she had turned me into a poet, too.

"Here you are," said Troy, pulling into the parking lot by the lighthouse.

"Did I ever actually tell you I wanted to come here?"

"Actually, no. We all knew about the note she left in your wallet. Man, do you think a thing like that can stay secret for long on this little island?"

"What made you think I would even bother to answer it?"

"If you're going to commit suicide, you'd do it before the most beautiful sight in the world, wouldn't you? Good luck. I've got to pick up a fare, but I should be back in about an hour. By the way, my wife expects you at six-thirty."

"I told you. I won't be here that long."

"You don't have a choice now. The last flight for New York leaves in an hour."

"The last flight leaves at five o'clock," I corrected him.

He unleashed that deep, echoing laughter that seemed to come out of a concert hall. "You're still looking at the weekend schedule, my friend."

"I've got a very important meeting at eight tonight," I cried.

Troy saluted me, gunned the motor, and took off. I yanked out my phone and banged out Dan's number.

"Why don't you just fuck me in the ass and put me out of my misery?" he exclaimed. "You can't do this to me."

"Sorry. Can't make it."

"It's ten million frigging dollars. That's not chump change anymore. Where are you anyway?"

I cut across the front lawn as I spoke. The lighthouse, painted a brilliant white, really wasn't that big, by lighthouse standards, but it did command the highest point on the island – highest being not much more than a few hundred feet above sea level. The landscape of Bermuda was practically flat; full of gentle hills gliding down to sandy beaches and a placid ocean. I stopped before the large, cast iron anchor sunk into the ground at the foot of the structure.

Gibbs Hill Lighthouse was built by the British in the eighteen hundreds, as most of the island's landmarks were. It was supposed to warn ships of the treacherous reefs that surrounded the land, but it didn't seem to have done too good of a job. Nearly 400 shipwrecks encircled the island, earning Bermuda the nickname, "Isle of Devils."

When I walked to the other side of the lighthouse, I saw a genuinely breathtaking view, though I was not in the state of mind to appreciate it: a vast, open field like arms sweeping outward, bequeathing to you the gently heaving ocean and blue skies. Miniature, white-roof houses dotted the land below, tracing the jagged, sandy shoreline.

"Cain?" The urgent voice pounded in my ears. "Where the hell are you?" Dan was still on the phone.

"I needed to take a breather."

"Buddy, ten million in venture capital is a lot to shit away these days. Tech stocks are falling on Wall Street like blind flies hitting the Zapper zone at a backyard barbeque. Bragdon's getting cold feet. He wants to look you in the eyes before he pulls the trigger. You want me to beg? Okay, I'm begging. Come on, Cain, I need you here."

"Keep the dinner date. I'll call in and close the deal."

"You're good. You're not God."

"Maybe I am. Maybe my whole fucking life is just a test of my omnipotent strength, to see if I can survive the challenges of my own creation."

"You're scaring me with that kind of talk. You've got to keep those appointments with your shrink. Did you know she called me here today? She said you've missed two sessions already."

"Why would she be calling you?"

"She's worried, Cain. I don't like this, either. Wherever you are, you've got to get back here. If not for the deal, at least for your own sanity. Well, at least for the deal."

I saw a movement down the hill, around one of the houses, and I watched, mesmerized, like a snake watches a mongoose. I remembered the voice on the phone.

"Dan, I can't stay. I've got to go."

"Don't hang up!"

"I'll call you tonight. Eight sharp. I'll close the deal."

My knees were going weak, my vision becoming blurry. The figure reappeared in the distance, this time closer up the hill. It was Kerry. She was dressed in a short, powder blue skirt and pink tube top. The top really wasn't the best choice of clothing for her upper body. Her heavy breasts bounced rhythmically within the flimsy fabric, repeatedly challenging the limits of modesty.

She walked awkwardly across the grass, but even in her awkwardness she was infinitely graceful. She wore sandals – totally inappropriate for the terrain – that kept slipping off her feet, forcing her to stop every few paces to adjust them. She made her way purposefully up the hill. I had the impression of a lioness stalking her prey. She had a sleek, powerful physique that weaved about, sometimes slipping behind the bushes momentarily, but relentlessly advancing. I could not tell if she had noticed me yet. But then, that was her style, to act as if nothing mattered to her in the world but what she was doing at the moment. Wasn't that how she fooled me at the White Horse Tavern? I had actually believed that she hadn't noticed me ten feet from the stage, and that made me relax; that made me think I had all the time in the world to get to her.

She stopped about twenty yards away. Her long blond hair whipped back in the wind and wrapped itself around her bronzed neck. She was flushed, perspiring slightly, beads of sweat on her forehead. Her skirt kept riding up her legs, billowing in the wind, forcing her to hold it down with one hand.

She grabbed her hair, twisted it into a long, single braid, and let it go again. Her arms appeared even more muscular than I remembered them to be, the skin taut and the muscles sharply defined. What was her latest obsession? Tae-Bo? Jiu-Jitsu? Anything aggressive, anything that toughened those sinewy limbs. I thought to myself that she wouldn't make an appetizing meal for a wild animal. Not enough fat on the bones.

She was looking at me now, not smiling, but glowering, as if inpatient with me: as if I was a nuisance, a pesky fly that would not go away, no matter how often she swatted at it. I wanted to grab her, hold on to her tightly until the police arrived. There would of course be a highly public trial. All my foolish and immature acts of desperation would once again be put on display for the world to see. People would say I got what I deserved. But even a bias court could not ignore the very legal fact that the money was mine. The world can continue to hate me, but at least I'd be financially solvent again.

"You fucked up my life," I exclaimed.

"Your own stupidity fucked it up," she returned.

Jesus Christ, I thought. She wasn't even the least bit remorseful. "I want my money back."

She brought her face to within inches of mine. Suddenly, my legs gave out from under me. I was on the ground, lightning bolts of pain shooting along the left side of my face. The bitch had slapped me.

Before I could respond, she grabbed my wrist and dragged me toward the lighthouse. I staggered along in shock and amazement. How often had I envisioned this moment? But I was always the one doing the dragging: dragging her into a courtroom, humiliating her before the judge – before the world itself.

She paid our admissions to the middle-aged woman behind the counter. *Paid with my money,* I thought. The lady smiled at her, apparently recognizing her, but regarded me with suspicions. Kerry led me up the narrow, winding stairs of the lighthouse. According to a sign outside the gift shop, there were 105 steps to the observation deck. I was out of breath by the 85th step, but she hadn't slowed down a single beat. We finally emerged onto the cramp, circular balcony, forty feet above the ground. The sight was really something to behold – the most beautiful sight in the world, as Troy had said. I could see the attraction of jumping off here. It was a peaceful place to die. The whole of paradise before me. But jumping wouldn't solve my problems. The fall didn't seem high enough to be fatal. Most likely, it would only maim me. That wouldn't do, to go through life as a cripple. A poor cripple.

"Take off your clothes," she ordered, hiking up her skirt. She wasn't wearing underwear.

I threw off my shoes and wriggled out of my pants. "All of it," she commanded, and I immediately ripped off my shirt and underwear, leaving myself completely naked. It didn't matter to me that we might be seen. She had that kind of effect on me, making me forget that there was always hell to pay for my actions.

"Go ahead, be a man and do it. Give it to me good," she said. "It's what you want to do to me, isn't it?"

"You bitch," I let out, and even as the words flew out of me, I realized that they did not carry much weight coming from a naked man. Clothes made the man – the business executive, the policeman, the soldier – gave him the strength to act, the strength to fight. But women were at their most powerful when they were naked. Something about their nakedness transformed them into goddesses, into omnipotent beings who could easily destroy the strongest man in the world.

She lunged for my crotch, but I stepped back quickly, out of reach. "I want my money first," I said.

She laughed. "You're like all men."

"If you mean, I like to keep what's mine, you're right."

"You're all talk, no action."

"Oh, there's going to be action, all right. In court. You're going to return all the money you stole from me."

She suddenly pounced on me, catching me by surprise, and pinned me against the wall. I reached for her hips, but she batted my hands away and pushed off me. I went after her blindly, under the influence of that insane, masculine urge, that primal desire, that bestial urgency to consummate the argument, to bend her to my will.

But I missed her. She dove into the stairwell, carrying something in her hands: my clothes.

"That's such a childish thing to do!" I cried.

Her footsteps echoed down the stairs, moving faster, growing fainter, mingling with her soft laughter, and then faded completely. I imagined a gazelle bounding down the stairs, though of course, a gazelle couldn't possibly negotiate such a narrow stairwell, or could it?

I ran after her, but as I neared the bottom of the stairs, the sound of tourists reached me. A young couple was talking to the lady at the counter. I stopped, remembering that my only claim to modesty were my cupped hands.

"Goddamn it!" I muttered, bracing for the inevitable.

The young couple began their giggly climb and presently came upon me. They immediately fell silent and politely eased past me. Once out of sight, they broke into laughter. I walked purposefully through the gift shop and scowled at the lady, who regarded me suspiciously, though not with much surprise. How many other men had Kerry left naked on the observation deck?

As I stepped outside, a crowded tour bus pulled into the parking lot. I hurried behind the lighthouse, praying that I had not already made a cameo in any of their pictures. Maybe, like most tourists, they'll never actually look at their vacation photos again. I just needed somewhere safe to hide, to bide my time until Troy's promised return, which I hoped would be soon.

Someone made a comment to the effect of, "My goodness, Lily, is that a…" but by then I was safely out of sight.

I looked down the wide, sweeping field to the sea below and caught a last glimpse of Kerry, far down the hill, near the shore. Out there stretched the immense blue ocean, and beyond that ocean was the universe and everything in creation. But all that mattered to me was that tiny, fluttering speck of humanity that was once my lover. It carried everything that could never be mine again in life. Including my pants.

3

"Thanks for the clothes."

"You can thank Kerry. She called to tell me where to find them. She said you'd been for a swim."

"In a sea of humiliation."

"Look at the bright side. You've given a busload of tourists something interesting to talk about. I understand some of them found you in their pictures and gave them to the local paper. You'll be in the early edition tomorrow. Don't worry, it comes out after your flight leaves the island."

"Why am I not surprised? Tell me again what your wife's cooking."

"Bermuda fish chowder to start, with a main course of fillet of Wahoo with green peppercorns and Bermuda oranges."

"I'll assume most of those things are edible?"

"They're very popular Bermudian dishes. Very tasty."

"What species of food is a Wahoo, anyway? Not that it matters. I'm sure you're going to make me eat it."

"It's a fish."

"You sure she doesn't mind my dropping in?"

"She's dying to meet you. She knows all about you. And you know what, she actually feels sorry for you."

"Now I'm really worried."

Troy's house was typical of the compact and functional, three-bedroom cottages of Bermuda's working-class. It was constructed of locally harvested limestone, called Bermuda stone, making it one of the older, more authentic structures in the neighborhood. With supplies running low, newer houses used concrete blocks.

The chimney protruded from the front of the house like a stepped pyramid: large and flat at the bottom, tapering to a long neck that rose high above the stone roof.

Despite its outwardly compact appearance, the house was quite spacious inside, with wide windows that let in the ocean breezes. Troy's wife, Annie, was 35 years old, but she could easily have passed for 25. The physical opposite of her dark, beefy husband, she was delicately featured, with brown eyes, long black hair and rich, brown skin. She had done some modeling as a teenager, according to Troy – and she looked like she still could.

Annie regarded me with great interest as she showed me to a seat. The living room was sparsely furnished, with only the essentials of a sofa, loveseat, chair, and end table. A stereo sat on the shelf, but no TV. Various magazines were scattered about on the coffee table. Among them were the *Audubon Society*, an old copy of *People*, and a recent issue of *Travel Agent* magazine.

"My friends saw you at the White Horse Tavern," said Annie. She regarded me sympathetically. Or maybe with pity. Right now I'd take either one.

"I'm sure there are witnesses even when I take a piss on this island," I said.

Annie disappeared into the kitchen and returned with a tray of drinks. "We call them dark and stormies. Black rum with ginger beer. It's our national drink," she explained.

"Later, I'll introduce you to the Bermuda rum swizzle," added Troy.

"One poison at a time," I said, attacking the drink. It was already five o'clock. Earlier in the day, I had spent two hours naked at the lighthouse, moving about from bush to bush, trying to keep out of sight from the parade of tourists that wandered about the grounds. At the point when the whole thing seemed like an exercise in futility, Troy appeared with my clothes.

"Do you have somewhere to go tonight?" asked Annie. "You keep looking at your watch."

"Actually, I have to make an important call at eight sharp."

I downed my second dark and stormy. Annie took my glass, disappeared into the kitchen, and returned with a refill. I drank that one down in a single gulp.

"She's on your mind, isn't she," said Annie, sitting on the sofa next to me. "You know what Kerry was doing when I met her? She was a hostess at one of the restaurants in the hotel. It seemed kind of odd to me at the time. If she had stolen as much money as they said she did, why was she working at such a menial job?"

"She likes to do unexpected things like that," I responded. But even as I spoke, I realized that Annie had raised a good point. As far as I knew, despite the $8.3 million in the bank, and other hundreds of millions from her previous victims, allegedly, Kerry had yet to go on anything resembling a wild spending spree.

"Wasn't she a trader on Wall Street?" asked Troy.

"Yes. That's where I first saw her, on the floor of the New York Stock Exchange. You've got to be tough-skinned to work in the pit, and she commanded a lot of respect. People were in awe of her. Or maybe it was fear. Beauty, brains, ambition, maybe even thievery... Dating her was like handling explosives. It took me six months to find out she was dangerous, and not through any particularly brilliant insight of my own, as you know."

Despite my initial reluctance, I found myself enjoying the Wesleys' company. They were genuinely sincere and kind people. Life had never been very kind to me, growing up alone as I had in my aunt's house. My parents divorced when I was eight and I never saw my father again. A year later, my mother was struck and killed by a drunk driver, or so I was told. I was never quite clear about the circumstances, as I didn't attend the funeral. My aunt didn't feel I could handle it. My aunt herself died of cancer three years later, leaving me to fend for myself in an orphanage, too old for adoption.

Growing up alone, money was my only reliable friend. I clawed my way through an education, working full time at night, and gravitated toward Wall Street early in my career. Money was my security blanket. It never abandoned me, except of course when I made stupid trades, so I did my best to be worthy of its loyalty. I made a lot of money quickly, and I grew my portfolios into some of the largest in the world. And my personal fortune piled up nicely into several sizeable accounts.

I told all this to the Wesley's as the dark and stormies kept coming, my mind growing confused and clouded. I knew there was something important that I had to do, but try as I might, I couldn't recall what it was.

Presently, Troy handed me my cell phone. I looked at the instrument, trying to divine its purpose. "You said you had an important call to make," he explained.

"Yes, of course." I took the phone, and by great effort, I recalled my conversation with Dan. He was meeting Norman Bragdon of General Partners to get his signature on the ClariTee account. Bragdon was his first critical investor in cellular technology, a new area of growth in which Dan and I saw potential. Now, I just had to remember where the meeting was supposed to take place.

I dialed Dan's cell phone and got a recorded voice. Either Dan had forgotten to turn on his phone or the location had no signal. Toggling through the address book, a restaurant name rang a bell. I called and asked for him. The young lady didn't say "Who?" but, "One moment, please."

"Jesus H. Christ!" said Dan. "I was about to have a heart attack."

"How did you know it was me? I didn't mention it to the girl."

"I wanted it to be true. I <u>willed</u> it to be true."

"Is he there yet?"

"He stepped out to the john. I'm sweating bullets here, buddy. Everybody's nervous with the NASDAQ taking another dive today."

"Yeah, so I've heard. All right, pass Bragdon the phone and I'll deal with it."

"If you pull this off, I'll burn incense on the shrine we'll erect in your honor at the entrance to our offices."

"It's a nice thought, but it may be in violation of the fire code."

"By the way, Dr. Blue called again. She wanted to remind you about your appointment tomorrow."

"Screw her. She's trying to have me committed."

"That might not be a bad idea. Sometimes I think you're racing in the Grand Prix without a steering wheel."

"Goddamn it, at least I'm in the Grand Prix. Most people are just sitting home, watching it on TV. I'm living it."

"All right. Just watch those sharp turns. I love you, Buddy, but if you're going to crash and burn, don't take us with you. Here comes Bragdon."

"Go to hell."

I waited, but I felt much too relaxed. Troy watched me, sipping his drink. Annie sat nearby, leaning back on the sofa, just as curious.

"Cain. The famous Cain Kahn?" shouted a deep voice into the phone. It was hard to understand him over the roar of the restaurant crowd. Eating in a noisy environment was the latest in Manhattan chic. The newly rich on Wall Street needed to shout their success to the rest of the less fortunate world.

"Bragdon, how's the new Bentley?"

"What?"

I spoke louder.

Bragdon said: "It's a beauty. Everyone ought to get one. In fact, if you want world peace, give everyone a Bentley. Beautiful machine, get behind the wheel and it calms you right down. By the way, how are you feeling?"

"As well as can be expected. Why do you ask?"

"Dan said you were in some kind of wreck? That's why you couldn't make it tonight."

"Yeah, you can call it a crash of sorts. But I'll live."

"Are you calling from a hospital? Sounds like you're under heavy sedation."

"I *am* taking something to kill the pain. But listen, Bragdon, let's cut to the chase. You've got ten million. We need ten million. I think that's a perfect match, don't you?"

"Jesus, didn't they ever teach you social skills? Don't you want to know how my kid is doing first?"

"She's not the one who signs the checks, is she?"

"No, thank God. She hasn't figured out a way to get at my money yet."

"Give her time, she's only six."

Bragdon laughed. "Seriously, Cain. The shit has been hitting the proverbial fan lately. I know this was supposed to be a signing ceremony, but things have been changing pretty fast. I need some kind of reassurance. Can't just go to the Board with a good story about you this time. Doesn't hurt, but I need a little more."

"I thought of that. I've put together a report that should satisfy them. I'll email it to you first thing tomorrow morning. All the numbers are spelled out. And they make sense. Cellular is the next big thing. ClariTee's got solid 2G technology based on real-world applications. No vapor ware shit. Two years from now, ClariTee sells out to AT&T or Verizon and everyone goes home with a bigger bulge in their pants."

"Believe me, Cain, I don't doubt you. But the report will help. It's a formality, you understand? Some of my Board would prefer to put their heads up their asses and wait out the tech bloodbath right now."

"Understood. Dan should be pulling the agreement out of his pocket by now and shoving it delicately toward your hand."

"Well, I think I should see the report first, don't you?"

"It's not a contract, just a goodwill acknowledgement of your interest. We don't need your check yet. ClariTee's got creditors breathing down their neck. Nothing major, mind you. Just a couple of family members and the pizza joint down the block. Can't write revolutionary programming without all-night pizza delivery. Honestly, very minor debts. The report has the details. Your name in the vicinity of their CEO's name will calm everyone down. I just need you to get back to us within a week. They'll be restless again by then."

"Understood. Hope you feel better."

There was a pause. Moments later, Dan got on the line. "How would you like the inscription to read on that shrine?" he said.

"Something simple: 'He died for our sins.'"

I hung up, or more accurately, I passed over the phone to Annie, as I was completely confused about how to work it further. She listened to see if anybody was still on the line and then shut it off.

"You're telling me," said Troy, "that you've just negotiated ten million over the phone, right here, in our living room?"

"Are all Bermudians this nosey?"

"It's not every day that we get to entertain in our own house an actual barbarian from the gates," said Annie. "You know, I've got a nice girl I want you to meet, seeing that you're now single and all."

"I've never met a nice girl that I liked."

"I didn't say she was a virgin. I was referring to her social skills."

"Let's discuss this over dinner," said Troy.

I followed them to the dining room, where the food was already spread out on the table. Annie ladled out steaming portions of a reddish, lumpy soup that she identified as Bermuda fish chowder and directed me to lace it with rum and sherry pepper. I poured in the rum.

"The fish's already dead," said Annie. "No need to kill it again."

I fell to my meal, the smell instantly waking up in me an incredible appetite. The last time I ate anything resembling solid food had been on the plane: two complementary bags of peanuts. The prospect of seeing Kerry again had driven all thoughts of food from my mind. Spending the afternoon in the buff by a popular tourist attraction had also proven to be a real appetite suppressant. I held out my empty bowl to Annie, who filled it up again. This time, she sprinkled the rum in herself and kept the bottle out of reach.

A few minutes later, Annie whisked away my empty bowl and presented me with a plate of Wahoo fillet, served with the traditional green peppercorn and slices of oranges.

"My recipe is famous on the island," she said. "Even the restaurants want to buy it from me."

"As long as it's edible."

"You're skirting dangerously close to getting your ass whooped," she said.

"Listen," Troy spoke, "tomorrow's Bermuda Cup Match. Stay with us for the next few days. They'll be lots of drinking, lots of gambling, lots of irresponsible behavior. Like a typical day on Wall Street. You'll be right in your elements."

"My ticket is for the six o'clock flight."

"What's so important back in the States that you've got to be there tomorrow?"

I had to think about that for a moment. "Goddamn it," I said. "I'm drunk."

Annie looked straight into my eyes. "Take a break, okay?"

My resolution wavered. "If I said yes, will you at least let me finish my meal in peace? I've never known people to talk so much."

The conversation soon turned to a discussion of Cup Match and other matters about the island and the kinds of people who lived there: the dark-skinned former slaves and the bleached white British descendant who were their original masters. Bermuda was one of the first Caribbean islands whose black slaves gained independence. Today, the island was still technically a subject of Great Britain, but only as a formality. It could become fully independent any time it wanted to. However, Bermudians were reluctant to sever their ties. The British connection was great for tourism.

After finishing my meal, I rose from the table too quickly and staggered to the door, disoriented from the alcohol. Annie showed me to the spare bedroom, where I was soon fast asleep.

I awoke early by habit, but I realized, as Troy had said, that there was no pressing business to rush to. Annie was still sleeping. Troy was already on his first shift. Costs of living were high on the island, and most people had to work two jobs to stay afloat. I stepped out into the cool morning air. The sun warmed the land, the grass shimmered with dew, the trees swayed in the breeze. Birds fluttered on the branches, their wings beating desperately, their small bodies flying through the air, casting quick shadows across the lawn. I was thinking that this was a place I could retire to, lose myself forever; forget my wounded pride, my deceased bank account.

I shook off my morbid thoughts and took a shower. By the time I emerged, Annie was puttering about the kitchen. She was wearing a red, almost shear baby doll pajama, startling me that she should feel so comfortable around me in such an outfit. Her dark hair fell in thick, loose strands down her back, emphasizing her long, slim figure. She was a stark contrast to the typical Bermudian woman, who tended to be tall, almost Amazonian in stature. She was probably not originally from the island. Then again, who was?

"Sorry about last night," I said. "I wasn't a very good guest, was I?"

"You had your moments."

"You guys are great people. I may not show it, but I really appreciate it that you let me stay over. By the way, dinner was delicious."

"The compliment's late but still appreciated." She poured me coffee. "Marie will be here in about an hour. She's got tickets to the Cup Match finals."

"I'm not really into sports."

"Don't worry. You don't have to be." She set a basket of muffins and fresh fruit before me. "Marie's a nice girl," she said. "You'll really like her."

"So I've heard. But let me get to a computer, first. Got to send out a couple of emails."

"Use our studio downstairs."

I disappeared for about half an hour, checked my emails, and sent off the report on ClariTee. Upon returning, I found Annie at the kitchen table, reading the *Wall Street Journal*. She had changed into a light green, one-piece dress, a hotel uniform of some sort. "Another One Bytes the Dust," said a front-page headline in the *Journal*. It referred to another major Internet firm that had declared bankruptcy. Another bad day for tech stocks.

I picked up the *Bermuda Sun*, one of the island's local papers, and was momentarily startled by the picture on the front page. A naked man by the lighthouse. Oh, yeah, I remembered now. There was an adjoining picture, much smaller, at the top of the page. It was of Kerry. I turned to page three as directed, where I learned that she had just donated twenty thousand dollars to a local charity. It seemed the spending spree had begun. *Twenty thousand less I'll be getting back,* I thought.

Moments later, Marie arrived. She was a tall, long-legged girl in her mid-twenties, solidly built, with a dark, playful face, deep-set eyes, and breasts that swelled out of a tight, red blouse. She was certainly enough woman for any man.

"Come on, you two," she announced. "We're meeting my friends at the stadium."

"Sorry, can't make it," said Annie. "I've got to work the morning shift at the hotel. You'll have to settle for just Cain."

Marie looked me over, frowning. "Well," she said. "It's going to be three girls and you. Think you can handle it?" She appeared to have been drinking already. A good sign of a bad ending.

I looked back at Annie.

"Don't worry. Marie will protect you from them," she said.

"Her friends aren't the ones who worry me."

Marie laughed, sent me back a long, exaggerated wink, and gestured for me to follow her. I did so hesitantly. I hadn't been joking about my fear of her. Getting into her car didn't help matters either. It was old and started up with some uncertainty. Then, she kept pumping the brakes in a weird way as we negotiated the narrow roads. Not a good sign. The car needed new brakes, for sure.

A noisy wind whipped about us as we approached the stadium. I thought, at first, that Marie had taken a wrong turn. We were supposed to see a game between the top two professional teams on the island; yet we were pulling into a bare, muddy field that resembled someone's back yard. People packed the grounds in a scene reminiscent of a Medieval fair. Every person was dressed more colorfully than the next. Many wore team colors of blue or red, with cars and scooters flying their flags from antennas. Tents had been erected throughout the field for a board game called "Crown and Anchor," in which players rolled dice with symbols that corresponded to those on the board. Food vendors sold everything from conch stew, mussel and beef pies to fish chowder and codfish cakes.

A large screen over the stadium entrance followed the live action inside. The teams, which were going through practice, were oddly dressed and swung a long, flat bat at a ball that the pitcher bounced toward them. It took me several seconds to realize they were actually playing cricket, a sport I knew absolutely nothing about. No one had thought it necessary to explain to me what sort of event I was coming to see. Not that it mattered much. I barely followed sports of any kind anyway. I would have had an equally miserable time watching baseball.

The biggest surprise was the behavior of Bermudians. I had come to think of them as sober and well-mannered people. The two days of Cup Match, however, were the exception. The annual competition between the island's West End and East End cricket teams was as much a sporting event as it was a major excuse to party. It was the only time of the year when gambling was permitted in Bermuda; and like a mini-Mardi Gras, public drinking and openly outrageous behavior by the locals were the norm.

A group of women across the field waved us over. Marie's friends, they were about the same age as she was, in their mid-twenties; all tall, wearing colorful blue or red skirts and blouses. They studied me like shoppers checking out the ripe fruit on the supermarket shelf, and I feared they liked to squeeze the merchandize.

As Marie reeled off their names, I was thinking that I didn't want to be here. The sound of happy people depressed me. I longed to be back home, in the comfort of my own little hole in the ground, where no one could see my misery.

"Well, you can keep brooding or you can party with us," commented one of Marie's friends. She was almost as tall as I was, with a gently rounded face and bright green eyes. Her hair was cropped short, emphasizing a strikingly long and graceful neck. Her hand held out a bottle of beer. I thought it too early to drink, but was reluctant to decline the offer.

"I'd like to play with him, too," said a companion.

"Honey, take a number."

"Well," chimed in the third, "there's enough to go around for everybody, so I've heard."

Considering the nature of their banter, drinking beer at ten in the morning wasn't so bad, I decided. I liked the way they treated me, as if I were a wet, mangy puppy that needed comforting.

I took a long swig of beer, eliciting cheers from the girls. The youngest one grabbed the bottle and downed the rest of its content in a single motion. Her hair was pulled back into a ponytail, revealing a smooth forehead. Marie looked on approvingly, snatched a bottle from another companion, and put it to my mouth, urging me to take another drink. She then took a drink herself. Not a dainty sip, but a long and deep inhalation, draining half the bottle in seconds.

"You go girl," said the third friend.

It started to drizzle, but no one bothered to take shelter. Sudden rain showers were common on the island. Called liquid sunshine by the locals, they were too brief to interrupt activities; afterward, the land shimmered brightly, as if sunlight had indeed fallen to earth in liquid form.

Marie agreed with her friends to get me drunk. One bottle was barely drained before another one magically appeared, plucked from the ice chest, the cap already flying off. She always took the first swig, like the royal taster, before handing me the bottle.

The rain left behind one of those vivid days for which Bermuda seemed to hold a patent: vegetation that sparkled in the sun; a fresh breeze that mixed the fragrances of jasmine and oleanders with the salt of the sea. Above was the boundless brilliance of the blue sky. Around me was the endless expanse of the turquoise ocean. I wondered why Bermudians had not invented 200 words for "blue," like the Eskimos had for snow. There were probably 200 words on Wall Street for greed.

I followed the girls like a dog on a leash, happy to be in their company. They took enormous pleasure in introducing me to people and watching their reactions. I didn't mind it. It had been a long time since women had treated me with anything resembling affection.

The noise level rose steadily as we neared kick-off time – or whatever the start of a cricket match was called. I looked across the sea of people and imagined that I saw a familiar figure at the far end of the field, then realized that it was not my imagination. Kerry was drifting through the crowd toward a group of cricket players in uniform. She approached a tall, burly young player, who shook her hand bashfully.

I started toward her, but Marie's youngest friend, whose name I now remembered as Rachel, suddenly slipped her arm around mine as Marie held on to the other. The third girl, Vanessa, pushed me toward the entrance and into the current of people, which carried us through a tunnel and out again to the bleachers. Fans were already standing for the national anthem.

The game soon began, and the wild and drunken mob broke into cheers as the first batter took his position. That's as far as my comprehension of the game went. I assumed one player was the pitcher and the other the batter, although after a while it seemed that there were two batters on the field, running back and forth between stakes in the ground. The mysterious ritual stirred up the crowds, which cheered and booed with equal fervor at what appeared, to me, to be the same things.

Half-way through the game, I felt an overwhelming urge to urinate and started to do so over the edge of the bleachers. I used to hold my liquor better before. When the crowd below me finally realized that a clumsy spectator wasn't spilling beer on them, they threatened to punch out my lights.

Marie pulled me away as the girls laughed uncontrollably. She hid away the offending appendage and dragged me out of the stands, took me to the men's room, and waited irritably at my side as I completed my task. I felt incredibly stupid, like a misbehaving child, and hoped no one recognized me.

Someone said, "Hey, look," and I turned my face away, burning with embarrassment. Then I realized the remark had been aimed at the presence of a woman by the men's urinals.

My task completed, Marie started back to our seats, but I pulled her to the side, suggesting instead that we get some fresh air.

"You might have noticed that the bleachers are already in the open air," she said.

Nevertheless, she followed me out of the stadium. I passed the spot where I had last seen Kerry, not so much expecting to find her still there, but simply to satisfy myself that I had made the effort. There was a cab across the field, parked alongside Marie's car. Its driver was listening intently to the game on the radio, and he waved us over.

The driver had a small, compact body and dark, animated face. He looked to be in his mid-fifties. Someone hit a home run, or whatever it was called in cricket, and he cheered.

"Mr. Kahn." He shook my hand. "I'm Joey."

"Joey," said Marie, "give us a ride home." Apparently, they already knew each other.

"What about your car?" I asked.

"Leave it for the girls."

"Great game," commented Joey.

"I wouldn't know," said Marie, eyeing me wearily. "No wonder."

"No wonder what?" I countered. "If I embarrassed you so much, why didn't you just leave me out there?"

"I promised Annie I'd take care of you."

"Why do people keep assuming that I can't take care of myself?"

"Of course. It's not like you ever do anything stupid to give them such an impression," she said. "Kerry was too kind."

"I'm allowed to make an idiot of myself. It's my goddamn right. That doesn't entitle anyone to steal my money."

"A fool and his money are soon departed."

"That's 'parted.' If you're going to insult me with clichés, at least use proper grammar."

"I'm an English major. I meant departed."

"Then what's the significance of what you said?"

"You're killing yourself. And if you don't succeed, someone else will do it for you."

"I just don't get it. I'm the victim here. Why does everyone keep blaming me, like it's my fault? Like I'm the criminal? Is this world so screwed up that it can't see the distinction?"

"As if," said Marie.

"'As if' what?"

"You said, "Like it was your fault." The correct expression is 'as if it was your fault.'"

"Yeah, yeah. It's all a big joke to you."

"Mr. Cahn," chimed in Joey, "my friend Troy asked me to take care of you, too, if I saw you. That's why I followed you here."

"Doesn't anyone here know the meaning of privacy?"

"He told me you might try something foolish. I was to give you a free ride if you had to get away quickly."

"I can take care of myself."

"Apparently not. You keep pissing people off," said Marie, unsmilingly.

"Ha, ha."

"Take us home," she told Joey, who immediately jumped behind the wheel.

At her house, she attempted to undress me.

"I can do this myself," I said.

"You're drunk."

She started the shower and threw me into the cold water, letting it hit me full strength. I tried to wrestle the hot water knob from her grasp, to adjust the temperature, but she adroitly batted my hand away.

"Damn it, it's freezing."

"Trying to wake up your ass," she said, slapping water against my body.

I finally pushed her away and adjusted the water to a more tolerable temperature. Upon finishing, I padded out in a towel.

She said, "Your phone rang and I answered it. A man said he was John Denver and asked you to call him back. I thought he died in a plane crash."

"Did you ever think maybe you should let the phone ring? Maybe you should respect my privacy?"

"You're naked in my apartment, with only a towel between me and your lily-white ass, and you're asking me to respect your privacy?"

"Do you mind giving me the message?"

"He wants to talk to you. He says it's urgent. You've got a cute body."

"It comes with instructions, too."

I dialed Denver's cell number. It sounded like he was in a car.

"John, don't come to Bermuda, if you're looking to get laid," I said. "Caribbean women are friendlier."

"Isn't Bermuda in the Caribbean?"

"Don't let them hear you say that. Bermuda's thousands of miles from the Caribbean islands – in a world of its own. What's going on? Are you afraid your VC's are going to pull out because of what's happening on Wall Street? Don't worry. They're in my pocket."

Even through the static, I heard his raspy, uncomfortable laugh. "No, I trust you. It's not that. Listen…." He gave another uncomfortable laugh. "I hope you're not mad at me, but I saw Kerry."

"Who?"

"Kerry. Kerry Daniels."

"You couldn't have. She's here in Bermuda. I just saw her about an hour ago."

"I mean, I saw her last night," he clarified.

"Impossible. I saw her yesterday, too. In the afternoon. There were no flights out of the island last night. Are you in Bermuda?"

"Actually, no. I'm in New York. I chartered a plane for her. She wanted to see me right away."

"What are you talking about? What do you mean she wanted to see you? Kerry knows you?"

"Well, yes, professionally. She wanted some advice about investing her money."

"_Her_ money?"

"I just wanted to let you know. With you getting me that funding and all, I thought I owed you that much."

"I'm glad to hear there are still some people out there with scruples."

"I'd understand if you feel like pulling my funding. I hope you don't. But I'd understand."

"You're not serious? You're actually willing to risk losing $27 million and personal bankruptcy just to help Kerry? Christ! But, you know what? Go ahead! Give her the benefit of your brilliant financial mind! What do I care? Come to think of it, since you're so eager to clear your conscience, there *is* something you can do to help me. Lend Kerry $8.3 million of the funding you get so that she can pay off the money she owes me. You can afford to be generous. You've got $27 million coming to you."

"You mean, pay you the money people say she stole from you?"

"John, it's not 'people' who say she stole it. The law says it. For Christ's sake, she's a wanted fugitive. Why do you think the police are after her?"

"It doesn't necessarily mean she's guilty."

I hung up the phone; or, rather, I punched the "End Call" button repeatedly until odd error messages appeared on the screen. The entire world was going crazy right under my nose. John Denver never struck me as a fat, diluted little fool, but there it was. I banged out Dan's number and caught him at the golf course.

"Cain, anytime you want to talk to me, I'm yours, buddy." He had obviously been drinking. He enjoyed a couple of martinis before the first tee. And after the last tee, too. And in between.

"I need a favor from you," I said.

"Fire away."

"Cut off Denver's funding. The deal is off."

"What? You're joking, right?"

"The guy's an asshole."

"Yeah, but Cain, this is business. What do you care about his personal life?"

"Cut him off, all right?"

"Cain, you don't just say 'no' to $27 million. Especially with what's going on right now. Did you know we made the *Wall Street Journal* with that deal? We're the talk of the town."

"This is not a discussion, Dan. I'm sorry. You know nothing's going down without my support, right? And I'm not backing this deal."

"Goddamn it, where are you, in some kind of hashish stupor?"

"Do it, okay?"

"Cain, think this through. Take a breath. A big, long breath. I'm going to give it to you warts and all because I care about you, buddy. So far, investors have been willing to trust your judgment because of your track record, but you're very close to wearing out your welcome with them. You see, people already know you're unstable. They know Kerry still has her grip around your dick. Sorry I'm being so blunt, buddy. But you're driving me to it. People are just waiting for you to fuck up. Any kind of inconsistency like this, especially in this kind of financial climate, just once, and the VC's will drop off from you like shit from an elephant's ass. You understand what I'm saying? Right now, it's your winning reputation that's holding this deal together. But you show any sign of breaking and you're going to hit bottom faster than a queer in a fag bar."

"Your analogies are not politically correct. I'll call you back later."

"Goddamn it, Cain, do you understand what I'm saying?"

"I'll call you back."

I stared at Marie. She was sitting across the living room, watching me. In the interim that I talked to Dan, she had changed into something more comfortable, a baby doll pajama. Did they sell any other kind of sleepwear for women on this island?

The scene before me was disquieting. She waited by the sofa, a drink in hand, leaning back, her long dark hair falling across the front of her face, partially covering one eye. A sleepy look, reminiscent of Kerry, a languid smile on her ripe lips. She was breathing deeply, slowly, expanding her chest to fill out the delicate satin bra that did no more than rest on her full bosom. Her skin was smooth and unblemished, glowing in the darkened room.

I gazed out the window for a moment, simply to take my eyes away, to rest them and get a bearing on my position. They fell upon the splash of white clouds across the afternoon blue of the sky. A bird landed on the window sill, hung precariously from the small ledge, then flitted away. I was thinking that *that* was what my life was all about; seeking out a ledge and barely hanging on. But unlike that bird I could not let go so jauntily. I could not trust my wings to save me from certain death.

"Honey, you've got to give it a rest," she said.

Christ, I thought, everyone treated me like a child. "Don't you get it?" I pleaded.

"If you don't make a move soon, baby, *you* won't get it," she said.

Out there, the world carried on just fine without me, and inside me, every cell of my body stood poised, waiting to breathe out again, waiting to let the blood flow once again through my veins; waiting for the normal routines of living to resume. Chasing after Kerry, my body hung in suspense, holding on for dear life, unwilling to take that leap into the unknown of life without her.

Later that afternoon, as the waning sun threw slanted rays of orange light through the window, I rose from her bed and padded naked to the back door, into the weakening day of Bermuda. The ocean shimmered quietly as it caught the soft tints of the sun. A single, thick band of light ran up the middle of the water from the shore to the horizon. It seemed to leap up toward the pale blue sky, to the incandescence ball that hung just out of the reach of the lapping waves.

I returned inside and dressed. Marie stirred momentarily. I glanced at her, feeling that I was being watched, but couldn't tell whether she was awake or not. I scrolled through my contacts for Troy's number, and about ten minutes later, the van pulled into the front yard. I thought about Marie as we pulled away.

"You're a stupid man," said Troy.

"That's why I called you," I said. "To knock some sense into me."

"You want me to turn back?"

"You didn't succeed."

Back at the hotel, I stood at the window and watched the trembling rim of the sun dip into the fiery pool of the ocean, and even after it had disappeared entirely, the colors remained hemorrhaging across the horizon. The view could have been a scene from a cheap dime-store oil painting, but it was effective in drawing the emotions from me. Room service brought me dinner and I ate in silence, watching the final light of the day sink away into the black puddle of the ocean.

A voice came to me, demanding a response. Finally, I realized that I had dialed Giancarlo Galilei's number. He wanted to know who was breathing so hard into the phone.

"Hey," I said. "It's me."

"Cain, I'm glad to hear your voice. You're all that people are talking about up here: that you're losing it again. Did you know that your bare ass at the lighthouse made the Jumbotron in Times Squares? Have you ever seen what a hundred-foot-high screen will do to a person's ass? Your pimples were the size of watermelons."

"I want you to help me catch her."

Giancarlo grunted. The world's most celebrated public relations practitioner was pumping iron. A complete gym occupied a corner of the basement of his three-story townhouse on 28th Street. The floors above contained a high-tech office, an ultra-modern broadcast facility, a control room, and a conference center. The theme song from Rocky II was blasting away in the background.

Despite his Italian name, Giancarlo was Spanish, from Castilian parents who traced their family line back to Spanish royalty. Supposedly, he was a direct descendant of the brilliant astronomer who bore his name, Galileo Galilei. He had the press release to prove it.

He was a lean, dark haired, six-foot-one, 34-year-old powerhouse of highly focused energy, both physically and mentally. His dark eyes burned with enough intensity to turn anyone who stared at him for too long into a pillar of salt. That was in his press release, too.

"It's my pride," I said. "She's flitting about like some exotic bird of paradise, and I'm pressing my nose against the glass, watching the insanity of the world as it eats up every word she says like she's the Mother Theresa of Wall Street."

"So that's what my press releases sound like. I'm no English teacher, but those definitely couldn't all have been consistent metaphors."

"I need to see you tomorrow. Say about noon?"

"Now you're talking."

I placed another call. A female voice came on the line.

"Bambi, you've got a minute?"

"Well, if it isn't the famous Cain Cahn. You know, the meter's still running on your sessions. You've never officially cancelled them."

"I need a minute of your time, not your sarcasm."

"I'm with a patient right now. I've got an eight o'clock cancellation. Drop by then."

"I'm in Bermuda. I've got to talk to you now."

There was a pause. "I hope you've got your pants on."

"Ha, ha. Can we talk seriously now?"

"Let me get back to you. Give me ten minutes."

I checked the drawers one last time to make sure I'd packed everything. Not that I came with much. I hadn't expected to stay overnight. A full moon peeked through the window. Every once in a while, a trembling line of dazzling bright surf snaked across the darkness, marking the shoreline. Little tufts of white foam, called boilers by the locals, bubbled offshore against the rocks and on shallow reefs.

The phone jarred me from my musings. Dr. Blue was back on the line.

"You'd better make it worth my while," she said. "I just cut short a session with an Arab sheik, a very expensive and, may I add, reliable patient."

"Do you think I'm crazy?"

"Do you want my professional opinion or personal one?"

"I want to know what you think, personally."

"Personally, I wouldn't call you crazy. Foolish idiot comes more readily to mind."

"Where did you get your license to practice? Groucho Marx College?"

"You asked for my personal opinion. A girl dumps you, and you're carrying on about her, stalking her, beyond what normal people would call normal."

"She stole $8.3 million from me. I thought you understood that."

"Oh, well, I thought you wanted my personal opinion. My professional opinion? The court ruled in your favor. That gives you the permission to make a fool of yourself to try to get it back from her."

"What makes you think I'm making a fool of myself?"

"Running around naked near a phallic tourist attraction so heavily laden with male symbolism that Freud would orgasm from the opportunity to analyze your actions – that would do it in my book."

"Oh, you caught the Jumbotron edition?"

"It was on the front page of *The New York Times*, too. Remember when they actually used to print news?"

"Did I really come out looking that bad?"

"You might as well have put on a clown nose to complete the picture."

"I remember now why I stopped coming to you."

"Hey, you wanted my personal opinion."

"All right. All right. I need you to cure me of my insanity once and for all. Teach me how to at least keep my dignity in public."

"It's very simple. Leave her alone."

"Let her keep my money?"

"I said, 'leave her alone.' I didn't say give up your money. Go after it the right way."

"How do I do that?"

"Are you really ready to listen?"

"Yes."

"Come by tomorrow, six-thirty. Dress sharp. Black tie."

"Black tie?"

"Let me be more specific: black tie *and* pants. I've got two tickets to a charity function at the United Nations. My girlfriend cancelled out on me at the last minute."

"She won't mind me going out with you?"

"Honey, Kerry's emasculated you to the point where you've practically joined the Sisterhood. Besides, this is purely professional. You need to start circulating again, surround yourself with respectable people. Attending a charity function suggests that you care about other things in life besides yourself."

I hung up, walked over to the balcony and strained to see deep into the night. In the distance, revelers on the beach went through a slow, silent dance by a small bonfire. Missing that kind of carefree life, longing to know what it was like, I stepped out onto the cool sand and followed a path down the hill. The moon was bright enough to light my way along the shore. The dark crags of the dunes ensured the same light didn't give me away. The voices grew louder, the faces more distinct as I neared the fire. The revelers consisted of nine or so people, most of them middle-aged. A yacht bobbed tranquilly some thirty yards offshore. Several dinghies rested on the sand, away from the lapping waves.

She was there! I shut my eyes and opened them again to make sure that I wasn't imagining things. No, she continued to be there, dancing by herself, waving her arms languidly, but not necessarily following the beat, as if she danced to her own music. A stout, middle-aged man struggled into view, trying to keep his balance in the soft sand. His efforts were made doubly absurd by the fact that he was obviously drunk.

"The little…" I began, but words failed me. I resisted the urge to run over and knock his head off.

Denver approached Kerry, offered her a bottle of beer, which she refused, and did a few awkward moves around her that were meant to pass for dancing.

I should dump all the money on his head – every penny of that $27 million – so that that little tramp can steal it from him, too, I thought.

An old man turned unsteadily toward the rock that I was hiding behind, apparently to relieve himself. The light of the bonfire lit up his face, and for a moment I thought he looked familiar. Most likely someone I had met briefly or read about in my former job. Bermuda attracted a lot of Wall Streeters.

I inched away from the rocks, off the beach, to the small path that returned me to the hotel. I looked back at Kerry one last time as she slowly writhed in the glow of the fire. Her body did not seem real, but I knew she was real enough. At one time, I had possessed her, taken off her clothes, felt her bare skin against mine; felt her breasts pressing against my chest. That was a long time ago, but I could still feel her, I could still taste her. When will the taste turn sour? No, it remained sweet, disturbingly, gently sweet. It lingered in me in much the same way as the Bermuda night, which seemed to go on forever.

4

I woke up early the following morning, showered quickly, and made the first flight off the island. Three hours later, I was in a taxi on the Van Wyck Expressway, fighting rush hour to get to the office. The driver complained bitterly throughout the trip. He cursed the increasing number of bad drivers who didn't seem to understand the universal rules of the road, himself exempted, of course, as he cut off other drivers to advance through traffic.

An hour later, I staggered into the company cafeteria, where Dan looked me over. He poured me a cup of coffee.

"You weren't serious about breaking off the funding for Denver, were you?"

"It was just a joke."

"Good. I'm glad to see you're back on track."

"I'm so much on track, I'm hugging the rails," I said.

"That's what I like to hear."

"Glad it is. I have no clue what it means. I just heard it in "Pretty Woman".

I carried the coffee back to my desk and fired up the computer. Tech stocks were headed for the toilet again. This was the Big One, I realized. The last two times, when techs took a nosedive, they swung right back up again within a week. Now, Wall Street was into its fifth straight month of freefall. Stocks couldn't seem to find solid ground. They smashed through floor after floor, a long way from the basement.

I began to do something that I hadn't done in a long time. What did they call it? Oh, yeah, "research." I checked to see how fast my clients were burning through their cash in relations to their target date to go public.

I called my investors to gauge their conditions, see who needed a little handholding. Some were already on their second bottle of antacid; others on the stronger stuff. Not that they needed the excuse. I was especially keen to hold on to PipeStation backers. Dan's words were fresh in my mind. This was the Big One for me, too. I couldn't afford to crash through any more floors.

I left a message at Denver's office, letting him know his ass was still covered. I didn't expect him to be in. The bastard was probably still in Bermuda. His secretary would relay the message. Who would be in his bed when he got it?

I shook away the thought. What business of mine was it whom Kerry slept with now? Hadn't I just hopped out of someone else's bed myself?

At lunchtime, I grabbed my jacket and headed to Giancarlo's office, where I was immediately ushered in.

The first thing one noticed about Giancarlo was his two-piece suit. A marvel of tailoring technology, it fit his trim, six-foot-two body like Spandex on a professional cyclist. The second thing one noticed was his face. It could have easily belonged to Spanish singing sensation Ricky Martin – youthful, sharp-featured, burning black eyes, short dark hair spiked like the quills of a porcupine. His full, animated mouth frequently broke into that famous smile immortalized on the cover of *Time Magazine*, *Forbes* and *Fast Company*. His legendary prowess in public relations had earned him the nickname, "The Spinning Spaniard." In the middle of the infamous Catholic Church child molestation scandal, he could have gotten a priest his own show on Nickelodeon.

"Cain," he said. His voice had the perfect pitch: deep, resonant, gentle and yet firm, a foreign accent somewhere in the mix that was vaguely reminiscent of European aristocracy, though he was from the streets of the Bronx. "It's been a while," he continued. "Although, in the past few days, I've gotten to know you better than I've ever cared to before."

"You've been busy yourself, I gather, protecting your tech clients' reputations."

"Tell me about it. With so many Internet companies tanking lately, I feel like Rumpelstiltskin at the weaving machine, working late into the night to spin cotton into gold. I have to explain to the media that my clients' businesses aren't failing; society is failing *them*. The financial community's growing lack of faith in the Internet is creating a hostile environment that practically guarantees even good Internet companies will fail. Facts have become almost irrelevant. It's all about perception."

"Of course, it has nothing to do with the fact that most of these companies are burning through millions of dollars a day of investors' money to fuel celebrity-studded parties in Hollywood; or the fact that executives are leasing helicopters to commute back and forth to their summer homes. And they're doing all this before they've secured a single customer or developed an actual product to sell."

"You're talking about my competitors' clients. I handle the ethical ones."

"We all have our crosses to bear. I help the greedy, you help the needy."

"Between the two of us, we make one honest man. That should count for something in heaven."

"We'll have to arrange to die together."

We regarded each other across the sleek, stainless steel desk. Giancarlo and I had known each other since second grade, when he helped me make friends with Gina, my first boyhood crush. He put in a good word for me by slipping her a note, extolling my skills at solving math problems and spelling words. It was his first press release. With its success, he found his true calling in life, going on to write notes for other kids in school in exchange for their lunch money.

A bank of video monitors lined the walls, covering different time zones. Not a single piece of paper marred the surface of his desk or any furniture in the room. He did everything on his computer. He didn't believe in leaving a paper trail.

"Let's cut to the chase," he said. "The least of your problems is that Kerry's got your money."

"If that's the least of my problems, what's the worst?"

"She's had it for so long, everyone's come to think that she's legally entitled to it. Who debates anymore whether George Bush, Jr., stole the election from Al Gore in Florida?"

"Luckily, there's no statute of limitation on theft."

"To a point. But a defendant's behavior can have a major impact on the court's decision, too."

"Nothing can change the fact that the money is legally mine," I said.

"We're not dealing with earthly laws here. We're dealing with a higher authority."

"The judgment of God?"

"No, the court of public opinion. If Kerry had been jet-setting around the world, swimming topless in Monaco, or stumbling drunk out of night clubs, showing her private parts to the Paparazzi, you might have had a case. Instead, she seems hell-bent on doing some damningly responsible good deeds, like visiting hospital wards of terminally ill children, volunteering at animal shelters and senior citizen centers, and harmonizing with Willie Nelson at farm aide. What were you doing with your money before she got a hold of it?"

"Whoring, boozing, partying. You were there with me for many of those nights, remember?"

"That has to change. For you, of course."

"Kerry was recently photographed visiting an orphanage in Bermuda," I said. "I guess that constitutes a better use of my money."

"She's also lent her support to "Make a Wish Foundation" for children with fatal diseases who only have a few months to live. Children always hit the spot with the public, especially the cute ones that are dying. But where she's really blowing you out of the water is by backing a really stellar cause: finding homes for those adorable little puppies and kittens rescued from the animal mills."

I shook my head bitterly.

He continued, "In other words, the problem we have here is that Kerry doesn't seem to be spending your money irresponsibly. Any attempt to sully her good name presents great risks. You might as well bad-mouth Mother Theresa or throw a puppy in the trash. The public will cut off your balls."

"If you haven't noticed, they already have."

"No, I mean literally. Right now, you're just a laughing stock. Harmless and even loveable in a bedraggled, wet puppy sort of way."

"Thank you. Your words bring me comfort."

"I'm just giving you the facts."

"So you're saying I'm screwed? I was too stubborn to listen to you when I should have. Now Kerry's reputation is untouchable."

"Not at all. I just gave you my two-dollar speech about all the obstacles we're facing to help put into context my absolutely brilliant mind when I succeed. I give that speech to every company that needs to justify a million-dollar retainer to their Board of Directors. The fact is, you've got an ace in the hole."

"There's hope?"

"Yes, you still have the law on your side. It's still legally your money."

"You just said that that doesn't mean anything. It's all about public perception."

"Right. Negative public perception is the Grand Canyon of obstacles. Success is not about the big leaps, but taking the baby steps."

"What are you saying, in plain English?"

"You don't try to confront her *mano-a-mano* and go Evel Knievel on her, like you've been doing. She's too sympathetic a public figure. She also has an uncanny knack for anticipating your next moves."

"I'm closer to understanding, but I need a little more information."

"In simple terms, you've got to get yourself a mule and take the long, winding road down to the canyon floor, then another long, slow journey up the other side."

"Heaven help me, I understand that. You're telling me we've got a chance, but it's going to be a long, slow process?"

"Yes, we've got a chance."

"What should I do?"

"Go home, get yourself ready for tonight."

"How do you know about tonight?"

"I move in mysterious ways. That, and your therapist called me about it."

The city seemed brighter that night. The smell of gasoline in the warm Manhattan air was sweeter than Wal-Mart perfume on a teenage girl. I dodged the prostitutes in Alphabet City with a spring in my steps and climbed the smelly stairs to my apartment as if I was entering paradise.

My cluttered closet contained another one of the few possessions to survive my fall from grace – my tuxedo. This was the first time I'd be using it since then. It was wrapped in plastic and still clean.

Bambi looked positively radiant in her pure white Versace evening gown that night. She moved gracefully even when standing still. Not a single fatty lump of imperfection spoiled the taut, limber frame of the former stripper. She was as exotic as they come, of some kind of Oriental and German mixture, with long and straight black hair, large almond eyes, thick, sweeping dark lashes and a small, heart-shaped mouth that would have done Betty Boop proud.

As the lead dancer at Baubles, the City's premiere man's club, she used to earn ten thousand dollars a night. That was on a slow day. She left the trade for a career as a licensed therapist.

Launching her practice came easy. Her night club patrons – many of them powerful public figures, celebrities and religious leaders – simply switched over from their own therapists. They were already accustomed to telling her their problems. She just cost less them now, though she no longer came with benefits.

At five feet, ten inches tall, she commanded attention everywhere she went. In high heels, she gave me serious competition. Our entrance created an immediate buzz; she with her drop-dead beauty and me with my bemusing reputation.

"You know," she began, "I like the way we electrify a crowd. My girlfriend and I are getting married soon and want to start a family right away. I'll be in the market for donor sperms, and I was thinking…"

"I've already had my balls squeezed dry," I said.

She suddenly yanked me onto the dance floor and circled languidly around me, slowly undulating – you couldn't call what she did dancing. The only couple on the floor, we got plenty of stares.

In the next instant, a familiar face emerged from the blur of the crowd. It was Giancarlo, who sent me two thumbs up. My view was then blocked abruptly by a photographer, his camera whirling away, flash popping furiously. I glanced toward Giancarlo for an explanation, sensing that he'd had a hand in this, and got another thumbs up. The photographer presently took a bow and slipped away; and then, so did Giancarlo.

"Did you see that?" I asked Bambi.

"These kinds of events attract all sorts of people," she responded, as if indeed she'd been through this countless times before.

She took my hand and led me to the open bar, where she requested a glass of white wine. "You're a Daiquiri man, now, aren't you?" she said.

"As a matter of fact, yes, I switched from whiskey sour. How did you know?"

"It was my job to know."

"Is there a significance to the kind of drink a man orders?"

"In your case, Daiquiris are a safer form of whiskey sours, made with rum instead of whiskey. It reflects the fact that you've gone soft since Kerry. You've lost your confidence."

"That skill must serve you well in your new profession."

"You'd be amazed at how much of my stripper experience was transferable to therapy."

"By the way, I noticed another strange thing tonight," I said. "A lot of men keep nodding at me as if they know me, but I've never seen them before."

"It's for me, sweetheart," she said. "Notice that their wives are usually not looking when they do."

"Thank God, I thought maybe my fly was open and they were trying to warn me."

"You're the picture of modesty."

"Who are these people, anyway?"

"Respectable and highly influential members of their communities." She indicated a balding, middle-aged executive, who nodded back. "Beryl Kolsky, shipping tycoon. He likes to wear diapers."

"That was an unnecessary piece of information."

"Van Dorf," she said, indicating another guest, who was collecting *hors d'oeuvre* for his wife. "He blew through $2 million at the Bellagio on a single night several years ago. Now, they comp him a $30,000-a-night suite whenever he's in town. He thanks them by never losing less than $100,000 per visit. He doesn't want to seem ungrateful."

"How considerate."

"Campbell," she continued, nodding toward a robust elderly man in a custom-tailored Italian tuxedo. "He once flew me over First Class to his suite in Vegas, where he had a bathtub filled with mud waiting for me."

"That appeals to you?"

"It wasn't for me. He likes to play the part of a bad little boy who rolls around in the mud and gets himself all dirty, then mommy yells at him and has to clean him up."

"Where do you find mud in Vegas?"

"You can find anything you want in Vegas. As long as you've got the money. But it wasn't real mud. Too unsanitary."

"Of course."

"They used the stuff from the beauty salon, over 100 bottles of it, at $200 a bottle. That wasn't even the expensive part of the evening."

"Certainly."

"Guess how much he had to pay the service staff to keep them from babbling to the tabloids?"

"You know, when I asked about the people around us, I was referring to their professions, not their kinky sexual habits. How much did he have to pay the service staff to keep them quiet?"

She arched her brow and smiled. She enjoyed talking about herself – or rather, about her former clients. At many of our sessions, I had to continuously steer the conversation back to my own misery; otherwise she'd veer off-topic and never return.

By now, the number of men Bambi had known in her former life no longer shocked me. An avowed lesbian, she could nonetheless reel off a litany of lascivious liaisons with high-powered businessmen that all shared the same theme of kinky sex in strange places and the use of unusual paraphernalia. But sex seemed hardly the right description for what she did. Her encounters typically involved an extraordinary degree of coordination with people, venues, and sundry suppliers. Summit meetings among world super powers were less complicated.

A brilliant administrator, she knew an impressive number of people in high and low places and had an uncanny ability to solve the most challenging problems of logistics. She pooled every resource with effortless ease, brought everything together perfectly for that one incredible evening. With time precious and in short supply, these powerful clients wanted to do it in style whenever they had a chance to. And when style was involved, coupled with world-class service, discretion, and sophistication, only Bambi fit the bill.

"The more elaborate the occasion," she said, "the more likely it was that we didn't have sex. Role reversals were the most popular requests. At their jobs, thousands of people and billions of dollars hang upon their decisions. For once, they wanted someone else to run the show."

My usual response was, "Can we get back to my own problems?" Even so, I took great satisfaction in knowing that other men were as equally pathetic as I was in the amount of money they spent on women.

"I once got a million dollar pair of earrings as a present, but had to return them," she said.

"Not your style?"

"They were beautiful. Problem was the client picked them up from his wife's collection. She reported them stolen to the police, and so he had to return them. He fired the maid to explain their sudden reappearance."

"The maid lost her job because of you? Who said escort services are a victimless crime?"

"You're a funny guy. I made him give the maid a $50,000 severance package, off the books, of course"

"Aren't you violating your professional code of ethics or something, telling me all these personal stories?"

"You're right. I'm being a naughty girl. You'll have to spank me tonight."

"I'm tempted to get a paddle out right now."

"Pump out some sperm and splatter 'em my way while you're at it. For a worthy cause, of course."

"That's a pretty disgusting image."

"I'm dirty when I wanna be."

"You never did tell me what this function was for anyway?"

"Amnesty International. Tens of thousands of people are in jails around the world, victims of political and religious persecution. Even our own U.S. jails overflow with victims of social injustices. Did you know that there's a black man in South Carolina who's been in jail twenty years for stealing an orange from a fruit stand?"

"Lucky they didn't catch him picking it off the tree. He probably would have been hanged for destruction of private property."

"That's not far from the truth."

As we danced and drank the night away, my admiration for Bambi grew. Dancing, of course, was her forte, but she was smart enough to tone down her movements considerably, to appear no more agile than other women. The few occasions she forgot herself, her body would suddenly take on a life of its own and gyrate in ways that seemed impossible for a human body to move. In her natural elements, unfettered by convention, she had a lascivious, dirty way of dancing, as if her body would fling the dress away any second and simply dance naked and free. At those moments, she caught every man's eyes, even as their women pursed their lips into tight, impatient grimaces. Fortunately, she rarely forgot. She moved gracefully, but with a subdued and quiet charm that went unnoticed unless you stared straight at her, which I did often.

I also learned something new about Bambi that evening. In the company of powerful men, she was the ultimate conversationalist. She possessed a vast wealth of knowledge on many subjects, and was especially fluent in world affairs. Every time she bumped into an acquaintance, whether in banking, in finance, in politics, or in science, she'd toss off a witty, insider *bon mot* that drew an instant laugh. They'd retort with their own obscure witticism, following which they'd all erupt into laughter.

Bambi surprised me in other ways. She wasn't the type to drape herself all over a man when she talked to them. She always maintained a respectful distance, so that a casual observer wouldn't have thought there was anything more than the most professional relationship between them. But the tips of her fingers sometimes brushed the surface of their hands, or ran lightly over the fabric of their suits, and these seemingly incidental gestures would electrify them.

As the evening wore on, I noticed something else. Many of the ladies who had glowered at me when I first arrived now rewarded me with gentler, kinder looks. Maybe it was the alcohol – on my part and theirs – or maybe they were simply grateful that, because I stayed close to Bambi all evening, their men were less likely to stray in her direction: I kept the competition in check.

When the function ended, we said goodbye to a considerable number of well-wishers, both men and women. The handshakes were hearty and sincere, a stark contrast to the cold reception we had received upon arrival. Quite a few women actually gave me a look that I hadn't seen in a long time: one that I could swear was flirtatious. Again, though, it could simply have been the alcohol talking.

I dropped Bambi off at her condo on the East Side and made my way home to my little hole in Alphabet City. But I no longer felt so alone in the world. I did something that night that I hadn't done in a long time: I went to sleep without cursing Kerry's name. I still dragged around that dull ache of my financial loss, but it did not hurt so much at the moment. When I awoke, Kerry was not the first thought on my mind. At the office that morning, I went a full hour into the job before her name rose to my consciousness again. Even then, it was prompted by an outside development: a call from Giancarlo.

"It's begun," he said

After taking a moment to gather my thoughts and identify the caller, I asked him to elaborate.

"Did you see this morning's *New York Post*?" he asked.

"It's not my usual routine."

"On Page Eight, there's a picture of you dancing with Bambi."

"How will this get to Kerry?"

"First, we needed some decent photos of you out there in circulation. Until now, the media has been using that grainy, shifty-eye headshot of yours that makes you look like a convicted serial rapist. This new batch makes you look positively handsome, even more so because you're alongside a beautiful woman."

"Fair enough. But I hardly think I'll get to Kerry with my good looks alone."

"If a picture is worth a thousand words, you just spoke twenty chapters."

"I guess I'm still deaf to your meaning. Explain to me again, how will my good looks get my money back?"

"Patience, grasshopper."

The other line flashed. I placed Giancarlo on hold. "Hello?"

"You piece of shit," said an angry female voice, and the line went dead.

I stared in shock into space. Finally, I forced myself back to work, my hands still shaking. The phone rang again.

"I lost you there, buddy," said Giancarlo.

"I totally forgot about you!"

"Those are not the words I like to hear in my profession."

"Guess who just called me?"

"Kerry?"

"She sounded really annoyed."

"Your picture with Bambi in the *Post* probably had something to do with it."

"But she isn't the jealous type."

"You learn something new every day."

"It's more than that. That's the first time she's ever actually called me directly. I used to do all the calling when we were going out."

"Then maybe it's the fact that you went to a charity function for Amnesty International," he said.

"Why should that matter?"

"She recently became their spokesperson."

The afternoon brought damp, dark clouds to the skies of Manhattan. The weather was cold and wet. The wind blew pedestrians about like leaves in autumn. But I was walking on sunshine. All I could think about was that Kerry had called me. I had stirred up enough emotion in that dark and devious, cold-blooded heart of hers to make her pick up the phone. It was a minor victory, by most standards, but in my case, it was monumental.

Only one thing worried me, and that was Giancarlo's parting words as he hung up the phone: "Brace yourself."

I soon found out why. Passing a newsstand during my lunch hour, I caught sight of a familiar face on the cover of the late edition of the

New York Post. It was Kerry. She was announcing a donation of $100,000 to PETA, People for the Ethical Treatment of Animals. Supermodels Naomi Campbell and Kate Hudson flanked her to the left, while actress Pamela Anderson flanked her to the right. All were naked, legs crossed demurely and arms draped strategically across their breasts.

The caption read: "Animal Attraction. $100K in the Kitty."

I hit Giancarlo's number. "Yes, I saw it," he said. "Brace yourself."

"You said that already."

"I want it to sink in."

"They can't accept the money. It's not hers legally."

"Obviously, they didn't read the fine print."

I suddenly felt the chill in the wind as gray clouds plunged the city into darkness. The drizzle turned to heavy rain. I considered going home early, when the phone vibrated. I took a deep breath and pulled it out. It was Dan.

"I'll be in the office in ten minutes," I said, "If it's about John Denver's funding, don't worry. I've got all our ducks in a row. We can go to closing with the investors before the end of next week."

"That's good news. I really appreciate all the effort you've put into it."

"I'm working on another high-tech firm. The market's rather rough for these babies, but that's the challenge, right? So far, this one seems to have a genuine profit arc."

"Well..." he began.

That didn't sound good. "Don't tell me Denver's out? I put my ass on the line for him."

"No, he's fine. It's just...."

"Let me call you back." I knew I needed time to brace myself.

"Cain..."

I hung up and ducked into a Starbucks, where I ordered a latte Grande, double. Finally, I screwed up the courage to call him back. He answered the phone himself, not his secretary, who usually screened his calls. Not a good sign. I braced myself again.

"Cain..." he said. "Buddy...I'm going to have to let you go."

"Say that again."

"Well, it's just that..."

"I heard you the first time. This is a joke, right? You can't afford to let me go. I'm the only one making deals."

"Believe me, this isn't easy for me to say."

"Dan, you're scaring me. You couldn't wait until I at least got back from lunch? What's going on?"

"Sorry, Cain. Look, finish your lunch first, okay? When you come back to the office, you'll have to start clearing out your desk. Actually, security's already done that for you. You'll find your stuff in a box by the receptionist's desk outside. If you don't mind, I'm keeping the stress ball. It's company property, anyway. I need something stronger than these damned antacid pills I've been popping."

I hung up before he could get another word in. I was about to speed-dial Giancarlo when the phone rang. It was him.

"I'm impressed," he said. "Kerry's front-page stunt is gaining traction. The last person I admired that much had embezzled $20 million from his company. He got probation *and* a promotion. He's now the CEO."

"I just got fired," I told him.

"Really? Well, that's the least of your problems."

"Kerry's pledged the rest of my money to Save the Whales Foundation?"

"It's even more serious than that. Your therapist, Bambi Blue. She's been shot."

When I got to the hospital, Bambi was sitting up on a gurney in the emergency room, surrounded by three police officers and two doctors, all male. One of the doctors was bandaging her arm, looking puzzled, as if overwhelmed by the complexity of the task. Otherwise, no one else appeared to be doing anything of particular significance.

"Are you all right?" I asked.

"I'll live," she replied.

"Sir, you'll have to wait outside. We're in the middle of an important investigation," said one of the policemen.

"Are three of you needed for this?" I asked.

"You must wait outside," chimed in a doctor.

"It's all right. He's a patient of mine," said Bambi.

"I knew Kerry was upset. But I never considered her homicidal."

"It wasn't your precious Kerry. It was my girlfriend, Kris. I forgot to tell her I was going to the function with you. She got jealous over our picture in the *Post*."

"Is it serious?"

"Just a scratch. Luckily, she was too worked up to shoot straight."

"Sir, I must remind you that this is a criminal investigation. If you continue to interfere, we'll have to arrest you."

"It's all right, Sergeant," said Bambi. The officer swelled with pride at being addressed by his professional title. Bambi added, "Now that Mr. Kahn is here, he'll take me home."

A policeman went for his gun, but she lightly touched his hand. "He's not forcing me. I asked him to," she assured him

A doctor moved in. "We really must advise you to remain here for a few more hours of observation, Ms. Blue."

"I appreciate your concern, doctor. But I really must go." She sent all the men a look of genuine gratefulness, and each felt as if she had addressed them personally.

Suddenly, a man with a massive head wound staggered into the room, disoriented, dripping blood. A nurse, chasing him with a blood-soaked towel, finally cornered him, wrestled him to an empty gurney, and applied pressure. The doctors and policemen looked on, fascinated, none considering that they should perhaps help out.

"Doctors!" called the nurse, irritably, indicating the struggling patient.

One of the police officers and a doctor finally seemed to shake off their confusion and hurried over to lend a hand.

Outside, the temperature dropped steadily, until it was now uncomfortably cold. I waved down a passing taxi and helped Bambi to the back seat.

"I hope you don't mind me crashing with you for a few days," she said.

"Of course not. We'll swing by your place to pick up some clothes."

"No, I can't go back there. Not yet."

"Don't worry about your girlfriend showing up," I said. "The police have the place under surveillance. If she tries to come back, they'll catch her."

"Actually, she's there now."

"Impossible. They have a policeman guarding the door. They would have caught her the moment she got close."

"The truth is, she never left. I hid her in the closet before the police arrived. It was the safest place for her. I knew they'd be looking for her everywhere outside, but not inside."

"She had just tried to kill you and you were worried about making sure she was safe?"

"She didn't mean for the gun to go off. She was just trying to scare me."

"So what are you going to do? You can't hide her in your apartment forever."

"We'll work it out, eventually. I'm just not ready to see her again until she comes to her senses."

"'Comes to her senses!' She almost killed you."

"She was just trying to make a point."

"A bullet through your head isn't the best way to make it."

"She missed."

"You're crazier than I am. At least the girl I'm obsessed with doesn't go around shooting people."

"This really isn't funny. We were finalizing our wedding date and picking out a date for the baby's conception."

"You've found a sperm donor?"

"We have a short list to work through but, you know, you can always cut to the front of the line. Just say the word."

"I might take you up on your offer. My sperms are just going to waste, anyway."

"They'll get a good home."

"They'll definitely appreciate the upgrade in accommodations. By the way, did I mention that Kerry called me this afternoon?"

"Really? She's not the type to initiate a call."

"She saw our picture in the paper and went ballistic."

"Who said the print medium is dead? What did she want?"

"Nothing. Just to curse me out."

"Interesting."

"It means something?"

"Yes, she's the jealous type, too."

"She's not that type."

"You didn't think she was the type to steal your money, either."

The Manhattan street life rolled by the window. I was always amazed by the sheer number of nationalities that inhabited such a tiny piece of real estate without descending into civil war. They were all too busy fighting for their promotions on the corporate ladder. This was the place to do it. The Financial Capital of the World. Free enterprise really could bring world peace.

Bambi studied the bandage on her arm and smiled at me. I could go for her if she was straight.

"I'm not available," she said.

"Excuse me?"

"I've seen that look before."

"But you said you wanted my sperm."

"In a tube."

"I think my compensation should be more tangible. You had no problem when it was business and, in a way, this is business."

She smiled. "This isn't business, but you're right. I'll make sure you get a night you'll never forget."

"Hold that thought."

"Can't hold it too long. The offer has an expiration date. My girlfriend's clock is ticking."

"I thought this was for you."

"The first one, yes. But she wants to give it a sibling from the same daddy."

"You mean to tell me I'm looking at a two-for-one?"

"You're looking at a 'one.' She'll give you a hand with the second."

"You know, you're just as screwed up as the rest of us."

"Of course. That's why I'm so good at what I do."

"By the way, I got fired today."

"Really? Why? You're the best one there. No one else is pulling in the money like you."

"Tell me about it. Cameron just called me up. Didn't even have the decency to tell me in person."

"Could our picture in the *Post* have anything to do with it?"

"I don't see how that's possible. The two have no connection to each other."

Arriving at my place, I helped her up the stairs. She didn't seem to notice the mess in the hallway, or maybe she didn't care.

Something about her hinted at a hard life in her younger days, and I suspected she had seen worse.

I gave her a quick tour of my little hole in the ground before excusing myself to hurry back to the office. I had no intention of speaking to Dan or anyone else but, upon my arrival, Crowley suddenly popped into the reception area and slowly circled me like a wary hyena around a still twitching carcass.

"Tough break," he said.

"Thanks for the sympathy."

"By the way, I took the liberty of picking up your leads, if you don't mind."

"How did you get access to my files?"

"The IT guy. Standard procedures."

"Have you considered that what you did is an invasion of my privacy?"

"*Tu casa es mi casa.*"

"What is that supposed to mean?"

"Company property, good buddy. Everything on that computer belongs to the company."

"You want to know something else? This fist belongs to my hand. Every second you spend in front of my face, you're that much closer to losing your teeth."

"It's business. Nothing personal."

I stared at him until he slithered back into the office. The receptionist shook her head. "Cheeky bastard," she said. She was British. She pointed to a box in the corner. "Mr. Cameron left that for you. I'm sorry."

"It's just business. Thanks, Julie."

I started for the box when Dan, skulking out for a burger, appeared at the door. He halted, eyeing the long stretch of lonely highway that ran past me to the elevator. Finally, he gave me a sad, hangdog look, as if to inform me that he was as much a victim of the situation as I was. He started babbling that he was sure I understood, but I simply glowered at him. I was too irritated to engage him in conversation.

I noticed, for the first time, that he had a nervous twitch on the left side of his mouth, under his pencil-thin mustache. The mustache was something he picked up when he entered the corporate world, to give himself less of a pretty-boy look. The twitch was probably indicative of an impending heart attack. Or perhaps it was a sign that the toxic financial environment was taking its toll on him.

I remembered that in the months after Kerry, I too suffered from a nervous twitch in my left eye. Maybe that's what happens to all men after they've been kicked in the balls and dumped upon, either by fate or a woman.

Fate, however, seemed to have been kinder to Dan, at least from a physical perspective. Signs of wear were creeping over his face, but he was still a handsome devil. The monotonous routines of life can play havocs with our physical appearance, but the genetic lottery can still soften the blow.

I took my time picking up my box to make sure Dan caught the elevator alone. Later, as I rode home in a cab, the phone rang. It had actually been ringing all day. It always did. I just rarely felt like answering it these days.

"How do you feel?" asked Giancarlo.

"How does dung feel when it's pushed through a cow's anus?"

"That's a nice quote, but I don't think I can use it for public consumption. We'll say, instead, that you're very concerned about Kerry's wild spending sprees. You're especially appalled at the organizations that are accepting her money, which courts say she stole. It's the same as if they accepted donations from a convicted bank robber."

"You're writing a press release?"

"Round two."

Even with Bambi waiting for me, I wasn't in the mood to return home yet. I directed the driver to Washington Square Park, where Greenwich Village's once flourishing Hippie population still congregated. Long haired and aging, the former flower children sat crossed-legged on the grass, strumming guitars and singing folk songs, while acrobatic street performers entertained the crowds. A fountain attracted homeless men and children, who seem to have a lot in common in terms of urinating in the water. I absently crossed in front of a performing mime, and he immediately leaped behind me to imitate my walk, delighting the crowd. Realizing I was their source of amusement, I quickly slunk away before they had a chance to recognize me.

I tried to hate Kerry, to convince myself that I would like nothing better than to squeeze her pale, slender neck and watch her die a slow, agonizing death. But I kept letting go of that smooth neck, caressing it rather than squeezing it. I kept bending low to inhale her breath, so elevating and fleeting, like the clean smell of nature after a thunderstorm.

Yeah, she made me a poet, too. She wrenched it out of me.

"So, you're saying," began Bambi, after listening to my ramblings for half an hour that night, "that you still love her."

"Surely, you wouldn't call my feelings for her love?"

"It's close enough. You can't seem to get her out of your mind."

"But it's all about sex and violence. It's not about caring."

"Do you think that she thinks of you in the same way?"

"No, for her, it's never been about sex. Nor violence. It's always been about money."

"Then why is she giving it away?"

The sun was setting, and everything in the room soaked up the dark orange hues and radiated them back out, as if glowing with their own inner energy. The noise of traffic subsided, commuters having long ago inched their way cross-town to the Lincoln Tunnel. Residents were reclaiming the neighborhood. They wandered the streets, filled up the restaurants, purchased their grocery. Dusk made Alphabet City somewhat habitable. For the moment it seemed like a real neighborhood.

Soon enough, however, night would swallow up the streets and the drug dealers and prostitutes would reclaim their turf, like rats issuing from their holes after the lights were turned off.

Bambi made few attempts to interrupt me – a rare thing for her. This time, she had her own problems. I closed my eyes for a moment and fell asleep, dreaming of no one else but Kerry and wondering whether I'd ever find anyone else like her.

Bambi was gone the next morning to start her sessions, which began at 5:00 am. Powerful business leaders were early risers, and this was the time they roamed the earth. The apartment already felt empty without her, which is what a woman will do to you if she hangs around you long enough – any woman, even a lesbian therapist. In the short time that she had been here, objects like coasters had already popped up on the coffee table. A vase of flowers materialized on a wall shelf by the foyer, and I didn't even know I had a wall shelf or, come to think of it, a foyer.

The phone rang. That was never good at six in the morning.

"Did you see the *Times*?" It was Giancarlo.

"It's six in the morning."

"No, the paper, *The New York Times*?"

"Why don't you fill me in?"

"The Opt-Ed page. The editor is reacting to news of Kerry pledging a hundred thousand to Amnesty International. He points out, and rightly so, that that money is not for her to give away. More importantly, it's unethical for any organization to accept stolen money. It's more or less what you told me yesterday."

"You got the *Times* to say that? I thought no one could buy them off."

"The way they keep jacking up their prices, they'll soon get their wish."

"That's quite impressive, considering they were my biggest critics during the crisis."

"Compliment accepted."

The Times officially changing its position on an issue was like getting nature to rescind the law of gravity. Their editorial launched a wave of heated debates over the ethics of any organization knowingly accepting potentially stolen money, no matter how noble the cause. Late-night talk shows chimed in with their theories. Jay Leno said that stealing people's money to fund wacky projects already had a name. It's called taxes. David Letterman said he didn't see anything wrong with organizations accepting stolen money. Wasn't that how General Electric, his parent company, got started?

Suddenly, I was the talk of the town again, but this time, in a good way. People notice me on the street, and some even sympathized with me. "Stay with it, buddy," they said.

The next day, the *New York Post* ran a picture of Kerry buying herself a pair of designer jeans. The headline read, "Hot Pant$!", noting that the jeans retailed at $1,800 and insinuating that she was buying it with stolen money. They neglected to point out that she was buying them at Filene's Basement at 80 percent off. *The National Enquirer* followed with a front page exclusive of a waiter at Cipriani complaining that Kerry walked in with a gaggle of girlfriends in tow, spent more than $2,500 on lobster and Champagne, and stiffed them with only a two percent tip. Toward the bottom of the article, as if a minor after-thought, they noted that the waiter wasn't absolutely sure it was her, just someone who had a slight resemblance.

A few days later, the *New York Post* noticed that Kerry was turning into quite the jetsetter. The headline, "High-Flying," followed up with accounts of her frequent trips to Bermuda, as well as her numerous trips throughout the U.S., to the estimated tune of $37,000 a week. At her rate of spending, the *Post* projected, she would burn through all her ill-gotten loot in two years – at least the $8.3 million for which she was convicted. Who knew how much more she had squirrelled away, allegedly.

Kerry made the cover of the *New York Post* again the following day, in a photo showing her eating ice cream in the company of John Denver, with the tag line, "Pipe Dream?" The implication being that she was a gold digger angling to marry the plumbing magnate. I had no clue as to how Denver got into the picture.

Amnesty International was on the defensive by the end of the week. At first, they refused to comment, insisting they hadn't yet gotten around to confirming the contribution. But *The New York Post* uncovered an email in which the director thanked Kerry personally for her generosity. In response, a spokesperson explained that the "thank you" was just a general acknowledgement of appreciation, and not an official acceptance of the contribution. However, a photograph surfaced of Kerry and the director having lunch at Nobu the day before, suggesting they had met in advance to discuss her donation, and the spokesperson conceded the subject may have come up, though the director couldn't precisely recall.

With public pressure mounting, the board finally ruled that the organization could not accept the donation because it failed to meet their strict criteria, though they didn't elaborate on what those strict criteria were.

Following this, Kerry plunged back into seclusion, wearing dark glasses in public and shielding her face from photographers. Meanwhile, a candid video of me went viral on YouTube, showing me kneeling before the altar in St. Mark's Church, praying. Apparently, an E! Television crew just happened to be in the neighborhood and found me alone, my head bowed in thoughtful meditation, and shot the footage. Why they would think to enter a church in pursue of celebrity scandals was not made clear.

"She didn't seem to have the same pity for you when the shoe was on the other foot and society was vilifying you," observed Giancarlo.

We were sitting in an outdoor café on Eight Street several weeks later. I could not recall the last time I had enjoyed eating out in public. Occasionally, a passer-by recognized me and gave me the thumbs up sign. More demonstrative fans reached across the barricade to pat me on the back.

"I can't help it," I said, "I've been there myself and understand what she's going through. I want to win, but fairly. All that negative publicity leaves out pertinent details that would make things less scandalous."

"Yes, I think I remember the Times Square Jumbletron running a disclaimer under your enormous ass, explaining that things weren't what they appear to be. We should ask the tabloids to extend the same courtesy to Kerry."

"Well, that was different…"

"She hasn't given you back your money," he continued. "Am I missing a pertinent detail here?"

I swelled with resentment at the mention of my money. Prospects for another job anytime soon looked bleak. The dot-com meltdown had poisoned the financial sector. Wall Street looked like a scene from Zombie Apocalypses, with bankers and analysts haunting the streets like shell-shocked survivors of a global catastrophe, futilely seeking haven.

The word "recession" was now making the rounds. I couldn't even get a job for a salary that would have barely paid my entertainment bill in the old days. I would soon be forced to cut down on non-essentials like eating.

"Better you don't," said Giancarlo.

"Better I don't what?"

"Get a job."

"How did you know what I was thinking?"

"You were talking out loud. I heard every word you said."

"I've been doing a lot of that lately. Why don't you want me to get a job?" I asked.

"Media celebrities like you can't mingle with the common folks. Everyone watches when you sneeze or take a crap, then sell their stories and pictures to the tabloids. The next day it's all over the tabloids that you don't cover your mouth or wash your hands. A job among the masses can undermine every ounce of goodwill I've built up for you in the public eye."

His phone rang. A smile slowly broke across his face as he listened to the caller. "We've got a meeting with Senator Harris tomorrow," he said to me. "He's working on legislation giving congress authorization to track down your money and get it back from the foreign banks. We're going to pry it lose from her, even if it's from her cold, dead hands."

"I don't want to hurt her in the process."

"When you get back your money, feel free to be magnanimous and give all or part of it back to her."

"Haven't the court's already ruled in my favor? The judge can just garnish her bank accounts."

"U.S. courts don't have jurisdiction overseas. This legislation will freeze all her assets globally and force the banks to return them, no matter where they're located."

"If the police had done their jobs right in the first place and caught her, we wouldn't be in this mess today."

"Great. Blame those incompetent bastards, the cops. That'll really inspire them to spring into action on your behalf." He gulped down his margarita and flagged down a cab. "Got to go," he said. "I'd invite you to share an evening with my date's twin sister, like the good old days but, you know, it's not the best thing for you right now."

"Yes, I know. It's not good for my public image."

"Actually, I just don't feel that generous tonight."

I finished my coffee and then I, too, finally headed home. The blinking light of the answering machine greeted me, but the apartment offered no other sign of life. Gone were the pitter patter of Bambi, who had found herself another place, and the smell of warm food on the table. She sometimes got into the homemaking mood and ordered Thai, and I would come home to its redolent aroma. I hit the play button. It was Kerry.

"That was a shitty thing to do," she said.

She had never left me a voicemail before, anywhere. I replayed it. There was no mistaking the voice, and it wasn't in a conciliatory mood.

The ringing phone woke me early the next morning.

"Turkey."

"All right."

"I mean, your little sweetheart is taking off to Turkey."

"The country?"

"Yes. You have to go after her."

"Turkey's a big place. I'll never find her there."

"My people will keep her in sight until you arrive."

"Why don't we just grab her at the airport here, before she leaves?"

"Too risky. Could cause a scene. Won't look good – a big brute like you manhandling a delicate damsel like her, even if that delicate damsel has the teeth of a cobra. We'll get her on the other side. Less chance of bad publicity."

"How is it that she's able to fly in and out of the country without getting caught? I thought there was a warrant out for her arrest?"

"I've been asking myself the same question."

"So, I just stare at her from across the aisle for 17 hours until we get to Turkey?"

"No, you're on a different flight. She's on Turkish Airline. You're on Delta. Oh, I forgot to mention. A warrant will be issued for your arrest this afternoon, so you have to get out of the country anyway."

"Why? What did I do?"

"She accused you of sexual assault."

"That's absurd! Where's that coming from?"

"You tried to force yourself on her at the lighthouse."

"It was the exact opposite! And, anyway, what evidence is she offering?"

"Video grabs from the Jumbletron."

"She's out of her mind."

"No, she's out for blood."

5

Arriving at Atatürk Airport in Istanbul, I retrieved my belongings and strolled out to the passenger loading zone in search of transportation. Within seconds, a driver jumped out of an idling car to grab my luggage. I was about to object when he addressed me by name, explaining that Giancarlo had sent him. No sooner was I in the back seat than he floored the gas pedal and we lurched forward, swerving around the "lazy dogs" blocking the intersections. He was referring to the pedestrians, though they clearly had the right of way.

We soon reached the open road, where broad stretches of scruffy green hills floated by, interrupted by the occasional, dark patches of forest and farmland. In the distance, Muslim women bent over their crops, wrapped in their colorful garbs. The men wore tightly twisted turbans and loose, flowing tunics.

An hour into the drive, clusters of apartment buildings broke the monotony of the landscape. They seemed to sprout right out of the ground, with no visible infrastructure of roads leading to them. From a distance, they appeared to be luxury condominiums, but drawing closer, the colorful clothing hanging out to dry, rusting appliances on the terraces, and broken bicycles littering the dirty courtyards revealed them as the homes of the country's working lower class. Turkey's rural population was on the move, slowly abandoning the fields and farms of their ancestors for the city life. They accumulated the trappings of Western civilization along the way, as well as adopted the Western habit of discarding unwanted appliances and other equipment instead of repairing them.

As the city crept closer, mosques in every size and shape sprung up around us. Their shiny domes, flanked by one or two long, pencil-thin minarets, blazed against the pale blue sky. The minarets were rarely wide enough to accommodate human beings and were probably simply decorative. Few people ascended the towers anymore to issue the call to prayers. Large speakers now pumped out the familiar chant at regular intervals.

The center of Istanbul met us with remnants of the defensive brick wall that once made the city impenetrable and helped it survive thousands of years and three world empires. Portions of the crumbling structure still jutted out from the ground many stories high. Often overgrown with weed and wild flowers, they lay quietly deteriorating in backyards and playgrounds and along the road.

To the right of us loomedthe waters of the Bosphorus Strait which, along with the Sea of Marmara and the Dardanelles Strait, formed the boundary between Europe and Asia. Ships were lined up for miles, waiting patiently to cross the narrow channel. The Golden Horn, an inlet of the Bosphorus that divided Istanbul, was the legendary passage from the East to the West through which ships had been sailing for thousands of years. Even today, water traffic was so heavy that a wait of several days was the norm. Tugboats pulled the larger ships across, helping them avoid the treacherous shallows and currents that could easily smash them against the shore.

Across the Bosphorus rose the crowded skyline of the Old City of Istanbul, dominated by the twin mosques of the Hagia Sophia – or St. Sophia – and the Blue Mosque. They were reminders of a time in history when empires challenged one another to erect the grandest monuments to their faith.

The fall of the Ottoman Empire in the early 20th century brought Turkey into the modern age and opened it to Western influence. Istanbul today was a large, sprawling metropolis, teeming with people from every walk of life. It teetered between the old and the new, between those who embraced Western culture and a dwindling population that still clung to the traditions and values of Islam.

The cab traveled now along a four-lane boulevard that could have easily belonged to any European city, except that occasionally women strolled by in full Muslin garb, covered from head to toe in the familiar burka. The Bosphorus Bridge, linking old and new

Istanbul, swarmed with people fishing off its rails. Boats hugged its sides, bobbing in the choppy waters as fishermen hawked their day's catch.

At first impression, the newer part of the city seemed the oldest. The main road was lined with decaying tenements and abandoned storefronts. The driver said something to me in broken English, pointing in the direction of the Old Railway station. It was the Pera Palas Hotel, where Agatha Christie wrote "Murder on the Orient Express." The station was the end of the line in Istanbul for the famed spy-laden train.

After traveling through miles of crumbling tenements, the cab finally broke into a wide traffic circle and brought me to the Marmara Hotel. A slim, modern glass structure, it rose high above the squat eateries and storefronts around it. Narrow escalators carried me to the second level of the hotel to Reception, where I signed in.

I dropped my luggage off in the room and stepped outside to hunt down dinner. Restaurants were plentiful in Turkey, serving every variety of food imaginable. Happily, one could also generally recognize the food groups here, unlike other regions of Asia, where one couldn't always be certain of their origin. My eyes caught a sign, rounding the corner, which flashed the name "Hajji Baba," a restaurant recommended by the bell boy. I ascended a flight of stairs to the second floor, where it was located, and found an unassuming establishment much like a diner. It was a popular place, judging by the crowd.

A waiter motioned to the many dishes on display behind a glass counter, from which I came to understand I should assemble my meal. I pointed to my choices and took a seat, and when the food arrived, fell to it with pleasure.

Night had fallen by the time I finished eating. The streets were swollen with residents on their way home from work. Vendors plied their trinkets to tourists, who enjoyed mingling with the locals. A store's window display of lingerie, an unusual sight in this conservative environment, reminded me of Kerry, who had a particular fondness for Victoria's Secret.

I bumped against someone in my musings and quickly apologized. A young woman – thin, tanned, with ringlets of dark hair falling across her eyes – stared back at me. She was unusually close to me, and I quickly pulled back, mumbling another apology, and put a more comfortable distance between us. She was obviously a country girl, judging by her modest clothes, and I did not want her to think me a rude and presumptuous tourist.

"I know you," said the girl, who came uncomfortably close to me again.

"I'm sorry..." I began, inching back.

"You are the famous Mr. Cain," she said.

I admitted that I was.

"I am a big fan of yours. I hate Kerry Daniels, too."

"She isn't so bad, really," I said.

"She is terrible. I am sorry, I have to go."

She abruptly broke away before I could respond, and I watched her small figure recede into the darkness.

Back at the hotel, I pulled out a map of Istanbul, curious to see how far Kerry was from me since her last reported sighting. Even if I caught her, I considered, what would I do with her? I couldn't just drag her to a bank and force her to transfer the money back to me – or could I? Turkey gave men a little more leeway in their treatment of women, and might consider it an appropriate form of action on my part.

The phone rang. It was Giancarlo.

"Finished your sight-seeing?"

"It's a great county. I wish I could enjoy it."

"Don't get soft. It's important to keep your guards up. By the way, don't worry about the warrant."

"The judge threw it out?"

"Kerry withdrew it at the last minute."

"Of course. It was totally baseless."

"Yes, but it could still have held you up a few days. It's as if she was just trying to chase you out of the country."

"But why get me out now? She should have known that, if I was going to go anywhere, I was going to go after her."

"I considered that. It's as if she wanted you to follow her."

"That doesn't make sense."

"Everything makes sense. You just have to find the motive."

"I know my motive. Getting back my money. So how do I catch her?"

"It's not about catching her yet. It's about the chase. We don't want to reveal our hand too quickly. This time, she doesn't have public sentiment on her side. Even women's groups are reluctant to continue to paint her as the victim. The public is asking: if she's got nothing to hide, why is she running away? The more she runs, the more suspicious she seems. So, let's make her run a little more."

"I find it amazing and frightening that you have the power to manipulate public opinion so easily, even with mixed metaphors. Thank God you're on my side. So what's next?"

"A good night's sleep. One more thing. Tell me right away if anything unusual happens. Don't take anything for granted."

"It's been uneventful so far."

"Good. Whatever you do, don't talk to anyone."

"What do you mean?"

"Keep to yourself. Don't even look at anyone, especially another woman."

"I think I already did."

"Oh, Christ."

"It happened in a flash. I never saw her before. It all seemed coincidental and innocent."

"How old was she?"

"You're beginning to frighten me."

"Never mind. I can guess. She looked very young, right?"

"Yes."

"Brace yourself."

"Why? What's going on?"

"I have a feeling we'll find out soon. Catch *Fox News* in about an hour. Whatever it is, just remember, it's only a flesh wound."

The line went dead. I turned on *Fox News*, where I was assaulted by their usual smattering of finance, slanderous conservative politics and celebrity gossip. About an hour later, a familiar face stared back at me. My name was mentioned by the narrator, and I realized I was staring into the eyes of the girl at the store. She was identified as Lale Baykaktar, a 14-year-old who had recently migrated with her family to Istanbul from the rural parts of Eastern Turkey. She had been missing for several days and her distraught parents feared that she had been kidnapped or even murdered. They now learned that it was possibly even worse; her virginity may have been compromised by the notorious Cain Kahn.

The phone rang again. "See what I mean?" came Giancarlo's voice.

"I bumped into her by accident. I had no clue who she was."

"Pure genius."

"You think Kerry had a hand in this? Why would she do such a thing?"

"To weaken your credibility. But don't worry, it's just a bump in the road."

The next morning came the bump again. Newspapers had splashed pictures of me on their front pages, my face just inches from the girl and smiling at her. Headlines proclaimed, "Did sly fox catch innocent rabbit?" and similar queries. I had no clue how the picture had been taken.

As I made my way to the breakfast buffet in the hotel restaurant, men winked at me, women gave me dirty looks. I was back in my elements.

"Mr. Cain, you're very macho," said a waiter, grabbing his crotch.

"Disgusting," said a female tourist.

After a quick and uncomfortable breakfast, I ran the gauntlet of admirers and detractors to get to the street, where I hailed an idling cab. The driver – in his mid-twenties, clean-shaven, with short, dark hair – was dressed in counterfeit Levy jeans and an oversized Tommy Hilfiger shirt, also counterfeit, judging by the misspelling.

"Where to, Boss," he said, saluting me.

"Just head toward the Old City."

Now, more than ever, I wanted to catch Kerry. The incident with the girl had changed the rules. I wanted to clamp my hands around Kerry's delicate throat and never let go, just to watch the look of terror in her eyes. Chasing after her had been an obsession. Now it was a mission. It was no longer about the money. It was about my survival. Well, the money still played a small role.

"Have you seen Kerry Daniels?" I asked the driver. At this point, I took it for granted that everyone in the world knew about her.

"I have a friend who saw her," he said, and I wasn't surprised. "She really made a fool of Mr. Cain. But he was very macho with that young girl last night, yes? There is still hope for him."

"You speak English reasonably well."

"I graduated from the Fashion Institute of Technology in New York."

"Don't taxi drivers have a university in their own country to graduate from?"

"I'm not a taxi driver. I'm a fashion designer. Aytug Bakan, at your service."

"Glad to meet you, Aytug. Where did your friend see her?"

"She was in his cab. He dropped her off at the Grand Hyatt, about two kilometers from here."

He studied me in the rear-view mirror.

"I assume you're going to tell me I look familiar," I said.

"As a matter of fact, yes."

"I'm sure all Americans look alike to you."

He chuckled. "You are the most famous man in the world."

And the poorest, I thought to myself. *A media celebrity, in Giancarlo's words.* "Can you take me to that same hotel?"

"Do you want to catch her?"

"Yes."

"Then, your best chance is at the Hagia Sophia. That's where she told him she was going today."

"All right, take me there."

"I cannot figure you American men out," he said. "Miss Kerry is beautiful, yes. But you obviously can get a younger woman. She is quite long in the tooth, as you say in your country."

"She's only 25."

"That is an old maid, in my country. Best marrying age for a girl is sixteen. However, our traditions are dying and today many modern women wait as long as 21, to graduate from college first. It's ridiculous how today's young people have no respect for traditions."

"How can you be criticizing young people? You can't be more than 25 yourself."

"I am 26, but I still respect my culture. My wife and I were betrothed at three years of age. We married at 18. Yes, a little old, I know, but I waited out of respect for my father, who was ill for a long time and could not attend the ceremony. I have five children today."

"You must have been in America most of the time you were married, getting your degree? When did you have time to make children?"

"I always made it a point to come home at least for one month every year during the summer to be with my family. I take no credit for such devotion, of course, because I really love my family, so I did not see it as a hardship."

"Your sense of duty is commendable."

"Thank you."

"You must be happy now, that you can see them every day."

"Unfortunately, I cannot. While I was away, my wife picked up too many bad habits from her nosy neighbors and became a big nag. I was forced to send her back home to live with my mother."

"I am sorry to hear that."

"It's not so bad. My father is dead and my mother is old. She cannot afford a maid to help her, but fortunately my wife is now able to do her chores and cook for her. In the end, it all worked out for the best."

"You are a fortunate man."

"Thank you. I cannot complain."

"How soon will we reach the Hagia Sophia?" I was eager to return to our original conversation.

"About 20 minutes. But please take my advice. Do not be offended, but you are foolish to chase this Kerry. You would be wise instead to marry this nice Turkish girl, make her a respectable woman. She will be very grateful and make you a devoted wife."

"May I remind you that Kerry stole my money?" It was always the same defense.

"Well, I ask you, why do you have so much trouble getting it back? Surely, a smart man like yourself with so much experience must know how to follow the money trail, as they say? I took a course in forensic accounting while in school, and understand all transactions are electronic and easy to trace."

"I tried, but she hid her movements too well."

"What about the SEC?"

"They hit a dead end, too."

"This Kerry must be a financial genius to outsmart so many smart people."

He had a point. I never thought it strange that she could do that. "She had a head start," I said stubbornly. "It was at least a month before the courts ordered an audit."

"Well, it's been more than a year now. Why cry over it so much? Mohammed would tell you that earthly possessions are illusions. Do not let yourself be unsettled by illusions."

"Mohammed never lost $8.3 million."

We reached the Hagia Sophia, where he hurried to my side to open the door. I walked away angrily, not with him, but with myself. And I didn't know why.

Another taxi driver, sipping tea as he leaned against his car some thirty yards away, regarded me with keen interest. He was short and stocky, a pendulous handle-bar mustache, common among older Turkish men, obscuring most of his face. He chugged back the tea and made no effort to hide the fact that he was following me closely, his mustache curling into a wide grin. Having grown accustomed to being stared at, I smiled back pleasantly.

Crowds of tourists perused the racks of cheap postcards and souvenirs at the small kiosks that lined the entrance to the mosque. I stepped into the cavernous inner shrine beyond the wide doorway, directly beneath the building's massive dome. Giant steel candelabras hung above, suspended on long cables from the ceiling. Each candelabra was easily over six feet in diameter. Dusty light bulbs, some of which were burnt out, traced their shapes.

Laughter exploded from a group of tourists nearby. They were milling around a large marble pillar, fascinated by a small hole in the structure, in which they took turns sticking their thumbs. Legend had it that making a full circle of your hand without lifting your thumb from the hole led to good luck.

I ducked into a high-ceilinged passageway to the left that curled upward along the wall of the mosque, leading to the upper levels. Sultans used to ride their horses through here in order to reach their thrones without having to dismount or touch in any way, the dirty peasant ground.

The interior artwork of the Hagia Sofia was as much of a creative achievement as the mosque itself. Gigantic mosaics lined the walls, depicting scenes from the Bible, with an image of Jesus Christ dominating the inside of the dome. Muslims, who did not believe in worshipping images, had plastered them over after seizing the city. After the overthrow of the Ottoman Empire, the government thought it more practical to turn the mosque into a museum and restore them, recognizing they would attract more tourist dollars.

I walked the entire length of the mid-level balcony, until I was back to where I started, with no sign of her. The upper level yielded the same result, and I was about to give up when I saw her. As if sensing my eyes on her, she looked up, directly at me. She seemed frozen in surprise, but I knew better. She was sizing me up.

I forced myself to stay calm as she moved toward the exit. I had to be careful. Any signs of haste on my part would draw the attention of the numerous guards in the area, who were already on edge about terrorism. They would shoot first and ask questions later.

She was gone by the time I reached the street, but I had done my job of getting her on the move. I was about to call Giancarlo for further instructions when I noticed Aytug milling about with the other cab drivers, treating himself to a strong cup of tea. Seeing me, he motioned me over.

"I heard her tell her driver to take her to Topkapi Palace," he said.

"I want to follow her."

Aytug laugh. "You've got it wrong, Mr. Cain. She wants you to follow *her*."

We threaded the afternoon traffic of the city, until we reached a narrow side street near the entrance to the famous landmark. A cobblestone path wound its way to the gate, where a guard stood by the ticket booth. Aytug was apparently on first name basis with him. They exchanged some pleasantries, and he then waved us through.

Topkapi Palace had been the official residence of the Ottoman sultans for three centuries. It sat upon the first hill of the famed Seven Hills of Rome, commanding a strategic view of the city and its vulnerable waters. The main building inside the wall was actually another fort, the second line of defense should the perimeter walls be breached. While the estate itself was expansive, the residential quarters, located within the inner fort, were surprisingly sparse and claustrophobic, by modern standards.

Aytug conjectured that Kerry was sightseeing, and if so, our best chance of catching her was to check each attraction methodically. He led me to a small room, where he said the sultans used to receive guests. Adjacent rooms used to house his harem. We went back outside, afterward, past a garden and into a stone cottage. It turned out to be a museum containing an extensive collection of antique jewelry, swords, Turkish suits of armors, and other artifacts of war. The colorful armor, representing various periods of Ottoman rule, hung against the walls and on racks anchored to the floor, while the jewelry rested inside glass display cases in the middle of the room. Holy relics, among them the golden chest believed to contain the mantle of the Prophet Mohammed, were also on display. Aytug maintained a running commentary through all of this, obviously enjoying the opportunity to show off his mastery of Turkish history.

As we joined the line shuffling past the exhibits, I turned to Aytug, "Are we actually looking for her or just sightseeing?"

"She's here," he responded, thumping me on the chest. He gestured across the room, where Kerry stood glowering at me.

Trying quickly to recover from the shock, I shot back my own version of a glower, but in truth I was filled with foreboding. She had an absolutely eerie way of materializing before me when I least expected it, more like an apparition than someone of flesh and blood. Her look of defiance always unsettled me. It made me feel as if I was the one with the need to repent.

Instead of running away, she headed straight for me, causing me to hesitate even more. People grumbled and cursed me openly, exhorting me to keep the line moving. I was about to comply, but realized that I might be playing right into Kerry's hands by confronting her.

As I considered my options, Turkish military policemen suddenly poured into the room. They ordered people out of the way and roughly shoved aside those who didn't move fast enough. One of the policemen pointed frantically at me, another one drew his gun, and people dropped to the floor, screaming. When no bullets flew, the crowd let out a roar, came to its feet as one animal, and surged toward the exit. A startled Kerry fought to avoid getting trampled, even as she remained determined to reach me. Aytug glanced around desperately, torn between loyalty to his Fare and fear for his survival. Apparently choosing survival, he clawed his way past the slower members of the stampeding crowd and out the door. It was then I realized that Kerry had also disappeared. Someone pushed me roughly from behind and, assuming it to be a policeman, I thought it best to comply. We reached the doorway, where a final push sent me stumbling outside, into a small garden.

When I finally turned around, I found Bambi standing over me, eyeing me quizzically.

"What are *you* doing here?" I asked, surprised.

"I've been following you."

"All the way to Turkey? Why?"

She ignored my question. "What are you doing on the ground?"

"You put me here."

"Not me. Let's go. You can't stay here."

"Who's objecting?"

With the sound of the police behind us, we ran through the inner courtyard and out to the large, grass-covered perimeter. She exhorted me to slow down, once we reached a safe distance, threw her arm over my shoulder, and smiled broadly.

"Act casual," she said, gesturing toward the guard at the front gate.

She flashed him a spectacular smile that visibly disoriented him, leaving him no other choice but to wave us through. Once outside, we broke into a run again, passing rows of attached houses with signs identifying them as bed-and-breakfast inns. We finally paused for breath at the corner, by a small park.

"The coast is clear," she said.

I discovered, at this point, that we were right behind the Hagia Sophia. I had assumed our cab ride to Topkapi had been a long one but, actually, we'd only made a wide circle, following the direction of traffic, and doubled back to get to the palace.

A street trolley rumbled by, impeding our progress momentarily. We then crossed to a low, unassuming building opposite the Hagia Sophia, the "Basilica Cistern." A set of stairs led us to the city's former underground water storage facility, constructed centuries ago, which now served as another tourist attraction.

Piped-in gothic music greeted us as we took the stairs to the lower level. A small concession stand offered rickety wired tables and chairs, and here we sat down to rest. On the far end of the facility, an upside-down Medusa head, carved into the concrete pillar, stared back at us.

"Got there just in time," she said.

"Just in time for what?"

"You were set up. Someone was supposed to slip an artifact from the exhibit into your pocket to make it look like you stole it. That's why the police came charging after you."

"You're joking."

"Check your pockets."

Inside my left pants pocket was a tiny stone arrowhead. It was similar to the ones on the tips of the spears adorning the suits of armor at Topkapi.

"It's just a small arrowhead."

"The Turkish government doesn't take kindly to their cultural artifacts being stolen. You're looking at several years in jail if you get caught."

"Christ! Who would do something like that?"

"That's a rhetorical question, right?"

"Kerry? I know she hates me, but she would never do that to me."

"Don't worry. It's a fake. Still, it would have taken some time for the police to figure it out."

I regarded her for a moment. "What are you doing here, anyway?"

"I figured you could use some company."

"Really, be serious."

"I'm on a mission for the CIA."

"Okay, I'll go along with the joke. Feel free to elaborate."

"My job as a stripper was a cover. I'm retired now, but I'm doing one last favor for the Bureau."

"I find that hard to believe."

"That I'm in the CIA?"

"That you would be stripping as a cover. You're incredibly intelligent. It would seem like a terrible waste."

"Compliment duly noted. But think about it: What's the first thing most foreign nationals do when they enter the U.S.?"

"Go to a strip club?"

"Exactly."

"Even if that was true, how many foreign spies can you intercept working in one of the hundreds of club in New York? It's not like they all make a stopover and meet at Baubles before continuing to their destination, is it?"

"I wasn't a spy. I was an envoy. I conveyed classified information between the U.S. and foreign leaders visiting the United Nations. All that secrecy for meeting them played right into our protocols to protect their activities here without arousing suspicions. Most world leaders are men. They have no trouble believing that their counterparts would go through all that trouble for a sexual dalliance, especially when they come from countries with conservative religious views."

"So you were never really an actual stripper?"

"I did strip. My cover had to look authentic. My call girl services, however, were a cover for passing them information. The sexiest thing I ever did in those hotel rooms was share a glass of wine and play Barry Manilow music. Celine Dion and Destiny's Child were also big."

"What about all those stories you used to tell me?"

"Scriptwriters. They created scenarios for me to use on customers. Made it all more authentic."

"They sounded so real."

"I had a good team."

"And you're not a licensed therapist, either? That certificate in your office is a phony?"

"No, *that* I am. I retired from the other business because the pay was terrible, and I couldn't keep the tips."

"What about all those powerful men you used to see – how could they still be your clients?"

"What can I tell you? I'm a good listener. A lot of times, they just need someone to talk to that's fully trustworthy and has no hidden agenda. One thing I never did was lie to them or pass on misinformation. I refused to, if I suspected the information was unreliable – for both sides. They appreciated that."

"What's so special about me that you flew all the way over here to protect me?"

"Well, you *are* special, but it's not exactly about you. It's about Kerry. I'm following a lead. That's all I can tell you, for now."

"So that's why you kept calling my office, trying to get me back?"

She nodded.

"You're playing with my head, right? This is all B.S. Part of your cure?"

"Do you want to know the truth?"

"No, because then you'll probably tell me that you have to kill me."

Her phone rang. "It's for you."

"You got out of there just in time," said Giancarlo.

"So I've heard. Luckily, Bambi pushed me out of the building before the police could get to me."

"I wasn't inside the building," she corrected me.

"*Someone* pushed me," I said.

"As long as you got out, that's all that matters," said Giancarlo.

"Bambi told me about the fake arrowhead they slipped into my pocket. What was the point of that? I would eventually have been exonerated."

"The PR value. Imagine the headline: "'Cain Kahn arrested for stealing priceless historical artifact!'"

"Even if it was genuine, it's just a small arrowhead. I can't see people looking at me as a hardcore criminal."

"It's not the crime. It's the act. They'll question your credibility, even more so because you didn't take anything of great value. You'll be seen as so desperate and down on your luck that you'd steal anything you can get your hands on."

"Maybe you're right. But when it's proven a fake, they'll know that I was clearly framed."

"No one will believe you. They'll assume you worked out a deal with the Turkish government to dismiss the charges."

"What could I possible gain by taking such a dumb risk?"

"People's sympathy. Anything to place more blame on Kerry and get people to hate her."

"This PR stuff is complicated."

"That's why it's best to leave it to the professionals."

"So what do we do now?"

"Bambi's taking you to a safe house."

"A safe house? Can't Bambi's CIA connection ring up the Chief of Police and explain the misunderstanding?"

"She told me she's working on that. For now, it's best to keep you out of their way," he said.

"By the way, how long have you known that Bambi used to be with the CIA? I didn't even know you two knew each other."

"We didn't, until about an hour ago. Mind-blowing, right? She's the one who got clearance for me and the photographer when I heard you were going to the U.N. Makes perfect sense, now."

"I still don't know how much of all this to believe."

"Just follow her lead. She thinks there's a reason why Kerry is going through so much trouble to get you arrested."

"It's obvious. She doesn't like losing."

"Losing what? She's already got your money. It's as if she's trying to get you out of the way. But what are you in the way of?"

"So your theory is...?"

"Well, it's Bambi's theory. She won't tell me, but judging by the amount of resources they've put at her disposal, it's got to be something big. For now, put yourself in her hands. I'll handle the PR. She'll keep you safe."

Putting myself in Bambi's hands wasn't such a bad idea. Her outfit was nothing special, just a modest, tasteful dress, in accordance with Muslim culture. With her body, however, nothing seemed tasteful.

"Hold that thought," she said.

"What thought?"

"You were talking out loud again. My love life may be in the dumps, but I'm still in the market for a donor. We'll discuss it when we get back to the States. Come on, let's get a bite. I'm starving."

We crept back up to the top of the stairs, where she carefully checked the streets to make sure we had not been followed. The coast being clear, she rushed me down the block to what turned out to be a small, private hotel.

Most of the buildings in the neighborhood originally belonged to wealthy Ottoman residents during the early part of the 20th century. Today, with Ottoman cuisine in vogue, many residents found a new source of income turning their homes into historical bed and breakfasts.

We ate in a meticulously restored dining room, with the landlady enthusiastically piling onto my plate, food that she boasted was authentic Ottoman fare.

"It's fit for a sultan," she said. "Did you know the art of cooking reached such a peak of popularity at Topkapi Palace that as many as 100 chefs would specialize on a single dessert for the sultan?"

"That's very interesting."

"Try this Raki," she said, pouring a clear liquid into my glass.

"It's their local drink," explained Bambi. "Anise and water. It's quite good."

The landlady filled my glass half-way with the alcohol and topped it off with water, whereupon the mixture immediately turned cloudy. It tasted rather diluted at first, with a strong liquorish flavor, but I warmed up to it after the second glass.

Bambi was on the phone again to Giancarlo, and after a few low-keyed words, she handed the phone to me.

"Do you still have that fake Byzantium arrowhead?" he asked.

"Yes."

"Your location's been compromised. Wipe your fingerprints off it, but don't let the landlady see it. Follow Bambi's lead," he said.

Bambi was already settling the bill with the landlady, who then offered me a bottle of Raki as a souvenir. A cab arrived moments later and we jumped in. As we drove away, several police cruisers pulled up to the hotel and immediately disgorged a group of uniformed men, who surrounded the startled woman. One officer noticed our cab, and he quickly jumped back into his cruiser and turned on his siren.

"Take the next left," Bambi ordered the driver, and he quickly steered the vehicle into an alley. "Wait a moment."

The police cruiser hurtled past us, after which she asked our driver to continue.

"The police wants the lady?" the driver asked.

Bambi pointed to me.

"Ah, yes," he said. "You are safe with me, Mr. Cain. The Turkish people love you."

"Perhaps they can take up a collection for me."

"You are a funny guy," he said.

I was serious. I literally had no money left, except for the cash in my pocket. As we traveled the narrow streets of the Old City, Bambi took the arrowhead from me and tossed it discreetly out the window.

"Where are we going?" I asked her.

"The Grand Bazaar."

"Are we meeting someone there?"

"I want to buy a carpet. They have great bargains."

"I'm sorry about your lover's spat, but you can't seriously be thinking of comforting yourself by shopping right now? Let's just book the next flight out of here."

"That's quite a sexist thing to say. Not all women use shopping as therapy after a fight with their lover."

"Isn't that what you're doing?"

"You shouldn't try to analyze me. You could get hurt without the proper training."

"How can that hurt me?"

"I know karate. I can knock you out cold with one punch."

It was called the Grand Bazaar, but the entrance to one of Turkey's most popular tourist attractions was anything but grand. One of the oldest covered bazaars in the world, it boasted more than 4,000 shops, all under one roof. Yet, there were no soaring archways or glittering neon signs to greet visitors; no vast parking lot of cars surrounding the stores. We entered from a quiet residential side street and followed a narrow, vine-covered alley to the interior of the plaza. The only indication that this was a world-famous attraction was an unobtrusive plaque on the wall. Otherwise, one could have passed the street a hundred times and not realized what lay through the gates.

As we entered the facility, peddlers suddenly materialized around us, from young boys to very old men. They entreated us to buy their products under threats that their families would starve otherwise. Vendors, sitting atop of spread-out carpets, were packed tightly together as far as the eyes could see, their colorful merchandise strewn before them on the floor. The more prosperous ones had actual storefronts, and these occupied the wall to the left. They sold everything from the ubiquitous "evil eye" pendants to packaged candies, postcards, clothing, glassware, kitchen utensils, bedding and, of course, every possible type, size and design of carpets.

They called Bambi "beautiful lady" and were all surprisingly respectful toward her. It helped that they were trying to sell her something. Free enterprise could not only bring world peace, it could also smooth out relationships between the sexes.

She paused before a storefront and, seconds later, the owner shot out with several glasses of tea, urgently inviting us inside. He addressed Bambi in Chinese, but getting a blank stare, he tried Korean. Like most peddlers in Turkey, he spoke a few essential words in almost every language, an important skill for doing business with an international clientele. After years of repetition, their pronunciations were impeccable.

She thanked him in Turkish, whereupon he unleashed an excited torrent of words in his native tongue. When she asked for the price of a carpet in English, he suddenly switched to a halting, though functional imitation of that language. He then pulled her inside, insisting he would not take "no" to an offered cup of tea.

We waited on a padded leather bench as he shoved his slowly moving assistant toward a carpet on the wall, which he urged the young man to take down immediately. He himself tore down another carpet and flung it on the floor before us with great flourish. His young assistant, whom he introduced as his son, quickly grabbed a similar carpet and sent it sailing through the air, to land noisily at our feet for inspection.

Throughout this theatrical performance, the two men maintained a running, passionate commentary on the significance of the patterns and designs of each rug. Bambi smiled, asked a question every now and then, and listened thoughtfully to the elaborate answers.

The owner's face lit up when she spoke, and he'd compliment her good taste and keen powers of observations. She'd nod appreciatively and, with a wave of her hand, indicate her desire to see the next carpet. Finally, she pointed to one that caught her eye and he immediately exclaimed: "Three thousand for the beautiful lady. I cannot go lower for I must feed my children."

"Too high," she said. "I will give you $1,500."

"I am already losing money. I will catch hell from my wife tonight. The carpet is worth much more. She will say I am not a good businessman."

Bambi remained unimpressed. He sighed, shook his head like a defeated man, and consulted with his son. He came back shortly.

"You are much too beautiful not to have all that you desire in life. I will give you this splendid carpet for $2,700. It is my absolute final price. You are taking the food out of my children's mouth."

"You're mocking me because I'm a woman," she said. "I would not give two thousand for it, although I must admit the pattern is exquisite and it is very well made."

"It's of superior quality. The best in all of Turkey, worth ten times its selling price. I sell it with great pain in my heart. I do not wish to part with it, but I must feed my children. I cannot go lower than $2,400. It is less than I paid for it, but when my children's stomachs are empty, I must fill them."

Bambi suddenly grabbed my shirt and pulled me up from the bench.

"I changed my mind," she said. "I wish to check another store."

The owner immediately panicked and begged her to sit down again.

"At least, the beautiful lady should not insult Kalim's hospitality and finish her tea first," he said.

"I'll finish your tea, but I have been insulted enough with such high prices for your carpets."

"All right. Only $2,200. Take it. You won't find a better bargain in all of Turkey. My children will not eat meat tonight but fill their bellies with stale bread. But I am a poor man, so what can I do? I must make a living."

Bambi downed her tea and handed him the glass. He followed her out of the store, mortified, desperately begging her to return. She remained firm, saying she was not interested. He finally slunk back to his store, a mortally wounded and defeated man.

The aisles exploded with laughter as the other vendors, having watched Bambi's dramatic exit, heartedly congratulated her for her keen powers of observation.

"Kalim's carpets are overpriced and of terrible quality," said one. "Come here, beautiful lady, mine are the best in all of Turkey. I will give you the best prices."

"Weren't you a little harsh back there?" I said. "He really was giving you a good deal."

"In Turkey, it's an insult to a storeowner if you don't haggle prices with them."

"Yes, but you took off on him rather rudely."

"I'm going to be paying him the greatest compliment one can possibly pay a shop keeper."

"Refusing to buy his product?"

"Believe me, I'm about to make his day."

She stopped abruptly, turned back toward the store, and walked inside. Everyone stared in wonderment as she reappeared with Kalim and shook his hand in front of the store. She gave him the shipping address in the U.S. to forward the carpet to. When she kissed him on the forehead, they went wild. His reputation was forever established among his colleagues; his triumph today destined to be eagerly recounted for years to come.

"Okay, that was weird," I remarked. "Although, I shouldn't be surprised anymore by the things you can do to men."

We weaved through the many intricate and random aisles of the bazaar, until finally I had absolutely no idea of where I was or where I was going. Bambi assured me she knew her way around. She had been here many times before.

We presently entered a narrow alleyway that forced us to proceed in a single file. Bambi took the lead, plunging confidently through every twist and turn like a seasoned explorer. At one point, however, she slipped around a corner and out of my line of sight. Just then, a hand clamped around my mouth and pulled me aside. I found myself in a smaller, darker side-alley, and twisting free, I turned to discovered that my abductor was a woman. And that woman was Kerry.

I recalled my vow to do something to her when I caught her again. Yes, grip her throat and force her to transfer the money back to my account.

"Follow me," she commanded, and I obediently fell in step behind her. The truth was that I would have followed her anywhere. She was truly a sight to behold. She had a lean and limber torso; long and muscular thighs that pumped furiously through the crowd in fluid and graceful symmetry. Her long hair, caught in the breeze of her rapid pace, whipped about her body like the mane of a racehorse.

She rounded the corner of one aisle, then another, and finally broke free to the light of the main aisle, near an exit. We emerged onto a small parking lot that was filled with empty tour buses. The drivers were clustered around a tea cart, sipping tea as they waited for their travel groups to finish their shopping. Up the street, a trolley pulled into the station. Meanwhile, next to me, a taxi drifted over and the passenger door swung open. The driver was the same one I had seen waiting at the Hagia Sophia.

"Get in," ordered Kerry.

"You're joking, of course. You just tried to get me arrested with that fake arrowhead stunt. Now you want me to willingly jump into a cab with you and go who knows where?"

"I want to show you something."

"A bank?"

"Don't be silly."

"Damn it, you've got all my money and you're asking me not to be silly!"

"Don't curse."

I grabbed her hand to pull her away from the cab.

"Cain, my driver has a gun under his jacket, and he won't hesitate to use it, if he thinks you're not cooperating."

"A gun! What's going on here?"

"You don't know the half of what you've gotten yourself in."

"What *I've* gotten myself into? I'm not exactly chasing you by choice."

She yanked her hand free. I was about to reclaim it when the driver suddenly revealed a glint of metal under his jacket.

Bambi emerged from the far end of the bazaar at that moment. Seeing me take some steps toward her, Kerry pulled me back violently. Before I could recover my balance, she shoved me into the back seat of the cab and the driver pulled away.

Bambi shouted something at me as she reached the curve that I could not make out, but her lips took on a familiar shape that I recognized as "shit!" It was apparently loud enough to be heard by the men around her, for they laughed and tipped their tea glasses to her, and she shook her head and walked away in frustration.

6

We drove to the center of Istanbul's Old City, and we pulled up shortly in front of a round and weathered brick structure.

"Where are we?" I asked.

"Follow me," she said.

Inside the building, a young boy stood by an open elevator and came to attention as we entered it. He smiled politely, pulled the doors close and started the creaking elevator's slow and painful ascent. Arriving at the top floor, he pulled open the doors and pointed across a dusty room. Kerry marched over and opened a small door and, as I followed, I noticed a sign overhead that identified the structure as Galata Tower.

The door led out to an observation deck, which commanded a dizzying view of Istanbul's waters and many of its mosques and cultural sites. Another time, I would have been impressed. At this moment, however, I was aware of who was standing next to me and what she had done under frighteningly similar circumstances at Gibbs Hill Lighthouse. I was not afraid of her. I was afraid of myself.

Below us, at the foot of the tower, Kerry's driver watched anxiously. His large mustache twitched nervously, as if on a hinge. He didn't like the situation, and neither did I.

"This tower used to serve as a sentry post for guards watching the water for approaching enemy invaders," she said.

"I read the same guide book."

"You know that I have family in Istanbul."

I narrowed my eyes at her and maintained a safe distance. "I don't know what you're up to right now, and I don't care. I just want my money back."

"Think of someone else besides yourself, sometimes. Try to listen to what I tell you."

"I'll be happy to listen to anything you have to say once my bank account is back to normal."

"You're disappointing me."

"I didn't know I had to meet your expectations."

I grabbed her arm and instantly knew it was a mistake. Below us, the driver dug into his jacket, and I let her go.

"Will you listen to me for a moment?" she said.

She averted her eyes and stared at the view. Her hair floated languidly in the warm breeze. The loose strands occasionally brushed my face. We were that close now.

The old feelings were resurfacing. She could still get to me. I braced myself, like an explorer marshalling his strength to plunge into that unknown jungle: where the possibilities, the rewards and the dangers where incalculable; where past and future all merged into a single state of being. Goddamn it, she was turning me into a poet again.

Yet, this time, there was something different about her that I had never seen before. She had always appeared in control. Now, she really did seem to need help. Then, again, my other, smaller brain might have been doing the thinking right now. Last time I followed its advice, it cost me dearly.

"All right, I'm listening," I said.

"I didn't want to take your money."

"Then I'm sure you won't mind giving it back."

"I can't."

"You mean, you won't?"

"No, I can't. I don't have it anymore."

"Try another line. That one's not going to fly with me."

"It's the truth."

"Then who has it?"

"John Denver. At least, he used to. I let him invest my money."

"_My_ money, Goddamn it! And how is John Denver suddenly in the picture again? He's apparently in every part of my life now."

"He was taking his company public and I figured it would be as good an investment as any."

I was gripped by a sudden wave of nausea. "We're talking about PipeStation, right? The same company that went public against my advice, resulting in a catastrophic IPO failure? The one that was chased into bankruptcy within weeks by nearly 30 investor lawsuits?"

She nodded.

"Why would you throw your money away on that train wreck? You, of all people? You've got your insider sources who would have told you it was way too early to go public. They would have told you the huge risk you were taking."

"Yes, I knew the risks, but I didn't care anymore. I was so mad at you, I just wanted to get rid of the money. Anything that reminded me of you."

"You're not that kind of emotional girl. Or that stupid."

"Maybe I am."

It occurred to me that she was leaning dangerously far over the railing, as if she was about to jump off.

"What are you doing?" I asked, and quickly pulled her back.

"That's what you'd like me to do, isn't it?"

"Of course not." I reached for my phone, but then remembered my service was not set up for Turkey.

"Use mine," she offered.

I dialed up Capital Partners. "Dan?"

"Cain! Christ! What the hell are you doing in Turkey? I've been trying desperately to reach you for the past week. I need you, man! I'm on my knees, Goddamn it. You've got to come back. Your place is here."

"Let me guess. Since PipeStation's implosion, everyone wants your head?"

"That's just for appetizers. For the main course, they want to rip my balls out of my scrotum and stuff them down my throat. The PipeStation debacle spooked all of my clients."

"That's what you get for not following my timeline. It was all there in my report. In fact, our major investors insisted upon that condition in their contracts. I can't imagine how you got them to go along with your decision."

"Well, they sort of assumed that you had given us your blessing."

"They knew you had fired me. I no longer worked there. It was front page news."

"I might have suggested to them that, since you felt personally responsible for bringing them in, you were still advising us on the sideline."

"Do you realize that was borderline illegal?"

"We're buddies, man. Water under the bridge, right? Now we issue a press release, call it a bureaucratic screw-up. You had clearly been against the IPO. The guilty have been beheaded. You're solidly behind all our other accounts a thousand per cent."

"You're joking, right?"

"I saved you the trouble of writing the press release. Just need your blessing"

"What drugs are you taking?"

"Not a drug, buddy. A dish. Humble pie. I'm eating it all, now, and proudly. You were absolutely right. There, I said it. I'm risking everything to take you back, but I don't care."

"Who's talking now, you or Denver?"

"What do you mean?"

"Denver put the screws on you to fire me, didn't he? He wanted a clear shot at Kerry's money – at my money – but had to get me out of the way, first. He knew I wouldn't give the go-ahead to take PipeStation public so soon."

"I'm hearing static, buddy. You're making noise, but no sense. What does Denver have to do with this?"

"Kerry's money was ripe for the taking. He got her to invest it all in the company."

"Check the prospectus. The only major investors on record were the ones you brought in. Her name would have come up at some point, with that kind of money."

I turned to Kerry. "When did you invest the money?"

"I wasn't an investor," she said. "I bought shares in the IPO."

"We would have seen that large a purchase, too," said Dan, overhearing her, "unless she came in near the end. By then, it was pure chaos. Day traders were buying and selling millions of shares to the penny, causing wild stock fluctuations. The SEC is still trying to sort out the mess."

"When did Denver confirm the trade?" I asked her.

"I don't remember. I wasn't paying attention. Hardly matters, at this point. The shares are worthless, right?"

"It *does* matter. I don't think he ever intended to buy you the stocks in the first round. He knew they would tank. In fact, he was betting on it."

"You mean he faked the purchases?" Dan queried.

"Something less scrupulous. My guess is that by holding off long enough to buy at the bottom, he was able to keep most of Kerry's money to pay off his personal debts and have enough left over to retire with. Putting less money in toward the end also kept the purchase under the SEC radar."

"Jesus, that's devious, but brilliant," said Dan. "Sorry, pal, no offense."

I regarded Kerry. "You're not that dumb," I said to her and, surprisingly, she almost seemed to smile. "You intentionally threw away my money, didn't you? You wanted to make sure you screwed me royally."

This time, she turned away, and she actually appeared saddened by the accusation.

"Hello?" called Dan.

"You're not off the hook, either," I said to him. "Why would you agree to the wishes of a jerkwad like Denver, at the risk of pissing away your company's credibility? What was in it for you?"

"It's a long story."

"Goddamn it! I'm missing an important piece of the puzzle here."

Dan was silent. Finally, he said, "You want me to cry, too? I can do that."

"That won't be necessary."

I snapped the phone shut and returned it to Kerry.

"You don't have a choice. You have to take your old job back," she said. "It's the only way to fight for your reputation — from the inside. No one else will have you."

"Since when did you start caring about my reputation? Something's going on here. It can't be that simple."

"You don't have a choice," she repeated.

"Were you fucking Denver?"

She suddenly pushed away from me and stared angrily into space. Finally, she turned to me again, her eyes narrowed, her breathing heavy.

"You keep disappointing me," she said.

At that moment, the frantic sound of my name floated up from below. Bambi, emerging from a cab, was waving me down furiously.

"What's that bitch doing here?" said Kerry.

I felt the old, familiar sense of dread again. Kerry suddenly sprung back inside the tower and leaped into the waiting elevator. The boy stared at her, mesmerized, until her urgent voice snapped him into action.

It took a few seconds before the significance of her behavior finally dawned on me. I gave chase, but reached the elevator too late. I ran back to the porch to warn Bambi, but it was a pointless move. Kerry's driver was holding her and her driver at bay with the gun. The two men were cursing each other out in Turkish. Despite the gun being pointed menacingly at him, Bambi's driver spitted out even more passionate insults. Finally, infuriated, Kerry's driver fired the gun into the air, freezing everybody in place.

Kerry emerged at that instant and leaped at her driver, slapping him on top of his head repeatedly and berating him for firing off the gun. She tore the weapon from his hand and waved Bambi back. She then dragged her driver into the car, jumped in on the other side, and they sped away.

The elevator returned at that point and I jumped in, needlessly explaining to the boy that I needed to get down. Bambi eyed me suspiciously when I reached her, punched me in the shoulder, and returned to the car. Her driver followed, sliding in behind the wheel.

"The police are right behind us," she said.

As if on cue, the distant wail of police sirens pierced the air. The squeal of tires taking a sharp turn in the narrow streets followed and, shortly, a police cruiser leaped into view a block away.

"Come on," called Bambi.

I jumped into the back seat. "How did the police find us so quickly?"

"Your precious Kerry tipped them off."

"It doesn't make sense," I said.

"Actually, it's making more sense than ever before," she replied.

We prowled the back alleys of the city for nearly half an hour, changing directions, doubling back on ourselves, making sure we were not being followed. Finally, we veered back onto the highway and sped up again.

"What happened back there?" I asked.

"There's been a hitch."

"That doesn't sound good."

"Kerry's pick-pocket accomplice, the one who slipped the fake arrowhead into your pocket, actually stole a *real* arrowhead from Topkapi. As far as the police are concerned, you're still a thief."

"I don't get it," I said. "Planting the phony arrowhead on me was perfect. No actual crime was committed. Why would Kerry then have him commit a real crime?"

"We think he acted on his own initiative."

"Why would he steal an arrowhead?"

"That's what thieves do."

"I mean, as long as he was at it, why not go for something more valuable, like one of those priceless jewels?"

"Our best guess is that he saw it as the perfect robbery. The police expected an arrowhead to be missing from the exhibit, and that's exactly what was missing. You're the suspect, so he's in the clear."

"Yes, but how much can he get for it?"

"For many people here, it's a year's worth of wages. It's also easier to palm off. More expensive historical items are too easy to track."

We fell silent as the car traced the shore of the Bosphorus. The day was waning as the sun retreated behind the hills. Lights sprung up in windows along the road. The noise of day subsided as the more subdued sounds of night took hold.

"Where are we going?"

"The airport."

"Won't the police be checking passports? I'm sure I'm on their wanted list."

"We're not taking an international flight here. We're going domestic, to Ephesus. I've got contacts that can get us into Greece, from where we can get home safely."

"What happened to chasing after Kerry?"

"At this point, we don't know who's chasing whom. It completely surprised us that she came after you today."

"She did it before, at the lighthouse; only this time, she brought someone with a gun."

"Was it her idea to go to the tower?"

"Yes, and I don't think her driver was very happy about it. They fought about it in the car."

"What did she want to talk to you about?"

"I'm not exactly sure. She told me she had given my money to that fat little scumbag, John Denver, and I completely lost it. I was really upset."

"Why climb the tower to tell you?"

"I keep asking myself the same question. In fact, looking back on it, I think that wasn't really what she wanted to talk about. I think she wanted to tell me something else, but I guess I was too angry to hear her out. Your appearance seemed to upset her, and that's when she took off again."

She passed the phone over to me. She had dialed Giancarlo.

"Sorry about that," I said. "I know it wasn't part of the plan to consort with the enemy."

"Not your fault. When a gun is pointed at you, nothing that follows is part of any plan," he sympathized.

"Well, I think, at least, that I was finally making progress with her."

"Yes, until you tried to kill her."

"What are you talking about?"

"Did you at any point hold on to her, maybe to pull her away from the railing?"

"As a matter of fact, yes. How did you know about that?"

"Ever hear of the Internet?"

"She looked as if she was about to jump. I was trying to hold her back."

"That's when they snapped the picture. It looks as if you were trying to push her off."

"How the hell did they get a picture like that? We were in the middle of nowhere."

"Someone must have used a telephoto lens from across the street. You were set up."

"It's just not like Kerry."

"That's the least of your worries."

"The stolen arrowhead?"

"It's really complicated things."

Bambi tapped my shoulder as the airport control tower rose into view. "Brace yourself," she said.

We approached the domestic counter minutes later to book our flight. The ticket agent clicked away on her computer, giving us a smile that I thought, in my paranoia, to be suspicious. I expected the police to descend upon us any minute, tackle me to the ground, and beat me to a bloody pulp before hauling me off to jail in handcuffs. It was not until we were on the plane and the dark landscape of Turkey floated slowly below us that I breathed easier. Bambi's eyes fell upon me as she shook back her hair.

"Bambi…" I began.

"I know that look. Don't get sentimental on me. Stay focused."

"I just wanted to thank you."

"That's acceptable."

"Would you believe me if I told you that my obsession with her is more than just about the money? I won't deny $8.3 million is a lot of money, but maybe there's more?"

"Even seven stories below, from the foot of the tower, I could see that you still felt something for her. It goes beyond the money."

"Do you want to know the truth?"

"When a man tells me that, he's usually setting me up for a really big lie."

"Don't think of me as a club client from your previous life."

"I never have."

"What I wanted to tell you was that the newspapers got it wrong about my affair."

"That's always a popular defense, and not necessarily a wrong one. The media isn't known for the scrupulous accuracy of its reporting, especially when it comes to celebrity scandals."

"Honestly, I was totally faithful. Except for that one time."

"Which 'one time?' The first or the 10th time?"

"Well, there was really only one time. It was a lie about the rest."

"Even so, that's just a technicality. If you were going to screw just one other person in the world, it didn't have to be her boss."

"Her boss blackmailed me into doing it."

"That's a new defense. Why didn't you mention it before?"

"I didn't know if I could trust you."

"Fair enough. So what's this deep, dark secret in your past that could force you to cheat on your girlfriend with her boss?"

"Not my past. Kerry's. I did it to protect her."

"Oh?"

"Her boss, Katrina Spelling, threatened to go to the SEC about Kerry's insider trading activities. She had evidence linking Kerry to a ring that manipulated stock prices. Kerry would have been looking at five to ten years if the SEC found out."

"So you valiantly had sex with Spelling in order to save Kerry's reputation?"

"Yes, I guess so."

"Even if that were true – and that's a big 'if' – after the scandal broke, why didn't Spelling do anything to defend herself? She got just as much blow-back as you, maybe even more. The media portrayed her as a man-hungry cougar. She was vilified by women's group for undermining the accomplishments of fellow sisters in the men's club of Wall Street. Not to mention, Human Resources condemned her for violating the sacred office policy against bosses having sex with the lovers of their subordinates. She resigned from her job in disgrace. That was as good a time as any to drag Kerry down with her. She had nothing to lose."

"I threatened to expose her blackmail scheme if she had. That would have opened her up to prosecution too."

"It would have just been seen as a wild accusation. You couldn't prove it."

"I had copies of all the emails and phone messages she left me."

"I'm surprised she was that careless."

"Some people lack common sense."

"You don't survive that many years on Wall Street by leaving a paper trail."

"Everybody slips up now and then."

"That's not a slip-up, that's a major stumble."

"Well, that's what happened."

"And *was* Kerry involved in manipulating stocks?"

"Yes."

"How can you be sure? The documents could have been faked."

"I know her signature. No one can fake that. I also checked the transactions against trading records to see if they were real. They were."

"You explained all this to her, right? She should have understood."

"She understood perfectly. The next day, she cleaned out my bank accounts."

I studied the misty terrain of Turkey until the plane hit a cloud bank and the scene faded.

"You're a very beautiful woman," I said.

"Tell me something I don't know."

"You're a great therapist. Probably the best in the world."

"That's a compliment worth keeping."

"How did you make the switch from dancer/super spy to therapist?"

"The better question is 'why?' To tell you the truth, stripping was fun for a cover, but it *was* risky. There was also an incredibly amount of paperwork. Government agencies are so anal about documentation that they can suck all the fun out of fun itself."

"How did you pick therapy to get into?"

"When I found out how much they paid 'real' therapists for the same advice I gave away free as a dancer, that sealed it. My girlfriend at that time – she's my fiancé now – had already been talking about starting a family and I needed a better-paying job. Even exciting spy careers are still government jobs, and government jobs don't pay too well and completely suck away your time."

A flight attendant, approaching us, placed her hand on my shoulder. "Are you Mr. Cain Kahn?" she asked.

"I am."

Almost instantly, two policemen materialized at our side, hands under their jackets. They gripped what I assumed to be concealed weapons.

"Please accompany me to the back of the plane," said one, squeezing my shoulder.

The other one threw himself into the seat next to Bambi, and quickly became flustered as she stared him into submission. "We only want to talk to your friend," he explained weakly.

I turned to the policeman escorting me down the aisle. "Are you going to kill me?"

"You have the wrong impression of Turkey, Mr. Cain. This is not *Midnight Express*," he said.

"I didn't steal the arrowhead. You can search me. You're not going to find anything."

"We know you didn't steal it, Mr. Cain. One of the guards chasing after you in Topkapi Palace recognized Ali Kerrk, a small-time thief who gets himself into mischief every now and then. He was right behind you. The guard saw him grab an arrowhead in the confusion. We caught up to him about an hour ago and recovered the artifact."

"If you know that, why are you arresting me?"

"For murder."

"Murder?"

"The murder of Mr. Kerrk."

"You just said you caught him with the arrowhead?"

"We did. Unfortunately, he was dead by then. Right now, you are the only logical person with a motive."

"What kind of motive could I possibly have? I didn't even know him?"

"It is not for me to think about such serious matters. I am simply doing my job. Our justice system will find out the truth."

"If I was after the arrowhead, why didn't I take it with me after killing him?"

"Perhaps you thought you did. Only, you did not realize it was the fake one."

The flight attendant addressed the policeman in Turkish; following which, he motioned for me to take an empty seat. The plane descended and rolled to a stop shortly, and passengers impatiently streamed down the aisle as if late for an appointment. We fell in line as, up ahead, Bambi shot me a mysterious glance. She motioned to the front of the cabin, where two male passengers stared hard at me.

The last of the regular passengers soon exited, except for the two men. They seemed particularly sluggish about getting their luggage from the overhead compartment. Bambi and I joined up again, boxed in by the two policemen. She nudged me slightly, trying to convey a message that I still could not decipher. At that moment, one of the two men suddenly threw himself between me and my escort. The other one lunged for the policeman in the front, knocking him into the seats and clearing the aisle for Bambi and me. I expected a frantic, bruising fight, perhaps even gun play, to follow. Instead, the four men stood at opposite sides of the aisle, flinging insults at each other. For all the world, they could have been a pair of bickering, long-suffering couples. Apparently, they've been through this before.

An hour later, Bambi and I were rolling through the hills of Turkey in a rented pick-up truck, into the blue-tinged mountains of Ephesus. Bambi handled the manual transmission with impressive ease, attacking the hills as if she had been driving a stick all her life.

The heat quickly overwhelmed the struggling air conditioning system, squeezing beads of sweat from every pore of our bodies. She was wearing a short-sleeve t-shirt, revealing surprisingly muscular yet shapely arms hewed through hundreds of hours of pole dancing. I craved a clean shower, but she still looked fresh and feminine, even as the sweat dripped from her pale skin. She was the Lara Croft of therapists.

"Did you know I'm actually wanted for the murder of the taxi driver?"

"Yes, we're working on it."

"Should I be worried?"

"Little league stuff," she said. Noticing my continued look of concern, she added, "I'm on it."

"Thanks," I said.

She laughed and kissed me on the cheek.

"What was that for?" I asked.

"You're an all-right guy. I could go for you if I was a man."

"That wouldn't exactly work," I said.

"Hey, that's how I roll."

"Where are we going now?"

"We attract too much attention together." She handed me an envelope. "Your ticket to Greece. The plane leaves tomorrow at 3:00 PM. We'll meet up on the plane. Don't try to make contact with me till then. If you see Kerry, call Giancarlo. He's our liaison. Don't try to handle her on your own again."

"I can't promise you that."

"If you had, I wouldn't have believed you, anyway."

She pulled the pick-up over by the side of the road, behind a faded and beat-up old taxi.

"That's your ride. Stay out of trouble."

She pushed me out and sped away in a cloud of dust. Minutes later, having gotten into the taxi, we lurched forward, and soon were rattling down the empty highway. Miles of green fields rushed past us, cut by large swatches of red poppy flowers. Farm tractors plodded along the hilly landscape, carving meticulous grooves into the mountainside. Groups of women, clothed in traditional Muslin garb, roamed the fields, scattering seeds before them. I finally closed my eyes and slept, until the driver shook me awake, explaining in broken English that we had reached our destination. His gold tooth stuck out of a bushy mustache, making it difficult for him to pronounce certain words. Short and scruffy, he ran to the other side to open the door for me.

We were at the entrance to one of the large, luxury resorts that were common along the Turkish Riviera, as this part of Ephesus was called because it bordered on the Mediterranean. The driver led me inside to the front desk, where he secured a room key and handed me a note.

"Speak to no one," read the note. "Lock yourself in your room until the driver comes for you tomorrow. His name is Erol." It was from Bambi.

Erol smiled and tipped his cap. "Tomorrow at noon, I pick you up," he said.

He left and, alone now, I realized that I had been booked into a surprisingly modern and opulent hotel. The reception area was wedged into a narrow ledge that looked down upon a giant indoor atrium, designed to convey the feeling of a Roman temple. Fake marble columns encircled a large, round pool surrounded by palm trees. The atrium roof was a mammoth glass dome that filtered and softened the light. The walls, also composed of glass, looked out to another, outdoor pool, beyond which was the Mediterranean Sea.

The hotel was popular with German tourists, who came down for long weekends, much like Americans who traveled to the Caribbean for a quick getaway. Tall, muscular, aglow with health, they roamed the hallways like giants among the smaller Turkish service staff.

Heeding Bambi's warning, I withdrew to my room and locked myself in. I switched on CNN to find my face on the screen, my exploits already big new around the county and, apparently, all over the world. A blow-by-blow recap of my rapid ascent from crime victim to cultural thief and homicidal suspect was the lead story, edging out Turkey's latest border skirmish with Iran. Yet, surprisingly, even Turkish officials appeared to be impressed by my exploits. They seemed to expect nothing less than to be given a run for their money by the famous Cain Kahn. They marveled at my ability to elude their sophisticated net of highly trained police officers. The fact that I was doing all of this in the company of an exotic beauty was an added bonus.

I could see Giancarlo's skillful manipulation behind the scene, as well as Bambi's web of connections to major police officials. It was sometimes too easy the way we eluded them. Yet it brought me little satisfaction. I was unable to shake the feeling that Kerry had tried to tell me something at Galata Tower, but I had been too stubborn to pick up on the clues. I finally fell asleep, desperately trying to hold on to the knowledge that she had once cared for me, and that she still could.

I awoke early the next morning to catch breakfast at the hotel's buffet table, located by the edge of the atrium pool on the ground floor. From my table, I could see all the floors of the hotel, which wrapped around the atrium like layers on a cake. The front of the reception desk on the third floor was already crowded with people and, among them, a familiar figure caught my eyes. She was tall enough to be another one of the many Nordic guests but, her back to me, I thought her stance intriguing. When she turned in my direction, there was no doubt. It was Kerry.

She was taking in the scene below and, as her eyes swept past my table, I braced for a sign of recognition. Yet, she merely turned again to the receptionist, accepted her receipt and, moments later, picked up her bag and walked away.

I sprang toward the escalator, thinking to intercept her, and watched in panic as she quickened her pace. In my haste, I stumbled and banged my knee, and when I looked up, she was gone.

It seemed a lifetime before I reached the hotel lobby, though it was probably just seconds. I brushed roughly against an elderly lady, who exclaimed, "How rude!" as she regained her balance. Bursting through the doors outside, I made it to the middle of the driveway just in time to watch Bambi's car disappear down the road.

"Follow that car," I said, jumping into an idling cab.

The driver regarded me warily and pointed to a set of luggage next to the cab. "I'm sorry, sir. I'm waiting for a lady who wishes to go to the airport."

"How many liras will she pay you?"

"Forty million."

"I'll give you twice as much."

The driver was short and lanky, with an overgrown handlebar mustache. He shrugged and eased out of the driveway. At the same time, the elderly lady sauntered out, a policeman trailing her. She pointed at me excitedly as several other officers joined them. They seemed to pause indecisively and, finally, at her insistence, they drifted into the middle of the driveway as my car turned into the access road.

"I wonder what Asis wants," said the driver, indicating one of the policemen in the middle of the driveway behind us.

"I'm in a rush. Can you find out later?"

"Of course. You Americans are always in a rush. You invented rush hour, but that is such a funny name. You are not rushing. You should call it slow hour."

"That's true."

"It's a funny joke. But it's funnier in Turkish. I'm Felix, by the way."

"Is that your real name?"

"No, but it's easier for Americans to pronounce than my real name."

"I don't suppose you studied comedy in New York?"

"As a matter of fact, I practiced on open mic night at Dangerfield's comedy club when I was going to school at Baruch College."

"It's good to know our American educational system is turning out such excellent cab drivers."

"Cab drivers are your best ambassadors."

"So I've been told."

"Anyway, I'm not a cab driver. I'm just making some extra money for my entrepreneurial venture, a bus tour company. I'm a natural, yes?"

"Absolutely."

By now, Kerry's car was no longer in sight, but Felix confidently drove on, apparently in no hurry to catch up.

"Are you sure you're going the right way?" I asked, finally.

"Of course. I have driven this road for 20 years. I show visitors all the sites."

"I'm not interested in the sites. I want to follow the American lady."

"I heard her tell Habib she wanted to see the sites. I know Habib very well. He always starts with the Roman ruins."

An hour into the ride, Felix turned into a small road and, presently, pulled over. Several tour buses and numerous cars lay scattered about on both sides of the road, as if abandoned *en mass* by the drivers. There was no one in sight, and nothing to account for interest in the spot. I regarded Felix skeptically as he motioned for me to cross the road and to head out into the field.

"I will meet you on the other end," he said.

I walked hesitantly in the indicated direction, and I was about to turn back, when a ticket booth mysteriously popped up in front of me, a young woman inside. She called me over and explained that I must buy a ticket, and I did so, wondering if I was the victim of another tourist scam. There were no gates or any kind of fencing to indicate an entrance to anything. I continued walking until a pair of marble Roman columns rose out of the ground, behind a small hill. Following a downgrade, I came across a group of tourists. Their guide was explaining that the columns once supported important government buildings. Large holes dug into the mountainside across from us were once storefronts, from which merchants sold their wares, he explained.

As I followed behind the group, the view suddenly widened to reveal the Roman ruins of Ephesus. Scores of marble buildings in various states of decay traced out an ancient metropolis, once a center of government and commerce in the country. The narrow marble road snaked past numerous crumbling buildings, chipped statues and columns, until it reached the façade of the famous Celsus Library. Once, it contained the most comprehensive store of knowledge in the world. Today, all that knowledge could easily fit on a computer disk. Across from the library, a combination Roman bathhouse and outhouse, and one of the first recorded brothels in the world, now lay exposed to the elements.

"A secret underground passage once connected the library and brothel. Husbands could discreetly slip away for hours of pleasure while their unsuspecting wives assumed they were hard at work among the books," said the guide.

Down the road from the brothel was the world's first known advertisement: a left foot and the figure of a lady carved into stone, indicating the brothel up the road, on the left. Farther down was the amphitheater where St. Paul the Apostle nearly incited a riot by preaching revolution against the government. Today, it was the setting for musical concerts and theatrical performances, hosting such international stars as Julio Iglesias and Botticelli.

The road finally spilled into a large field teeming with souvenir stands, the ubiquitous rug sellers, and food stalls. I came upon a stall that sold digital photographs of people walking among the ruins. Enterprising vendors snapped pictures of the tourists to sell to them as they exited the site, apparently taking their cue from amusement parks.

Recognizing my face among the prints, the vendor plucked my picture and offered it to me. I shook my head, seeing no need to waste money on myself. As he put it back, however, I saw another familiar face, and that was of Kerry. She looked absolutely radiant. The glaring sun of Turkey, so harsh upon the faces of others, imbued her with an almost ethereal glow. Her blue eyes regarded the camera, a thoughtful smile on her face.

"Has that lady seen her picture yet?" I asked, growing excited that perhaps she was still back at the ruins.

"Very pretty lady. She did not want it," he responded.

I had missed her. "I'll buy it."

"She will make a good lady friend," he said. "Ten dollars."

"I'll give you five." In truth, I would have paid him double, and only haggled with him for fear of insulting him. The thought of someone else taking the picture, or worse, the picture being thrown away, disturbed me.

I walked away looking at it, until Felix came over and studied it too.

"Beautiful lady," he said. "She was just by here."

"You saw her?"

"Yes, she left already with Habib. She is your lady friend? You had a fight and wish to make up?"

"No, she's not my lady friend," I said, and I feared that the words were all too true.

"Asis came by, too," he said. "He was asking questions about you. You are the famous Mr. Cain, yes?"

"Did you tell him I was here?"

"I told him I had dropped you off on the other side and did not know where you were at the moment, which was a little bit true."

"Take me to where she's going."

"It may not be wise. Asis knows you are after her. He may decide to catch you there."

I tore the picture in half, then into quarters, and finally into smaller pieces. Opening my hands over a wastebasket, I watched the pieces flutter in.

"Just as well," said Felix, "She would have broken your heart again. We go back to the hotel?"

"No, we continue."

Felix circled back to the original road where he had dropped me off and continued up the mountainside. The sky soon disappeared as we plunged into the thick forest. Every now and then we broke into a clearing and I'd see, far below in the distance, the town of Ephesus, sparkling like a miniature movie set. The road lacked guardrails and a moment of inattentiveness could send us over the ledge; so our lack of speed suited me just fine. It was a long time up, but a short time down, should we miss a sharp turn.

A parking lot greeted us at the end of our trip, a large sign identifying the site as Virgin Mary's House. Otherwise, nothing else explained why the area should be of particular interest to tourists.

"That's Habib's car. Your lady is here somewhere. He must be getting tea," said Felix.

He scanned the grounds further and finally pronounced them safe, noting that there was no other way to access the site except the way we came.

"Most likely Asis has stopped for lunch," he said.

"Good to know I'm not a high priority on his list."

"Don't push your luck. Hurry back soon," said Felix.

I wandered off behind a group of tourists who seemed to know where they were going. I soon found myself among souvenir stands and food stalls once more. Running the gauntlet of hawkers, I came upon a small stone hut, from which a Christian nun suddenly emerged. She was carrying a box in her hands and disappeared into a larger building nearby.

The hut was a Christian shrine, filled with pictures of the Virgin Mary, the mother of Jesus Christ. Followers believed that this was her final resting place and it was the destination for many pilgrimages. I entered cautiously, dropped a coin into a collection box and lit a candle by the vestibule, so as not to appear conspicuous. An adjoining room contained several pews, where the faithful knelt to meditate and, at the far end, an altar and a life-size statue of Mary. A second nun was at this altar, tending to another table full of candles. She replaced the melted candles and collected the change from the donation box. Several women knelt at the pews, shawls on their heads, bent in prayers. One of them caught my attention. Her dark shawl barely covered the profusion of blond hair that tumbled upon her shoulders. I approached her slowly, as if she was a wild animal that would bolt in fright at any sudden movement.

Kerry turned to me, caught my eyes, held them, rose, and slowly walked out of the church. I followed her down a shaded path, stopping before a stone wall that was completely blanketed with colorful pieces of scrap paper tied to strings.

"Every piece of paper represents a person's wish," she said. "People asking the Mother of Jesus for something."

"You got your wish, and you didn't even have to write it on a piece of paper," I said, and immediately felt guilty for those words and, as she had said before, irritated by the repetition.

"Are you going to call the police now and have me arrested?"

"My Turkish isn't that good. I wouldn't be able to explain exactly why I'd want you put into handcuffs and thrown in jail."

"You wouldn't have to explain it. The whole world knows our story. I saw the CNN report about us at Galata Tower. Don't act innocent and tell me you didn't intentionally set me up?"

She was silent for a moment. "You wouldn't believe me, anyway," she said.

I regarded her profile, her absolutely devastating profile; her long hair streaming languidly in the cool breeze. Sometimes the wind shifted directions and sent me a hint of her scent, something that was not from a bottle but directly from her skin. Even her sweat smelled good to me – a wild flower, pale and beautiful, clinging tenaciously to the barren mountainside of my life, the only miracle of nature I had ever known.

Now, before me, she was not defiant. She was tired, as if she was holding up the weight of the world.

"What are you doing here anyway," I asked. "You're not even religious."

"I've always been a spiritual person."

"Spiritual maybe, but not religious."

"All religions are spiritual."

"Tell that to Jesus Christ when they nailed him to the cross."

We sat on a bench, our faces just inches apart.

"If you had only given me a chance," I said, "I would have given you every penny I had, and gladly."

"You and a hundred other men. I couldn't bring myself to take advantage of your feelings any longer. I really cared about you. That's why I did it myself."

"Let me follow your logic here. You didn't feel guilty about stringing the other men along and having someone else steal their money for you because you *didn't* care for them. But you cared so much for me that you stole my money yourself?"

"Something like that."

"Let's start with a simpler problem. A man is dead and I'm wanted for his murder. You've got to straighten this out with the police."

"I don't know if I can."

"Sure you can. You just walk up to them and tell them the truth."

"It's not that simple. You'd better leave."

"I'm not going anywhere until we work this out."

"The police are here."

"What are you talking about?"

She motioned to a group of Turkish policemen marching meaningfully toward the chapel.

"Come with me," I said.

"No, we'll draw too much attention together. What time's your flight?"

I hesitated, surprised that she knew about it, then admitted, "I leave at 3:00 PM."

"I'll meet you there."

I took one last, frustrated look at her and walked quickly toward the parking lot. She turned the other way, into the forest.

A single policeman stood guard at the parking lot, but, unfortunately, he stood between me and the cab. After several attempts, I managed to get Felix's attention. He gestured toward the parking lot exit, indicating that he wanted me to run toward it. He approached the policeman and pointed into the woods and, perking up, the policeman drew his weapon and plunged into the bushes. Felix pulled out quickly, caught up to me near the exit, and slowed down just enough for me to dive in. The remaining police force emerged from the forest, at that moment. One of them sprinted after us; then, recognizing the futility of the chase, he pulled out his gun and fired in our direction. Quickly, his superior – Asis, as it turned out – gave him a swift kick in the ass, grabbed his gun and threw it into the woods. He slapped the policeman several times across the side of the head, until the man dropped to his knees, cowering.

"He must be a rookie," remarked Felix. "I have never seen Asis so angry with a subordinate before."

"You seem to know Asis pretty well," I said.

"He is my cousin."

"Is everyone in Turkey related?"

"Most likely. I have seven brothers, three sisters, 35 cousins, and 15 nephews. It's very difficult buying them presents for their birthdays."

"Really?"

"No, I'm just pulling your leg, as you Americans say. Every year, I just send them gift cards."

"You're a funny guy."

"Years of practice."

"I have to go back to the hotel for my luggage."

"It's not safe for you. I'll telephone my cousin to pick up your belongings and meet us outside the hotel."

"How is your cousin going to get my luggage?"

"He works reception."

"Of course. By the way, if you're Asis' cousin, why are you helping me instead of him?"

"The truth is that, with him hot on your trail, as you American say, he's getting a lot of media attention. In consequence, he is being considered for a promotion and has received many marriage proposals, as he strikes a very handsome figure on TV. It would not be wise for him to catch you yet."

"What will happen when he *does* catch me? Will he let me go?"

"No, then the justice system must make an example of you before the world."

"That doesn't sound very appealing."

"It's not."

We reached the airport an hour ahead of my flight. Felix told me many funny stories about his experiences in the United States, until his cousin arrived with the luggage. On his advice, I waited until the last minute to check in, when reception would be less likely to pay attention. I looked for Kerry on my way to the boarding gate, though I held little hope she would keep her promise. The boarding line moved slowly, but I wasn't there long before someone tapped me on the shoulder.

It was a woman, who lowered her shawl to reveal herself.

"Change of plans," said Bambi. "The police know about our flight and have their people on the plane. We've chartered a private plane to take us to the capital city, Ankara. There, we'll hook up with German contacts who'll get us to Berlin."

"Kerry is supposed to meet me here," I told her.

"I know. How do you think the police found out about our flight?"

I shook my head. "She couldn't have told them. We were going to talk, try to clear things up."

"Well, you'll have plenty of time to clear things up. We're taking her with us."

She pointed down the terminal, through which three figures advanced. I recognized the two men from the plane on the flight to Ephesus. Kerry walked between them, engaged in an animated conversation. She went cold, upon seeing us, and glowered back. She was back to glowering.

"I believe introductions aren't necessary," said Bambi.

"I thought you were really going to talk this time," I said.

She shrugged.

"As long as you're trying to clear the air, you might also be interested in another small fact that she failed to mention in your last meeting," said Bambi. "Her accomplice, Kerrk, spilled his guts about how she set you up."

"I thought he was dead."

"That was the initial assumption. It turned out that he had actually smoked too much hash and they revived him at the hospital."

I regarded Kerry. "You knew he wasn't dead, didn't you? At Virgin Mary's house, they were looking for you too. That's why you went into the forest instead of back to the chapel."

"It's a touching reunion," said Bambi, "but we have a plane to catch."

We left the airport to a waiting van, circled the facility, and arrived shortly at a small hanger. A twin-engine Cherokee sputtered to life, the pilot giving Bambi the thumbs up.

Soon, we were flying over the hilly terrain of Turkey. Bambi pulled out a granola bar and offered it to Kerry, who refused. She then dangled it before me, and realizing that I hadn't eaten since breakfast, I attacked it hungrily.

Kerry was irritated by everything I did, so I chewed quietly as she stared petulantly out the window. The two men, Aktuz and Kudar, shouted periodically to each other over the drone of the engine, planning some sort of social event. Apparently, they were related, possibly uncle and nephew. Aktuz was middle-aged, with a short, compact body and the prerequisite mustache of older Turkish men. Kudar was in his mid-twenties and clean-shaven, the preferred style of the young, with a sense of humor that the older man didn't always appreciate. I was curious to know how they came to work for the CIA, as they didn't exactly act like spies, but was too tired to investigate.

An hour into the flight, I woke up as the pilot shouted something about the fuel tank. After a brief moment of confusion, we finally understood that he had forgotten to fill up the tanks. He would have to make a stopover at Cappadocia.

We were shortly drifting over a spectacular vista of dusty, cone-shaped hills of every size and shape, scattered across miles of a sandy brown landscape. Deep ravines and canyons cut through the region, formed millions of years ago from the lava of massive volcanoes.

Cappadocia was once occupied by early Christians escaping persecution from Romans rule. Homes and churched were carved right into the soft rock of the mountains and into the porous earth. Elaborate secret cities, some hundreds of feet below ground, later served to hide the inhabitants from invading Arabs. Many of these underground communities were still being discovered today and were popular tourist attractions.

"I could use some earplugs," said Bambi, upon landing, and we set off for a pharmacy.

We entered the town of Avanos, famous for its pottery-making industry that went back to the Roman days. The pottery's unique red clay, considered among the best in the world, came from the Red River banks near.

At the pharmacy, Kerry said, "I need the bathroom."

Bambi stood at the door while she did her business.

"Me too," I said, and Bambi waved me in after Kerry emerged.

The bathroom, I discovered, was no more than a hole in the ground, over which I was compelled to squat. I came out shortly and found myself alone. A store clerk directed me outside, where I caught sight of Bambi and the two bodyguards running down the street. By the time I reached the corner, they were gone. I consequently wandered the town for hours, searching for them, and finally returned to the airport to wait them out.

By now, the plane's fuel tanks had been topped off and the pilot was eager to get going, as another client was waiting for him in Ankara. Bambi ran in moments later, the men trailing behind her.

"She gave us the slip," she said.

"She wished to pick up personal feminine products and we thought it impolite to watch," explained Kudar, flushing self-consciously from the memory. "It was only for a second."

"We must leave now," said the pilot.

"Change of plan. We'll spend the night here," said Bambi. "She's stuck here just like we are. We'll get her tomorrow."

She paid off the pilot, who quickly jumped into his plane and took off, and we scoured the streets of the town one last time before checking into a hotel. Bambi and I shared a room, the men another. Already accustomed to my presence, she moved about serenely in various stages of undress. She occasionally winked at me, but otherwise remained engrossed in her own private thoughts. She presently looked out the window one last time, as if hoping to catch sight of Kerry, then returned and sat by the bed.

"Come here," she said, padding the bed next to her, and I dutifully obeyed.

"Closer," she said. "I wasn't sure about this, but I guess now's as good a time as any." She pointed to her phone. It was opened to an email from Giancarlo.

"He has officially dropped you as a client. You're on your own."

I regarded the email for a long time, trying to absorb the news. Finally, I remarked, "Why didn't he tell me this directly?"

"Your situation is very volatile. He couldn't risk further contact."

"I didn't realize I had become such a liability to him."

"You've got it wrong," she said. "He's become a liability to you."

7

A cool breeze wandered over my face as I lay in bed the next morning. Someone moved across the room, threw open the window, and sent the blinding sunlight crashing against my face. A voice drifted toward me, soft, musical, almost ethereal, and I slowly opened my eyes to see Bambi next to me. She was waving a copy of the U.S. edition of the local newspaper.

I watched her move to a small table in the corner of the room, where breakfast had been served. Lifting the cover from one of the plates, she released the smell of toast and eggs.

"Are you sure that was his email?"

"It was encrypted and came with his electronic signature. Kerry must have powerful friends."

"What makes you think she's behind this?"

She again waved the paper before me, and this time peeled away the pages to reveal the top story, which speculated about my reasons for being in town. My own face, occupying a third of the tabloid-size periodical, stared back at me. I was in the tuxedo from Amnesty International and, truth be told, didn't look half-bad.

"We came in on a private flight. No one should have known you were here," she said. "Giancarlo's convinced that Kerry's being helped by another, very powerful PR agency. He recognizes the stories planted about you, and some of his contacts have mentioned getting information through anonymous emails."

"Giancarlo has never been one to back down," I pointed out.

"Yes, but this mysterious agency is playing dirty. They're the ones who got that picture of you at Galata Towers. They're now keeping police appraised of your whereabouts, putting you at risk. Dropping you as a client takes some of the pressure off them to keep you on the run. Without professional support, you're less of a threat, at least while you're here. We've have to move. I got word this morning that Kerry's trying to charter another plane to get her to Ankara."

She opened the window wider, revealing an expansive view of the moonlike landscape of Cappadocia. Long, intricately carved columns of stone, molded by the wind into elaborate and fantastic shapes, dotted the scene. The orange rays of the morning sun fell upon us and, as we ate, Bambi's phone rang.

"Damn it!" she exclaimed. "We've got to get out of here!"

We dressed quickly and ran out of the room. She pulled me to the stairwell just as the elevator doors flew open and disgorged a band of policemen, who ran toward the door. Reaching the parking lot in back of the building, Bambi remarked, "These guys are good. We can't go to the airport anymore. The police will be watching it."

Her phone rang. "Okay," she said to the caller; then, to me, "stay close."

We made our way through the crowded streets of town, dodging tourists who were already burdened with bags of merchandise. Store windows brimmed with pottery displays of all shapes and sizes. Craftsmen sat at their spinning wheels, shaping cups, saucers and bowls from the ubiquitous red clay. A number of American couples sat in tandem, one behind the other, in some of the windows, clawing at the clay. Since the movie "Ghost," recreating the famous scene with Demi Moore and Patrick Swayze had become a popular pastime, and shop owners were more than happy to comply.

Aktuz and Kudar met us on the other end of town, waiting by the side of a Fifties-era taxi, drinking tea. I recalled seeing the taxi on the cover of a *Lonely Planet* guidebook years before.

"Join us," said the driver.

Bambi hesitated, but then picked up the offered tea, and I followed her example.

"It's extremely rude to refuse," she reminded me.

"Ah, the famous Mr. Cain," said the driver, who introduced himself as Gulrepi. "Turkish people love America, but your values are a bit distorted, no offense. I tell you, if my woman stole my money, my whole village would hunt her down and stone her to death. Unfortunately, you Americans are too enlightened for your own good. That is why we feel sorry for you. We would not stand for such nonsense here. Allah made man the head of the household. That money would have been returned to you immediately. The woman would not have taken another breath upon this earth."

"It's a bit drastic."

"It is the will of Allah."

"Do not listen to the babbling of this old man," spoke Kudar, the younger of the group. "Turkey is much more enlightened today. Perhaps we would have flogged her, but not put her to death. That is a barbaric practice from the old days."

"Well, you young people have your ways," replied the driver. "It's a discussion for a later time over tea."

He continued, "Your colleagues have explained your dilemma. My cousin was a high-ranking general in the Turkish army. He has excellent connections throughout town and can find her for you, if you wish. His price is very reasonable."

Gulrepi handed me a creased and stained piece of paper as Bambi peeked over my shoulder. "That might not be a bad idea," she said, pulling her phone out. "We could use some help."

"I will introduce you," said the driver, taking her phone and dialing the number.

"Khaled? This is Gulrepi. You will not believe who I have with me. The famous Mr. Cain from America. He would like you to find Miss Kerry before she leaves town. Hold on, let me put him on the phone."

"Yes, this is Cain. Thank you, I appreciate the sympathy. No, don't stone her, if you find her. Just let us know where she is."

"He is a fast operator," said Gulrepi. "I can vouch for his self-control. He will not strike her."

"He didn't even ask anything about her. How will he know where to start looking?" I asked.

"She is here, of course," said Gulrepi. "It was on the news last night."

Bambi's phone rang. "It's Khaled," she said.

"I told you he was fast," said Gulrepi.

"Kerry's still in town," said Bambi, "but she found a way to fly out of here."

"How is that possible?" I asked. "The airport is crawling with police. She's wanted, too. She can't rent a plane any more than we can."

"Not a plane," said Bambi. "A balloon. She hired out a local operator who gives aerial tours of Cappadocia to get her out of here."

"She's crazy. You can't fly all the way to Ankara in a balloon...can you?"

"She doesn't have to. She just needs to get far enough out of town to rent a private plane from an independent pilot," said Bambi.

"My cousin runs a balloon concession," said Gulrepi. "Perhaps it is his balloon." He took out his cell phone, which glittered in the sun, its sleeves encrusted with flecks of gold.

"Ah," he exhaled, after a brief conversation with his cousin. "Miss Kerry did indeed rent out his balloon, but bad luck, they took off about half an hour ago. He has her in the gondola as we speak."

"Maybe we can catch her," said Bambi.

The driver's face lit up. "Chase scenes are my favorite part of your American movies. Don't need a plot. Just chase people around."

We jumped into the cab, but were compelled to navigate the congested streets carefully until we reached the edge of town, where the car picked up speed. Climbing into the hilly, torturous roads of Cappadocia's mountainous terrain, the driver kept up a running commentary about Americans' penchant for drama. He explained that our problem lay in growing up watching too many cowboy movies.

"You always think somebody's going to steal your horse if you're not careful. Me, my taxi is my horse. I never lock it up."

"Cowboys don't lock up their horses either," I said, amused.

"Quite true," returned the driver, thoughtfully. "But you also do not eat them. Quite a waste."

He knew the balloon's route and caught up to it about an hour later as it flew over the canyons. Taking the offered pair of binoculars, I confirmed that Kerry was indeed in the gondola.

"Use my gun. You might be able to shoot it down," said the driver.

I pushed away the offered weapon. "Are you crazy?"

"The balloon will not explode. It is filled with hot air, not helium."

"I'm not shooting anything down."

He shrugged and continued driving. The road traced the curve of the valley, along the same path as the balloon, allowing us to stay apace, but tourist traffic soon slowed us down and the balloon extended its lead again. It drifted serenely among the low-lying clouds, a rainbow of colors in the sharp-edged sky.

"There is an area near the Open Air Museum where it will fly low. We are coming to the site soon," explained Gulrepi. "My brother-in-law runs a concession stand there. He has a more accurate rifle that will give you a better shot."

"Nobody is shooting anything at the balloon!" I asserted.

"Don't worry. He is an excellent marksman," he maintained.

"Call your cousin in the balloon. Tell him to come down."

"That would certainly be less messy. However, he will not listen to me. We are not on good terms since he called me a black dog for spitting out his wife's soup the last time I was at his house. I would much rather shoot his balloon down," he said.

The Open Air Museum came into view, around which the canyon walls rose sharply to create a natural enclosure. Hundreds of people milled about the souvenir and food stalls by the roadside. The general flow of the crowd led inside through a natural gateway, to the monasteries and churches that had been carved right into the valley's porous rocks thousands of years ago.

"This used to be a thriving community. Now it's a popular tourist attraction," said Gulrepi.

"It's pretty far from town," I said. "Why would anyone build here?"

"Location. First of all, it's on a hill, so the enemy had to climb it to get to them, easily exposing themselves to attack. This particular area is also enclosed on all four sides by mountains, with only this narrow entrance to get inside, so it was easy to defend.”

“I assume you also give guided tour.”

“Yes, I was voted one of the top five best private guides by *Lonely Planets*. Come, let us take a tour.”

“Can we please stay focused? We’re trying to catch a balloon,” I said.

“Speaking of balloons. I think we are going to have a crash.”

He pointed to the sky, from which the multi-colored balloon was rapidly descending. It was about a mile away, headed straight for us.

“Is it supposed to be doing that?” I asked.

“I tried to teach my cousin how to drive a cab, but he was very bad at it and always crashed into people. I thought he would be safer in a balloon, where he cannot hit anything. I guess, except the ground!”

The balloon continued its steady descent, growing increasingly larger as we spoke.

“What a fool. He forgot to bring extra fuel,” said Gulrepi.

“Do you think they’ll make it this far?”

“We will know soon enough.”

It seemed, for a moment, that the balloon would just barely clear the ridge of the canyon. The two figures in the gondola, however, appeared to be doing everything but piloting the craft. They gestured wildly – I assumed in panic – until peering through the binoculars I realized that they were arguing heatedly. Kerry shook the pilot by the shoulders, pointed up at the dying flame, and tried to wrestle control of the lever for stoking the furnace. The pilot held it as far as he could over the edge of the gondola while fending her off.

“I hope she wins,” said Gulrepi, who was also watching the struggle. “My cousin will hit the wall of the canyon, surely, if he is at the control.”

“Kerry has never piloted a balloon before.”

“But I am sure she has more common sense.”

The balloon dipped suddenly, drawing closer to the ground, until another gust of wind grabbed it and flung it upward again. By now, the museum crowd had come to realize what was going on. They broke into cheers when the balloon safely cleared the rocky ground and soared high once more. It seemed it would stay up this time, until something happened to the furnace and the flame went out completely. An ominous silence fell upon the crowd as the balloon again drifted downward. Then it miraculously swept upward, hovered momentarily at the lip of the canyon some fifty yards behind us and, with barely six inches of clearance, made it over the edge safely. Now the danger was that it would plow into the spectators.

A woman screamed and everyone scattered. I stood transfixed as Kerry, realizing where she was, turned and stared straight at me. The gondola scraped the ground, headed in my direction, and Kerry reached out for me as if to be rescued. Our hands nearly touched, when the gondola swung up again and cleared the heads of frightened spectators in front of us.

As it looped over the archway that led inside to the museum, Bambi pushed me through the crowd. We made it inside just in time to see the gondola bump along the dusty ground, dragged by the long, deflated balloon, and come to a stop against a tree in the middle of the field. The pilot frantically fastened the craft down as Kerry jumped out and headed for the caves on the hillside.

"Let's split up," Bambi cried. "We'll circle the caves and catch her in the middle. Aktuz and Kudar will guard the entrance; make sure she doesn't sneak out."

"I have a few words to say to that knucklehead cousin of mine," remarked Gulrepi, walking purposefully toward the gondola.

Up on the hillside, Kerry shot past a group of startled onlookers and disappeared into one of the many tunnels that served as passageways between the carved-out dwellings. I reached the area shortly and jumped in after her, to suddenly find myself in total darkness. The tunnel quickly narrowed until it was barely wide enough for a single person, forcing me down to my hands and knees in order to continue. Heavy breathing and the excited voices of tourists echoed ahead, but Kerry's unmistakable voice rose above the din. She was arguing with a tourist over the right-of-way. One of them had to back up far enough to let the other through, and she was in no mood to be civil.

Following the voices led me to the dim illumination of a tourist's flashlight, and in front of the light, Kerry crawling furiously away.

She had somehow squeezed past the tourist, an old man, who seemed still shaken by his encounter with her.

Seeing me, the old man took off behind Kerry. I stayed close, to his dismay, until Kerry suddenly threw herself into another, connecting tunnel, which the old man, surprisingly, also took. Afraid of losing her, I grabbed his leg and pulled him back out, giving me a clear shot at her. He cried out in terror, but once released, he crawled away quickly, taking the light with him and plunging us into total darkness again.

I sped up immediately and bumped into someone in the darkness, but even blind, I knew it was her. The tunnel was a dead end. I instinctively grabbed at the air and finally clamped around her ankle.

"Aren't you ever going to leave me alone?" she cried.

"Maybe if you stopped running away from me, we could work this out."

"Haven't you figured it out yet, you idiot? I'm not running away from you. I'm trying to protect you."

In the middle of all the confusion, I couldn't help but laugh. She kicked angrily and forced me to let go, but I reached out and caught her wrist.

"You're not getting away that easily!" I said.

Surprisingly, she did not struggle this time, but lay on the ground quietly, not uttering a word. Concerned that I might have injured her, I spoke her name. A strange sound reached my ear and, in total darkness, I touched her face. She, unbelievably, was crying.

"I'm supposed to fall for that," I said, though I actually had.

"Go to hell," she returned.

We were just inches apart, but still I could not make out her face to confirm or disprove the sincerity of her emotions. I resented her and, yet, I also felt sorry for her. We sat shoulder to shoulder, leaning against the cave wall until, finally, she spoke.

"You have to stop," she said. "If I could give you back your money, I would. But you have to leave me alone."

I laughed again. The sound was strange, like nothing that had ever come out of me before. It was an empty laugh, because it lacked conviction.

"Feeling sorry for you won't pay the rent," I said.

"That sounded so lame."

"I know. It sounded stupid to me, too."

"Yes, stupid is a better word."

She suddenly grabbed my head and pressed her lips against mine, opened her mouth to suck me in, deeply, passionately, long and greedily. I tried to catch my breath, but she seemed determined to suck out every ounce of life from me, until I felt dizzy. Suddenly, she screamed and spat out a torrent of profanity. Someone else had seized her and was pulling her away. She resisted at first, but the effort proving futile, she relented, letting herself be dragged back along the maze of tunnels in the darkness.

I followed her, confused, until the blinding light hit us when we reached the tunnel exit. As our eyes adjusted, I recognized Kudar, who now sheepishly released Kerry. Standing above us was Bambi, who looked on somberly.

"We found you just in time," said Bambi.

"Who are you? How are you always able to find me?" cried Kerry. Surprisingly, she did not sound angry, but almost admiringly.

Bambi studied her for a moment. "I'm his therapist," she responded.

"The police are everywhere," said Kudar. "How do we get out of here?"

"I can distract them," said Kerry.

We all looked at Kerry for an instant, puzzling over her statement. Bambi peered over the mouth of the cave, to the bottom of the hill, where police were fanning out. Asis was leading them, frantically bellowing orders.

"You don't need to bother about distracting them," said Bambi. "They're separating, going in every direction but the right one. We can get out if we hurry."

"What do you mean? There's only one way out – the same way we came in, and they've got guards posted there," I said.

"We didn't all come in the same way," she said, and indicated the field below.

There, the colorful balloon, inflated again, was slowly nodding in the breeze, surrounded by all sorts of curious people, except the police. Lifting over the gondola, it began to steady as the flames beneath it intensified.

"You'd think that's the one thing they'd watch," I said.

Bambi smiled. "Let's move."

She led the way down, while I warily kept track of the movement of the police, who continued to search for us in all the wrong places, following Asis' directions. As we reached the balloon, Gulrepi pushed through the crowd to meet us.

"My cousin will be ready in ten minutes," he said.

"He has two minutes," said Bambi.

"This will get us out of here, but we'll still need a plane to get us to Ankara," I said.

"Miss Kerry was flying to a field just outside the Kaya camping area...." noted Gulrepi. "Perhaps she was meeting someone there."

"I know the place. There's a long stretch of level ground there, big enough to land a small plane," said Aktuz. He was rewarded with a curious look from Kerry, almost as if she had been pleased with his observation.

We climbed inside as Gulrepi quickly released the mooring ropes. Aktuz and Kudar stayed behind, the balloon unable to carry more than four passengers. In any event, the police weren't looking for them, so they weren't in any danger. The two men would catch up to us in the taxi.

The pilot furiously yanked on the pulleys to the furnace, sending short bursts of flame skyward. At the same time, the hills around us exploded into chaos. The police, almost as if on cue, had finally caught on. They were running down the hillside, knocking visitors out of the way, their desperate voices echoing through the site.

"Meet us at the field," Bambi called to her companions.

The balloon slowly lifted, drawing applause from the crowd. The police finally arrived, but too late, except for one particularly eager rookie who leaped onto a dangling rope and held on. However, realizing that he could not bring down the balloon by himself, and instead risked being hoisted dangerously high into the air, he swung away and landed awkwardly in the crowd. Scrambling to his feet, he pulled out his weapon, but Asis again quickly interceded, slapping him on the side of the head. The crowd roared again as we sailed above them and continued leisurely into the blue sky.

"They love you, Mr. Cain," said the pilot. "You are a big hero in Turkey."

"The people, maybe, but not the police. I'm a wanted fugitive."

"They were just putting on a show for the cameras. That was my cousin with the gun. He is a good actor, is he not?"

"Yes, very talented family."

"The way he is pointing the gun, looks very dramatic on TV."

The vast expanse of rock formations sprawled across the alien landscape of Cappadocia and swallowed the balloon as it soared silently in the sky. Huge, cone-like columns, worn smooth by thousands of years of wind and rain, reached out to us like witches' bony fingers. Other formations were even odder shaped, resembling inverted stalks of onions, with slim stems at the bottom and large, bulbous heads on top. Some sported windows, carved from the inside out like jack-o-lanterns by their former tenants. Sixty years ago, the government turned the region into a national park, making it off-limit to squatters, but every once in a while, people were still found living in them.

We completed the ride without further incident, with Kerry uncharacteristically quiet. As we slowly descended, Bambi motioned up ahead, where Gulrepi's cab was already waiting.

Aktuz and Kudar fanned out to meet us and grabbed the ropes as we neared the ground. The pilot was already visibly nervous, for the area had an unsavory reputation. Once we disembarked, he entreated us to take care of our business so that he could be on his way.

"We won't need you anymore. Thank you," Bambi informed the balloon pilot.

"I need to pee?" said Kerry.

Bambi regarded her. "All right, but don't try to escape again." She pointed across the field, beyond which the ground suddenly disappeared. "That's a sheer drop of 60 meters. I won't hesitate to throw you off it."

Kerry rolled her eyes as Bambi directed her to a large bolder nearby which, sunk into the middle of the field, gave just enough cover to protect her modesty, though not enough to facilitate an escape.

"That should work," she said.

The drone of a prop plane reached our ears shortly and, moments later, a single engine Cessna glided down the narrow stretch of dirt road that cut across the field. Kerry came running out from behind the rock, adjusting her dress. The plane hit the ground roughly, taxied along the bumpy track and finally stopped near us. The engine still running, the pilot furiously signaled us over.

"We must go. I saw police cars about a kilometer away," he said.

Climbing in, we quickly ascended into the crisp, clean air of Cappadocia. The daylight was waning, the sun growing large and reddish. It cast spectacular shadows below us that were truly mystical, and it easily explained how people could believe in gods and consider the place sacred.

Kerry dozed off, her head tilting onto Bambi's shoulder. Bambi regarded her, apparently considering what to do, and finally allowed her head to stay there. I too dozed off and, in about an hour, awoke to Bambi's voice. We were making our approach to Ankara airport. To avoid attention, we taxied directly into a hangar and entered the facility through the service doors. We thought it best to purchase our tickets at the last minute again, to keep our names out of the system as long as possible. A policeman nearby seemed to recognize us for a moment, but then turned away and resumed his duties. Even so, Bambi remained cautious.

"Wait here. I'll get the tickets," she told us.

As she started for the counter, the policeman lurched forward and caught up with her on the line. She dug into her purse and produced a small notebook, which he reviewed thoroughly. He pointed to a page and listened gravely as she responded. Finally, he stepped back politely, letting her proceed with her transaction. A moment later, she came back to us. I noticed the policeman going over to the reservationist and striking up a conversation, glancing in our direction several times.

"What was that all about?" I asked, concerned.

"He used to be on the security detail for one of the country's top public officials."

"He was trying to pick you up?"

"He wanted to book a session to discuss his marriage. He's going to be in New York for a law enforcement convention."

"Over there," said Kerry, pointing to a group of policemen who were heading our way.

"Just walk normally, but move quickly," said Bambi.

We looked around for a means of escape, when we noticed the policeman by the ticket counter pointing us down the hallway, beyond the escalators. We followed his sign to a door, through which he nodded for us to enter. A long, dark corridor greeted us, and following it as far as we could, we met up again with our friendly policeman.

"Quickly," he urged, pulling out a key and unlocking a door. "They will not come this way."

He led us down another long and narrow passageway and, after several more turns, we found ourselves at the foot of a large passenger plane.

"This is our flight!" Bambi exclaimed in surprise.

"I got your flight number from the receptionist," he said. "You can get on safely. I arranged to keep your names off the manifesto, so they will not look for you here. Do not forget me, Miss Bambi."

"I've locked you in," she said.

He shook our hands gratefully and watched us board, keeping an eye out for his colleagues. Later, he stood by the terminal window to watch the plane take off.

It occurred to me, and only after we were in the air, that Kerry and I had not exchanged a single barb or accusation since leaving Cappadocia. Even more astonishing, I had not thought about the money, though the source of all my suffering and anguish had been inches away all afternoon. If there was ever a time to think about the money, it was now. But maybe I had exhausted all my bitterness and, if so, that frightened me. Bitterness was good. Only bitterness would get me back my money.

In sitting down, Kerry could have placed Bambi between us; yet, she sat next to me without hesitation or any sense of irony. I braced for the worse.

Bambi must have been thinking the same thing. "For two people who've traded so much animosity in the media, you two have surprisingly little to say to each other in person," she said.

"I've already said everything I need to say," I responded, suddenly on edge.

"You haven't said the most important thing of all," said Kerry.

"You're joking, right? Am I supposed to apologize?"

"No, you're supposed to care."

"Yes, about my money."

"About me."

"I'd like to. I really would. But that's not how it works. You betrayed my trust. You got me right where it hurts the most."

"You did too."

"I've never taken a penny from you."

"I wasn't talking about money."

"What could I have possibly taken from you that could be of any value to you?"

Kerry suddenly went pale. She turned away quickly and hid her face under a voluminous canopy of hair. Almost simultaneously, Bambi's expression changed, too, as if she had also caught on to something that I was still too far away to grasp – or maybe I was too close.

"Kerry..." I said, hesitantly.

"I'm tired," she said. "I can't talk anymore."

Bambi was thoughtful for a moment. "I think it's best that I ended your therapy," she said to me.

"I'm cured?"

"No, I don't think I can help you anymore."

"Great, now you can insult me freely without violating your Hippocratic Oath."

"I'm not a doctor."

"Now you tell me."

Kerry laughed. "She *is* your therapist!" she said.

We landed in Amsterdam shortly, where we immediately boarded a flight to Bruges, Belgium. Bambi had hacked into the airlines' reservation system and bumped off three unsuspecting passengers. They would later find a confused reservations agent trying to explain why they were mysteriously rebooked on the subsequent flight and credited with 10,000 free travel miles for their inconvenience.

"How did you get access to the system?" I asked.

"I hacked the international database."

"What database? Interpol?"

Bambi arched her brows.

Kerry remained silent throughout the flight, this time placing Bambi between us. Even after we landed, and as we walked through the terminal, I continued to ponder the significance of our last exchange. She was the enemy, I kept reminding myself. She was up to something. Her unusual display was not based on feelings but on manipulation. She'd say anything that would get her what she wanted.

Even so, it was exhilarating to be next to her again; brushing accidently against her as we walked; hearing her voice; watching that perfect body glide through the terminal, creating a disturbance as she moved. She cut through the very molecules of the air and through the crowds around us like a speedboat across the glassy calm waters.

"Hey!" called Bambi. "Help me with this."

We were by the rental lockers, one of which she had opened.

"What's in there?" I asked, as she pulled out a canvas bag.

"Change of clothing. We've been wearing the same clothes for days. It's too easy for them to I.D. us."

"These are for us?"

"Just for you. We're going shopping."

She slipped an arm through Kerry's and led her to a women's boutique across the way. I had no choice but to follow, though I could think of worse ways to spend my time. I made myself comfortable on a bench near the entrance to the fitting room, as instructed, and reluctantly gave them my thoughts on their outfits as they paraded them before me. As expected, they insisted on my opinion and promptly ignored it, accusing me of lacking taste, which I couldn't deny.

They eventually walked out with four shopping bags between them and stopped to eat at the self-service cafeteria.

"The first thing we'll do when we get back to the States is talk to Denver," I said to Kerry. I had meant it in the most civil manner and thought it a good start toward reconciliation.

"Now you see why I left you!" she returned, irritably.

I hesitated, confused by her response, but before I could stop myself, I exclaimed, "Excuse me, you didn't 'leave me,' you ran off with my money in the middle of the night."

"We've already been through this," she said.

"I'll keep going through it until I get my money back."

"How are you going to get it back? Denver's already lost it in the stock market."

"You're assuming he was being honest with you. Maybe he never invested it like you think he did."

"I know he did."

"There's one way to make sure, and that's to subpoena his transaction records."

"Money, money, money. Don't you have anything else to talk about?"

"After I get it back, I'll be happy to discuss any other topic that strikes your fancy." I hated every second of our now-familiar argument, but I could not stop myself. A year of bottled-up resentment had been uncorked, and it was difficult to plug it up again so quickly.

"Good!" she declared. "You got that out of your system. Can you drop it, now?"

"Goddamn it, you take such a cavalier attitude toward eight million dollars. But it's my money. I spent years making it."

"I find it odd," said Bambi, "that you don't trust Denver about investing the money. Yet, you trust Kerry that she gave it to him."

"That makes no sense," I cried out, but at the same time, I realized that it made all the sense in the world.

Kerry shot Bambi a stunned look. She inhaled heavily, then slowly released a silent, smoldering sigh of frustration.

"Every financial transaction leaves an electronic trail," Bambi continued, calmly regarding Kerry. "All you have to do is show him the trail. Then he can approach Denver with more certainty."

"I don't have a computer handy."

"There's an Internet café down the hall."

"For security purposes, I'd rather not access my bank account from a public machine."

"Honey, where's the money?" said Bambi evenly.

Kerry reared up like a cornered animal, but Bambi simply shook her finger at her. "I've got a fourth-degree black belt in Karate and Jiu-Jitsu," she said. "You don't want to mess with me."

Kerry breathed heavily. "The money's gone," she said. "And that's it. I don't have to prove anything to anybody."

"I thought you've changed," I said. "I guess I was wrong."

"To tell you the truth," she said, "I don't care what you think any longer."

Just as I was about to respond, our flight to Paris was announced. "We'll finish this later," said Bambi, and led us silently to the plane.

A group of guards, loitering nearby for no particular purpose, tipped their hats to the two chic, smartly dressed ladies.

Half an hour into our flight, Bambi sprang up from her seat and led me down the aisle. "Let me show you something," she said.

We moved to the back of the plane, out of a direct line of sight from Kerry. "Kiss me," she told me.

I complied.

"Concentrate. We're being watched."

"I'm doing my best."

"You're distracted." She pulled my ear sharply. "The next thing I'm pulling isn't your ear," she warned.

"Goddamn it, stop kissing me then."

"Don't be such a baby. Keep it together." She rubbed her nose in my ear, breathing slowly and heavily. "Follow my lead when the plane lands," she said.

"What's going on?"

"It's a diversion."

"From what? Do that thing again with your tongue."

"I've had a private conversion with Kerry."

"When? You two never left my sight."

"Except for the fitting room."

"I meant to ask you about that. You two seemed like you were hitting it off nicely and becoming the best of friends; then we started talking about the money in the cafeteria."

"We're still good. It was just an act for the benefit of the people trailing us."

"Someone's trailing us?"

"Yes."

"And this is just an act, too?"

"Somewhat. They've got to think that we're an item, keep them from wondering why I'm helping you out. Let's head back to our seats. We can't overdo it."

"I'm sure it'll be okay if we overdo it at least one minute longer…"

"Stay alert and follow my lead. Get ready to make a break for it soon."

We returned to our seats, where Kerry regarded us quizzically.

"What have you been eating?" she asked me.

"Nothing."

She raised her hand suddenly to my face and I braced for the blow. Instead, she rubbed my lips gently.

"You missed a spot," she said.

"I didn't eat anything."

"I know."

The plane touched down at Charles de Gaulle Airport and pulled up to the gate, whereupon Kerry announced that she needed the bathroom.

"Why didn't you use the one on the plane?" asked Bambi.

"You're joking. Those places are always filthy."

Once past Customs and inside the terminal, Bambi said, "We'll wait for you here."

They exchanged a quick look as Kerry went inside alone. We waited several minutes before Bambi, appearing impatient, finally followed after her. She was out shortly, looking very upset.

"There's an entrance on the other side," she exclaimed, grabbing my hand. "Follow me."

She pulled me into the woman's bathroom and broke into a sprint. Patrons leaped out of the way as we weaved through then, but didn't seem much surprised at the sight of a man in their territory. I suppose the fact that a woman was dragging me along helped a little. Reaching the other side, we found ourselves near the revolving doors that led out of the terminal to the passenger loading area.

"Don't go out yet. We've got to time this right," she said.

We watched throngs of travelers surged in and out of the terminal; until, abruptly, Bambi pushed me through the doors. At that instant, a waiting taxi gunned its motor and sped away from us to the sound of squealing tires.

Seconds later, two men burst onto the pavement from inside the terminal and ran after the speeding car, shouting, "Stop! Stop!" It was a scene straight out of the movies. I wondered whether anyone being chased had ever actually obeyed the command to stop the car.

I finally recognized the object of their pursuit inside the receding car: Kerry. She looked briefly at the two men, then threw her head back against the seat as the car quickly disappeared into the twisting ribbon of roads that led out of the airport. One image lingered in my mind, and that was my last view of Kerry, who blew me a kiss.

Shortly, the two men trudged back in frustration, glared at us, and disappeared into the terminal.

"What was all that about?" I asked.

"Strategy," said a familiar voice. It came from the passenger of another cab, which had been idling nearby. The passenger stepped out of the vehicle, threw off his cap and tugged away at his fake beard.

"Giancarlo!"

"Everything's going according to plan," he said.

"Who were those two men chasing Kerry?"

"Local freelancers. They'll be well-compensated for their performance."

"That was all an act?"

"Part of the plan. Let's get ready," he said.

"Ready for what?"

"Your press conference."

"What press conference?"

"Don't you read your own press releases?"

"Unfortunately, as a fugitive, I don't get home delivery."

"No problem. It's all under control."

"We have to move," said Bambi. "We have a plane to catch."

"I thought you fired me as your client?"

"Part of the plan," he said, as we rushed through the airport. "We had reasons to believe our communications channels had been compromised. We needed breathing room to set up our trap."

"A trap for what?"

"My enemy."

"Your enemy? Are we talking public relations or counter-espionage?"

"Is there a difference?"

"I assume one uses a gun."

"My biggest enemy uses a gun."

"You mean rival?"

"A rival doesn't pack heat. I'm talking about Fabio Wallinsky, CEO of Wallinsky Worldwide. He carries a miniature gun, though it's actually a lighter. But cigarettes kill, too, so it's the same thing. And yes, I must grudgingly admit that he's actually good at his job."

"I've never heard you talk about a competitor in that way."

“And it pains me to do so, because he’s not the best example of our kind. We PR pros aren’t exactly known for our high ethical standards, but his behavior pushes the envelope and mails it out without a stamp. That’s why Kerry’s been able to deliver those rapid-fire upper cuts that have kept even a pro like me off-balanced so successfully. She’s had help.”

“Wallinsky?”

“He has an army of subordinates on his payroll worldwide, doing his bidding without question, all for minimum wage. I’ve got twenty people on my entire staff, not counting interns – whoever does! – and they all get at least double the minimum wage, or thereabouts.”

“So, getting back to your point, Wallinsky’s people have been trailing me and alerting the press for the past year? That explains why Kerry was always able to anticipate my moves; and the press, somehow, always got a picture of me in the most compromising positions.”

“Exactly,” said Giancarlo. “He recruits his people from the darkest, most desperate corners of the world, where respect for the law and the concept of fair play are nonexistent.”

“Job placement agencies?”

“Precisely. Superman has his Lex Luther. Batman has his Joker. I have Wallinsky.”

“I didn’t realize public relations was so violent.”

“It’s just like cooking. Every year it kills more people than cholesterol. You just never hear of that side of the industry. I should know. I had a chef for a client once who defaulted on his payments and I had to release him. Then he died.”

“He killed himself?”

“He committed career suicide. *The New York Times* food critic gave his restaurant a bad review a month after he broke his contract with me.”

“Sometimes I think you’re putting me on. You sound like you run a protection racket instead of a PR firm.”

“What can I say? I just happen to be good at what I do.”

“Can you two boys talk shop later,” interrupted Bambi. “We’re going to miss our flight if we don’t pick up our pace.”

“I meant to ask you: Why are we going to London? Why not return directly to the U.S.?”

"Timing," she said. "Wallinsky is just the bait. I'm after bigger game."

"Who?"

"Strictly NTK - Need to Know."

"Are you at least able to tell me why Kerry was wanted in Turkey, and why you let her go?"

"After intense interrogation, her taxi driver implicated her as the mastermind behind the arrowhead theft. But, actually, she's not really the bad guy."

"Of course she is. She stole my money."

"Yes, but she didn't steal it to get back at you for cheating on her."

"She didn't?"

"She stole it to save your life."

We reached the boarding gate just as the ticket attendant turned off her computer, signaling the close of boarding. Bambi quickly blocked her from leaving.

"We've got to catch that plane," she said.

The attendant regarded her and, after a moment's hesitation, returned to her terminal. Seconds later, she scanned our boarding passes and waved us through.

"Is it really that easy for you?" I asked Bambi.

"No, sometimes I have to slug them first."

Once on the plane, I turned to Giancarlo. "I really appreciate the great expense you're going through on my behalf, but I doubt that I'll ever be able to pay you back."

"Hey, we're friends. That, and the CIA also has a generous budget. You can thank your therapist for that."

Bambi took an exaggerated bow.

"In any event," continued Giancarlo. "They'll soon be plenty to go around for everyone. We just have to finesse the right people."

"As far as I know, the only 'right people' is Kerry. Or maybe Denver."

"Like the clouds lifting, everything will become clear soon," he said.

"That's close to a legitimate analogy, though slightly risky grammatically."

"Thank you."

"Couldn't you just tell me now and save yourself the risk of a bad analogy later?"

"It's like Christ at the Last Supper."

"See, I told you that you were taking a big risk with those analogies. I'm not sure that's a positive one," I said.

"Anything with Christ in it is good."

"He was betrayed the night of the Last Supper and later crucified."

"And look what it got for him? The crucifixion concept was pure genius."

"I'm sure you have a good explanation for that assessment."

"The crucifixion launched one of the wealthiest and most powerful religions in the world, next to Scientology — though, at least, Christianity was inspired by true events, more or less."

"That's the kind of disclaimer you'd find on a Hollywood documentary."

"Let's just say only man's expulsion from the Garden of Eden could hold a candle to the brilliance of the Crucifixion story; although, technically, they're really part of the same campaign."

"Again, losing paradise wasn't a good thing. It cursed mankind with Original Sin which, as you know, permanently shuts him out of heaven. As a result, millions of good human souls were stuck in purgatory for eternity, much like patients in a doctor's waiting room, waiting for the Messiah to free them. Jesus Christ had to die on the cross to finally give those unfortunate souls a way to enter heaven."

"Yes, but there's a catch, right?"

"Well, a person has to get baptized first to cleanse himself of Original Sin; then he can enter heaven. The sooner he's baptized, the better, because if he dies without getting baptized, he's stuck with Original Sin, and it's the eternal waiting room for him."

"Precisely. Christians are threatened with eternal damnation unless they sign a contract as soon as possible, vowing a lifetime of servitude to their God. That's what baptism is, a contract with God to serve him until death. It's the only way to get to heaven. The expulsion from the Garden damned the human race to purgatory. The Crucifixion gave it a way to be forgiven and get to heaven."

"I guess, if you look at it that way, it *is* a bit manipulative."

"Where do you think the cigarette companies got their inspiration from? Hook them when they're young and you have a customer for life."

"I've known you for twenty years, and you can still amaze me with the things you say."

"Really? Let's have this conversation again Friday night after I've had a few. I've heard I'm even more interesting then."

"Actually, I just realized that we *have* had these kinds of conversations many times before. It's just that we've never remembered them the next day. This is the first time we've both been sober."

"Well, let's not make that same mistake again. I really enjoy these conversations, and I wouldn't want them all to end because we don't think we have anything new to say to each other."

The plane shortly took a wide turn in preparation for landing. Bambi kept tapping away on her Blackberry, and finally she looked out the window and announced, "Be on guard."

"Is it really that dramatic?"

"Yes."

A taxi was waiting for us outside the Heathrow Airport and the driver, apparently without instructions, sped into the tranquil night of the London suburbs. We reached our hotel an hour later, a nondescript bed-and-breakfast, but instead of checking in at the front desk, we continued to the back, through a neighboring fence, and into a deserted side street. Bambi inspected a parked car and reached inside the driver-side fender, near the wheel, where a set of keys awaited her. She pulled away slowly, scanning the empty lot, studying the rear-view mirror, peering ahead past the headlights.

"Can I get a hint about what's going on?" I asked from the back seat.

"NTK," she said. "You should try to grab a quick nap."

"We have six hours before our next flight. Plenty of time."

"No, it's barely enough time."

An hour into our trip, Bambi turned into a small, unpaved road. It led us, after a number of twists and turns, to an impressively large and ornately decorated mansion, hidden away in the thicket of trees. It seemed out of place for the neighborhood, which offered more sedate, working class dwellings, and it took me a moment to absorb the view.

"Who lives here?"

"A patient of mine."

"Another sheik?"

"Actually, yes, an oil baron. He often conducts business from here. We shouldn't have any distractions."

"Distraction from what?"

"Normal stuff."

She ushered us into what appeared to be a plush and lavishly decorated home theater. Pushing a button lifted a wall to reveal an electronic console and a large monitor, flanked by numerous, smaller flat-panel displays. Banks of computers hugged the wall on the left, expelling miles of cable that snaked around the room. Following her instructions, Giancarlo logged onto his company's website and printed out numerous files, among them, a mailing list with about 50 names and a press release.

"This is a list of the world's most elite journalists, broadcasters and commentators," he explained.

"What am I supposed to do with it?"

"Invite them to your joint press conference."

"Joint press conference? Who am I joining with?"

"Kerry."

"Together? Does she know this?"

"She planned it."

"When will this historical event take place?"

"In a few days, somewhere in Manhattan. Time and place to be determined. Just follow the script we've prepared for you."

I started dialing while Giancarlo and Bambi poured over the press release. They debated every word, changed them, then changed them back again. I had ceased long ago to be surprised by Bambi's intelligence, but now I was impressed with her writing skills. She made bold, grammatical corrections to Giancarlo's writing, to the point where it hardly resembled his original document. He sulked like a petulant child when she deleted entire paragraphs and rewrote them in proper English, ensuring logical and consistent metaphors. She made comments like, "You're mixing your similes; or, "This is a dangling participle," to which he would reply, "I'm not writing the damned U.S. Constitution."

"You got to say what you mean and mean what you say."

"Yeah, well…" was his only defense.

Giancarlo finally pushed Bambi off the computer and said, impatiently, "That's fine. We're not writing for National Public Radio."

She shrugged. "It's all yours."

It began to dawn on me that this whole presentation was bigger than even I could have imagined. Journalists were knocking over their phones excitedly and diving for their tape recorders upon hearing my voice. They thanked me profusely, as if I had just generously given them the biggest scoop of their careers. Cut off from the news for so long, I was completely clueless about the enormous spectacle that my life had become.

We had picked up some sandwiches on the way and now devoured them quickly. Hours later, we piled back into the car and headed for the airport, Bambi driving again. No one had considered sleeping.

"Don't get a big head about yourself," said Bambi.

"What do you mean?" I asked, as the sun rose over the sleeping landscape of the city.

"Keep in mind that we're after more than just your money. I'm sorry for the secrecy, but it's government protocol. I'm depending on you to play your role perfectly."

"If my role is to act surprised at every turn, no problem. I'd gotten used to being treated like the punch line of a bad joke. It's good to be on the other side of the fence and actually be treated with respect. If that's helping your mission, I'm glad to oblige."

"Don't take it all for granted, though," said Giancarlo. The media is like a wild tiger. As long as you can satisfy their voracious appetite, you can have them eating out of your hands. But if you let your guard down, they'll rip your head off. I always take them out to lunch after getting a particularly positive story, but I check my pockets afterward– not for my money, for my cell phone. I can't tell you how many times reporters have asked to borrow my phone because, supposedly, they can't get a signal on theirs. The fact is, they're trying to find juicy pictures and emails that could reveal sensational stories."

Bambi reached under the seat for a small box, which contained six cell phones, numbered consecutively. "Tonight, we'll use numbers one through three. A half hour upon landing in New York, we'll switch to numbers four through six."

"Why do we have to switch phones?"

"The moment we land, reporters will be sweeping for our bandwidths to hack into our conversations. We can't afford any breach of secrecy."

"I thought hacking into people's phones was illegal."

"It is, but only if you get caught."

She distributed the phones, and then presented us with several vials of little white pills.

"What are these, cyanide capsules?" I asked, half joking.

"Caffeine," she said.

The sun rose as we approached the airport. Traffic sped at a maddening pace around round-abouts and narrow, crowded access roads, all of the cars driving on the wrong side. Bambi seemed perfectly at ease behind the wheel, while I was continuously startled by the sudden appearance of cars where I least expected them.

"This is going to be your crowning moment," said Giancarlo. "You're going to make history, like General Custer at the Last Stand."

"Didn't Custer lose that battle?"

"It was good for the Indians. Every battle has a winner."

"Tell that to the dead."

"You can't please everyone."

"Aren't you being a bit dramatic? It's just a press conference."

"It's the biggest event of the decade. This is bigger than Watergate and the O.J. Simpson trial combined."

"You keep using negative examples from history."

Bambi beckoned with her finger, indicating for me to come closer to her, and gave me a peck on the cheek. "We don't want you to get a swell head and lose focus."

"I've got to know," said Giancarlo, "Why did you try to push Kerry off Galata Tower?"

"Hey, aren't you on my side? You know it was a set-up."

"Don't be defensive."

"But it's true. I was set up."

"Conspiracy theories never go over well with the public."

"But you know it's true."

"That was a test. And you failed."

"Oh?"

"You're not taking this seriously enough."

"I am. I just keep forgetting that you're in your PR mode. Of course, that's like being surprised that a lion is in its predator mode."

"I like that. You did mean it as a compliment, didn't you?"

"Yes. But what was your point about the Galata question?"

"My point was to never suggest a conspiracy," he said. "No matter how credible, it'll always sound suspicious. I'll just leave you with one word: Ross Perot."

"That's usually considered two words."

"Ross Perot was a very successful U.S. businessman who decided to run for president in 1992 as an independent against George H.W. Bush and Bill Clinton. His down-to-earth, folksy style caught voters' imagination and, against all odds, his popularity began to soar. For one brief, shining moment it actually looked like he had a shot at the presidency. But he screwed it all up when he complained about a conspiracy against him to keep him from winning."

"That's true. I remember that."

"Another word: Clinton."

"You got the word count correct."

"At the height of his sex scandal, his wife Hillary accused the Right of launching a conspiracy to prove his involvement with Monica Lewinsky."

"He did have sex with that woman."

"That's not the point. The point is that he immediately lost his credibility with the public, and that nearly cost him his job. It's the kind of thing that will happen every time you raise the ugly head of a conspiracy."

"I think you mean 'ugly specter,' not 'ugly head.'"

"What's the difference, they're both ugly?"

"Isn't that what you want to prove? That there's an ugly conspiracy to get me? There is one, isn't there?"

"Of course, but you don't do it by whining about it."

"Why not? It's the truth."

"Consider UFOs and the whole government cover-up conspiracy theory...."

"Don't tell me now that there really are aliens?"

"No, it's just that the conspiracy theorists are relentless. At this point, the public just sees them as kooks."

"Aren't they?"

"Most likely, but that's not the point. PR is not about the truth or the lie. It's about public perception. If these alien conspiracy nuts would let up a little and not be in our faces so much, they might get some traction."

"They're still not going to find the bodies of dead aliens in underground government laboratories."

"It won't matter. Elvis is still dead, but it's fun to believe he's just hiding out somewhere in a hick town pumping his own gas."

"So what should I have said about Galata Towers?"

"In this case, the truth. She slipped and I tried to catch her. The camera happened to take the picture at that moment."

"They'll buy that?"

"Not necessarily, but your simple and honest explanation introduces enough of a doubt about the interpretation of the image to soften their cynicism. What about trying to rape her in Bermuda?"

"Wow, that's kind of harsh."

"So it did happen?"

"I love Kerry. I would never do anything like that to her. I have a great deal of respect for her."

Giancarlo threw Bambi a long, wide grin. "That's my boy!" he said.

"I got that one right?"

"You nailed it."

"I'm a fast learner." The truth was, I meant every word of it. I added, "I still have a lot to remember, though."

"That's where these come in handy," he said, indicating the cell phones. "We'll be using them to avoid danger."

"Actually, the phones are for us to remain in constant communication in the event of a sudden change of strategy," said Bambi.

"That too."

As we reached the airport, she turned to me again, "Watch your phone. Success could depend on a split second of action."

She handed me my passport.

"How did you get this back?" I asked.

"Don't be impressed. They're forged. Right now, it's all about getting back to the States. We'll get you the real deal later. We only have one chance to get this right. Any one of a number of things goes wrong and you can kiss Kerry – and your money – goodbye."

"Like what things?"

"I can't say anymore. Just know this: Nothing I say from now on is a joke. Everything is meaningful. Everything. It's a matter of life and death."

"Damn it, you're frightening me again."

"That's my intention."

As we waited on the Immigration line, Giancarlo and Bambi continuously scanned the faces of the crowd. *They work quite well together,* I thought. It's as if they'd been doing this all their lives.

The officer behind the counter eyed me suspiciously. He was rather tall, with a scrubbed, pink baby face and deep blue eyes. As tall as he was, his clothes were clearly a size too large for him. I did my best to smile pleasantly as he studied my passport and compared the headshot to the live version. He finally stamped the document and slapped it back on the counter.

I prepared to board when my phone vibrated. Bambi had sent me a message. "Don't look back," it read. "Walk quickly to Boarding Gate 10."

I followed her instruction and took my place in line, expecting them to join me shortly. The line advanced quickly, however, without any sign of them, and I let others ahead of me to delay my appearance before the ticket agent. Unfortunately, my turn came sooner than I had hoped and, inevitably, I was forced to endure the agent's questioning regard.

"Sir?" she asked.

Seeing that I didn't offer her anything, she provided more details, "May I have your ticket, please?"

I reluctantly complied and watched with alarm as she tore off her stub and directed me to move along. She snapped shut her large, black ledger and slipped it under her arm. "You need to step into the corridor, sir, so that I can close the door," she said.

I finally did so, wary of causing a scene.

"Enjoy your flight," she said cheerily, as I stared back through the plastic window of the door.

A flight attendant waiting at the end of the corridor called for me to move along again. I walked numbly through the passageway toward the plane, convinced that I had somehow made a catastrophic mistake and Bambi's carefully devised plan was now in jeopardy. I couldn't figure out where I had gone wrong. Maybe I had misunderstood her instructions and gotten on the wrong line. Or maybe the wrong gate. The flight attendants' uniformed were clearly not American or European. I couldn't be sure anymore of having read the number correctly. I paused before the door to the plane, afraid to enter and be flown to some unknown part of the world, separated forever from Bambi and Giancarlo.

"Sir?" uttered the flight attendant inside, who waited impatiently.

I braced to accept my fate, but just as I was about to enter the plane, a hand grabbed me from behind and pulled me back. It was the flight attendant I passed in the corridor. A side door suddenly opened and she pushed me through, instructing me to take a set of shaky metal stairs down to the tarmac, just under the nose of the plane.

"This way," said a small, bearded man at the foot of the stair, who seemed like a refugee from Middle Earth.

I followed him into a nearby hangar, where I was reunited with Giancarlo and Bambi. Their faces told me that things were not going according to plan.

"They found out about us, again," said Bambi. "I had to book us on another flight."

"Why can't we just take the flight anyway? It's not like they're going to shoot us out of the air."

"It's part of the strategy," she said.

"How can you be sure we're being watched?"

"I recognized one of Fabio's assistants behind you, on the line," said Giancarlo. "The panic on his face when you offered to let him pass you was pure gold."

"He *did* seem confused," I considered.

"Don't you remember passing him in the corridor? He was waiting to make sure you boarded," she said.

"I was too upset to notice him."

"Luckily, he let you get too far ahead, and the curve of the corridor hid the entrance to the plane from his line of sight for a couple of seconds. We had to work fast to take you away before he realized that you never made it in. It's to our advantage right now for them to think they know where you are. They're probably still watching the other gates as a precaution, so we have to be on guard."

Giancarlo pulled out of his pockets a baseball cap and fake beard. "I'll reconnoiter," he said.

"Where did you get those?" I asked.

"Standard part of the trade."

"What trade? The James Bond School of Public Relation?"

Bambi led us up a narrow stairway to the main floor of the terminal, where Giancarlo went ahead into the crowd, strolling and looking about him like an elderly man on a Sunday walk. Finally, he took up on a line and, after a few minutes, he tapped his forehead with two fingers.

"That's the signal for me to join him," said Bambi.

"You mean, you even have signals?"

She opened the door. "If anyone's still on our tail, we'll flush them out."

Making her way through the crowd, she joined the line several people behind him. Minutes later, she tapped her forehead and I quickly jumped into the stream of traffic and settled several paces behind them. We made it through without further incidents, but it wasn't until they inspected our tickets at the gate, stamped them, and waved us into the corridor toward the plane that I breathed a sigh of relief.

My eyes took several seconds to adjust to the unusually darkened passageway, and when my vision cleared, I noticed a strange figure at the far end, staring back at me. He started to advance when Giancarlo suddenly grabbed my arm and pulled me back. Bambi, too, jumped into action, but in the opposite direction. She ran toward the man, who was now joined by a partner, leaped at the wall, and caught an overhanging hook. Swinging her body in a wide arc, she launched herself lengthwise into the two startled figures. They instinctively tried to catch her, but she landed on them so hard that she knocked them to the ground. She was on her feet before they could recover, kicked them back down when they tried to rise, and ran back to us.

"Where did you learn to do that?" I exclaimed.

"Pole dancing."

We burst back into the terminal and ran toward the adjoining gate, which was already closed. An overhead sign flashed that boarding had ended.

"Keep moving," said Bambi.

"And what, smash down the door?"

"Don't stop!"

As we neared the door, a flight attendant flung it open and waved us through, into the corridor. We piled inside, after which she swung the door shut and bolted it.

"Hurry," she urged, leading us down the passageway and into the waiting plane. She then quickly secured the plane door and ushered us to our seats.

"Now what?" I asked.

"We sleep," said Bambi, who promptly proceeded to put her advice into action.

In the subsequent hours of the flight, I could only manage restless naps, in which my dreams spun about without logic or purpose. Every now and then I would look out the window, groggily watching the monotonous scene of clouds below us. I would then slip back into my dreams, but they weren't like any I had had before because, for the first time in as long as I could remember, they were not all about Kerry.

I finally woke up to find Giancarlo tapping away on his laptop. He had never bothered to learn touch typing, and so forcefully pressed every letter like a man squashing an endless procession of bugs. "I'm working on my next client," he said.

"And who would that be?"

"Fabio. He's going to need professional help, once I get through with him."

"You're pitching your services to your mortal enemy?"

"I like the challenge."

"He's devious, unethical, manipulative, and a cheap boss. I thought you only represented the honest ones?"

"He's honest in his fashion."

"You're not very consistent."

"I'm flexible. But I'll finish later. Now that you're awake, you have to prepare for your speech."

"I have a speech?"

"Of course. Media from all over the world are converging at Kennedy Airport, where you're going to give an impromptu press briefing."

"I thought the whole point to our giving Fabio the slip was to sneak into the U.S. without being noticed."

Bambi opened her hand to reveal a small electronic device. "You've had a bug on you since your last meeting with Kerry. We've known about it, but we had to put on a good show, make it look like we really believed we've been giving them the slip."

"I can't believe she could be so devious."

"It's part of the plan. We're counting on them to leak the news of our arrival at Kennedy Airport. It's going to give us the perfect opportunity to plant a distraction."

"They're playing right into our hands," said Giancarlo.

He handed me a sheet of paper covered with his nearly indecipherable script. "Your airport speech will be extemporaneous. This is for your major speech tomorrow. It's still kind of rough. We'll polish it up as we go along."

I reviewed the speech, which recounted an extraordinary tale of danger, betrayal, absolution, and redemption.

"This is quite a liberal interpretation of the facts," I noted.

"It's an approximation," he said, "for the sake of expediency."

"In your defense, there are small kernels of truth, if you look hard enough."

"The sincerest speeches have a bit of truth sprinkled over them."

"In this case, it looks like you used an eye-dropper."

"I try not to dilute the product."

"Let me take a look at that speech," said Bambi.

Giancarlo, mortified, reluctantly handed it to her, and after a few deft strokes of the pen on her part, she gave it back to me.

"This version seems closer to the truth," I said.

"Yes, but is it a good speech?" demanded Giancarlo. He snatched it from me and started furiously to amend it. Minutes later, he passed it back. "I think this works better," he said.

"I don't see that you've made any new changes from Bambi's version."

"Here." He pointed to the middle of the speech. "I changed 'terrible' to 'horrible.' Commit it to memory. You're going to have every reporter in your face, trying to throw you off-script, so it's important to know it backwards and forwards."

"That's great for tomorrow. How about today? I have no clue as to what I'm supposed to talk about."

"Today, just speak from the heart."

"You're joking."

"Of course." He handed me a small piece of paper. "I'm going to introduce you; then, you just follow my lead."

The seat belt sign started flashing as the plane circled for landing.

"It's show time," he said.

New York City soon sprawled below us in all its sparkling grandeur. Our descent slowly revealed countless highways, cars coursing through them like shiny corpuscles, going silently to their mysterious destinations. We landed shortly and taxied to the terminal. The windows of the lounge across from us throbbed mysteriously, and a closer inspection revealed them to be teeming with journalists, packed tightly and restlessly, staring back out at the plane. Suddenly, camera flashes went off rapidly and continuously, as if an electrical short circuit had been tripped. Giancarlo pulled me away from the window.

"Stay out of sight or you'll start a riot," he said.

As the plane rolled to a stop, the flight attendants moved quickly to clear out the passengers, until we were the only ones remaining.

"Go get 'em, Mr. Kahn," said one of them.

"How does she know about this?" I asked Giancarlo.

"It's the lead story on all the networks," he said.

She kissed me quickly and shyly on the cheek, catching me by surprise. Bambi pulled me away.

"That's not part of the show," she said.

"Are you jealous?"

"She was fishing in your pockets, looking for your speech. It's worth thousands of dollars to the tabloids."

I reached frantically into my pocket, looking for paper. She held it up to me, having taken it out herself before I rose from my seat.

"I'm beginning to lose my faith in humanity."

"About time."

"We paused at the exit to the plane, where two tall and beefy men immediately surrounded me.

"We've got the path all mapped out, Mr. Kahn," said the one with the shaved head and broader shoulders. "I'm Matthew. I'll take the lead. Mark here will cover our flank. Peter's waiting at the gate. He'll clear the trail. Stick close to us. We'll get you there."

"Can I call you Matt?"

"No, Matthew. That's my code name for this assignment."

"Stay focused," Giancarlo advised me.

"If you don't, they'll eat you alive," said Matthew. "I've seen this before."

"Right," agreed Giancarlo. "Eyes front. Don't smile. But don't frown. Look pleasant, but not happy."

"Maybe I shouldn't look at all," I said.

"You can close your eyes," said Matthew, helpfully. "I'll guide you."

"How can I see where I'm going?"

"Hold on to my shoulders. We'll get you there."

"You'd think I was the second coming of the Beatles."

"They at least had their music to fall back on," said Giancarlo. "You mess up today and you're toast. Aside from that, relax. No pressure."

"Was that supposed to be a pep talk? By the way, where's Bambi?"

"She's exiting from the back of the plane. Her presence would be a distraction. We want all eyes on you."

"How do I start?"

"I'll introduce you."

"Hands on my shoulders, head down," Matthew instructed. "It's show time."

"Go!" said Giancarlo.

"Peter, the Messiah has risen and shall enter the house of the Lord," Matthew declared.

"Now I understand your code names," I said.

Matthew regarded me in confusion.

"You're the three apostles. You're using Bible references," I explained.

"Peter, prep the gate," said Matthew, disregarding me. "Luke, position. John, back us up. In five, four, three, two…."

We plunged into the passageway, taking up a fast trot like a boxer about to enter the ring for a fight. Mark held shut the door to the lounge ahead of us and, just as we reached it, flung it open. Immediately, a tremendous roar rose from the crowd, causing the floor literally to shudder.

"Hold on," cried Matthew as another, powerfully built man came into view. The man parted the crowd like Moses before the Red Sea. Locking arms with Matthew, he shielded me from the bodies pressing against us and the extended hands that tried to grab hold of me.

I could barely see over people's head and felt like a salmon fighting my way upstream, tumbling inside the churning waters. A podium finally emerged above the crowd, propped up on a small, makeshift stage. Inexplicably, Giancarlo was already there, apparently having gotten through while most of the journalists were crowded around me.

A tremendous cheer filled the air as I approached the microphones. All the major television networks were present, their branded microphones and cell phones held up high to capture my every word, their reporters jostling for position. But it was the high concentration of women in back of them, jumping up and down ecstatically, that surprised me. They weren't protesting me as the devil; they were cheering for me, holding up signs in support, as if I were a beloved celebrity.

As I waited for Giancarlo to quiet the crowd, my phone vibrated. I glance quickly at the message, which simply said, "Go with the flow." It was from Kerry.

I looked up and there she was, all the way in back of the terminal, near the exit. Her face was barely visible inside a hooded sweatshirt.

I blinked and she was gone, and when I checked my phone again, so was the message.

"Ladies and gentlemen of the press," began Giancarlo, "this is quite an unexpected development. Mr. Cain Kahn was completely caught off guard. He had hoped to return to the states and go back to his quiet life without fanfare. But since you're here, he doesn't want to disappoint you and has graciously agreed to answer some of your questions. But before we begin, I would like to state, on my client's behalf, that Mr. Kahn has absolutely no knowledge of Kerry Daniels' rumored pregnancy and categorically denies that he's the father. He will therefore not be taking any questions on the topic."

As expected, the news struck with the force of a lightning bolt. The mass of bodies heaved and swayed like the restless waves of the ocean. Reporters pelted me with questions and nearly toppled over the stage, except the bodyguards pushed them back and glared menacingly at anyone who tried to challenge them.

"Cain!" one shouted. "If you're not the father, who is?"

"What?"

"Do you know the sex of the baby?"

"But she's not-"

"Will you still marry her even if the child's not yours?"

Giancarlo nudged me. I glanced at my phone for guidance and, luckily, found some.

"No comment," I said.

"Will you take a paternity test to confirm you're not the father?"

"This is the first-" I again attempted to explain.

Giancarlo motioned to the bodyguards, who immediately flanked me, lifted me off the ground, and whisked me away through a narrow break in the crowd. A waiting limousine swallowed me up as the journalists spilled out after me, continuing their fuselage of questions.

"What pregnancy are you talking about?" I asked, completely dumbfounded.

"A misdirection," he said.

"So, she's not pregnant?"

"Of course not."

"I wish you'd warned me about these kinds of things. I was caught totally by surprise by the question. I looked like a deer in the headlights."

"That was the idea."

8

The limousine looped around Kennedy Airport and picked up the Van Wyck Expressway to Manhattan. It seemed as if I had been on the road forever. Every night had brought me to a new destination, a new hotel – and I hadn't minded it at all. Maybe I had even enjoyed it. It had finally given me the opportunity to see and talk to Kerry again, even if not under ideal conditions. As much as it tore me up emotionally every time, I lived for those moments. Returning to the old routines was going to be difficult.

After battling traffic and emerging from the Mid-Town Tunnel, the limousine turned downtown several blocks to 28th Street and pulled up to a modest and unassuming three-story townhouse off Park Avenue, where Giancarlo lived. Looks were deceiving. He actually also owned the adjoining two houses, which had been carefully connected from inside. The buildings' facade hid a broadcast facility worthy of any major TV network. A press room dominated one of the houses, complete with auditorium-style seating and a stage; the second house had more traditional office space with cubicles filled with young people hurrying about, punching out messages on their keyboards, then scouring the many monitors surrounding them, searching for the results of their handiwork. A high-tech kitchen peeked out of a large, adjacent room, and this was already packed with numerous young men and women in uniforms that identified them as part of a catering service. A spacious auditorium dominated what would have been the third house. Its giant screen was split into multiple images beaming news from around the world.

"They're preparing for tomorrow's press conference," said Giancarlo.

"I meant to tell you, I think I saw Kerry at the airport," I said. "Weren't we supposed to arrive ahead of her?"

"There was a lot of confusion. You were probably just imagining things."

"She seemed real. She even left me a message."

"Let me see."

"It disappeared."

He gave me a look, and I had to concede that the whole thing happened too quickly, and during too much commotion, to support its validity.

I counted over forty people in the houses, and every one of them was busy. The world fluttered by on countless TV screens; the JFK airport press conference dominated the news cycle on nearly every one of them. The words "Breaking News" covered the screens, with hyperventilating news anchors delivering the shocking scoop. Speculation ran wild about Kerry's possible pregnancy. How many months? Could it be detected in the latest images of her? If I'm not the father, who is? Would that be revealed soon? Is Kerry accepting my denial or will she demand a paternity test? Assuming, for the moment, that I was not the father, why was I still reconciling with her? A thousand other, nonsensical questions were rapidly picked at and discarded, much like homeless men picking through garbage bins, pulling out and throwing away unwanted items, hoping to find something of value.

"It's frightening how easy it is to send the media chasing after clearly ludicrous stories," I said.

"It's like playing catch with your dog," said Giancarlo. "No matter how many times you take the stick from its mouth and throw it out again, the dog can't help chasing after it."

"Yes, but don't they realize how ridiculous they look?"

He shrugged. "It keeps them entertained."

"I hope you know what you're doing."

"Does it look that hard to do?" His arms swept the scene. "We're hooked up to every major network in the world. Everyone is waiting for you to speak again. You sneeze and it'll be front page news."

"This set-up must have taken weeks of preparation."

"I never leave anything to chance."

"You must have sunk a fortune."

"It's money well spent."

"You're a great friend."

"Don't be silly. We've got sponsors. We're making tons of money. It's a group effort, so we'll be splitting the profits evenly."

He pointed to one of the numerous monitors where, for the first time, I noticed a Coca Cola logo. In fact, most monitors flashed the logos of popular brands when they went into hibernation: Benetton, Campbell's Alphabet Soup and Lego were the most common. Music played softly in the background, and now I realized that the same one had been playing since my arrival: The Turtles' "Happy Together."

"Your reconciliation is a global phenomenon," he said. "We've contracted for more than thirty million in sponsorships and counting. It's so huge that Coca Cola is bringing back its old slogan: 'Things go better with Coke.' Get it? You and Kerry go better together."

"Thirty million?"

"Yes, and where do you think that money's going?"

"To charity?"

"Well, yes, you're giving a percentage to organizations serving battered women. I'm donating a part of my take to children's orphanages. Kerry's starting a nonprofit trade school in Africa to help women rescued from sex trafficking. When the dust settles, we should each have pulled in about five million clean."

"That accounts for your good mood."

"That, and the smell of blood. I'm finally going to take down my old rival. Only live coverage of the resurrection of Jesus Christ would have drawn a bigger audience."

"Incredible!"

"Hold your applause."

"No, I mean that girl, over there."

At the far end of the apartment, out of the tangle of television equipment and hyperactive technicians, a woman moved toward us.

She appeared to do so in slow motion, while the flurry of human bodies shuddered about her, like frantic drones around their queen bee. Finally, she broke free of the chaos and into the clearing. It was Kerry. Or so I thought.

She stopped just several feet away from me and smiled, but the expression on her face gave her away. She looked sweet, demure, sympathetic, gentle, and vulnerable – everything Kerry was not.

"It's not," said Giancarlo.

I tore my eyes away to focus again on Giancarlo.

"She's Kerry's stand-in, to run through some conference scenarios with you. I want you to become perfectly comfortable talking to Kerry. Scarily like the real thing, isn't she?"

"Almost."

She extended her hand. "It's a pleasure to meet you, Mr. Kahn. I'm Gabrielle."

"You two have to rehearse your spontaneous press conference," said Giancarlo.

I impulsively reached out to touch her, to convince myself of what I didn't want to know – that she wasn't Kerry.

"I'll be back in a moment," said Giancarlo.

Gabrielle too started for the door, but I grabbed her arm.

"Where are you going?"

"I was just getting my phone," she said.

I didn't want to explain that I was afraid to let her go. Even if she was a facsimile. Giancarlo returned shortly with several pages in his hand. "We typed up the script of your speech," he told me. "We've also composed some potential scenarios."

He addressed an assistant nearby, who was looking at a bank of TV monitors. "What's our spread in Vegas?"

"Five to one she's a no-show."

"Let the games begin."

9

Rehearsals with Kerry's double went on all evening, and it proved to be a uniquely pleasant experience. I had forgotten how it felt to be with Kerry for an extended period of time, under friendly conditions. I enjoyed saying her name out loud, touching her, watching her become the perfect woman, even if she was only an imitation. The conference room, meanwhile, was pure pandemonium. The random racket of carpenters and set designers, banging away on hammers and dragging furniture across the floor, made regular conversation almost impossible.

Everyone was shouting, and everyone had something to complain about to their subordinates.

A theme park designer obsessively rearranged the furniture. He placed props at strategic locations, then changed his mind and placed them somewhere else. At one point, he irritably scolded an assistant for leaving a flower vase on the wrong table – the one where, in fact, he had left it himself ten minutes earlier. "Am I the only one who sees that it doesn't belong there?" he asked. Apparently, he was. A fashion consultant argued over the color and placement of the curtains on the windows; an up-and-coming movie director rehearsed a group of actors, who would serve as greeters and ushers. An IT professional familiarized a battery of tech specialists with the dedicated communications system for the inevitable, critical moments when every technology breaks down. Meanwhile, several speechwriters furiously typed away: revising scripts, modifying stage directions, debating hypothetical conversations, questions and responses.

"You've got to look and act like a responsible individual, reflecting your status on Wall Street," said Giancarlo to me. "On the other hand, you can't look too conservative. They'll think you've got a bug up your ass, like someone who deserved what they got."

"How am I going to pull that off?

"I've got my best acting coach who will work with you on that. She'll be taking over from Gabrielle in half an hour."

I walked up and down the stage steps repeatedly at his instructions.

"You have to get to know every step by heart. I don't want you stumbling in the bright lights and creating a comical scene that will detract from your credibility," he said. "Also, stare at Gabrielle until you're completely comfortable in her presence. You can't seem obsessed with Kerry, like a stalker. You can't appear to ignore her either. You always have to act like a gentleman. In other words, be yourself."

"Being myself is hard work. I'm not sure I can remember all that."

"Don't worry. The instructions will be on the teleprompter."

"This is quite a bit of preparation. How long have you been working on this?"

"At least a week, round-the-clock. We're figuring this will run about an hour."

"Thank God. If this had been half an hour, you would probably have spent a month preparing for it."

"That's about right."

"I was joking."

"The shorter the opportunity, the longer the preparation needed. We only get one shot at this. You've got to seize the moment, strike while the iron is hot, deal the *coup d'état*, bring down the hammer, and close the deal air-tight."

"Your abundance of metaphors leaves me breathless."

"It's a gift."

"By the way, where's Bambi? I haven't seen her since we left the plane."

"She's taking care of other things for us."

"What other things?"

"You're only a third of the joint press conference."

"If it's a joint press conference with Kerry, wouldn't that make me a half?"

"Sorry, can't say anymore. Everything's on NTK. A couple of big bombshells are going to drop at the press conference. It's important that you look appropriately shocked. The element of surprise is our best weapon."

"What kind of bombshells?"

"We're not sure yet. We're working on several options."

Our conversation continued this way until the acting coach arrived. By now, I had resigned myself to his ambiguous responses. The day wore on until, finally, Giancarlo felt that preparations were complete. Gathering everyone together, he commended them for their exceptional display of teamwork and dedication to the tasks at hand and pronounced an end to the day. As they filed out, he reminded them to come back early and promptly tomorrow.

The house was eventually left empty, except for several technicians who wandered about picking at electrical panels with their plyers. One of them crawled under the desk of PR staff members – the night shift – who manned the international desks. They seemed oblivious to his presence, as if it was a common occurrence for people to crawl around their legs, fixing things. A quick glance around conveyed the impression of a movie sound stage ready for the first day of shooting. It made sense to treat the event like a big-budget production. The success of the conference strongly depended on the visual impact of the images that would soon be beamed to hundreds of millions of homes around the world. That, of course, put no pressure on me!

Exhausted, we too decided to break for the night and head to our separate bedrooms in the basement.

"We're flying without a net, aren't we?" I said as we parted.

"Into the clear blue sky."

"We're going to crash and burn."

"We're going to burn brightly."

"Please tell me you meant that in a positive way?"

"Of course. Nothing but clear sailing ahead."

"That's what the captain of the Titanic said."

I settled upon the knowledge that it would all end tomorrow, one way or another. The past year had been chaotic, unpredictable and relentlessly brutal upon my ego. And I was going to miss every minute of it.

I awoke in the middle of the night to the strange sensation of someone pressing against my body under the sheets. Kerry was by my side, but for a moment I wondered whether it was Gabrielle, as I couldn't make out her face clearly in the darkness. Her lips brushed against my skin; she guided my hand to a warm and familiar place, and I knew it was really her, after all.

Later that evening, I said to her, "Even at my lowest points, I never thought of telling anyone the truth about you. I had copies of all the documents proving your guilt. I could have released them at any time. But no matter how cruel you were to me, and how much of a fool you made me look in the eyes of the world, I never did. That should have counted for something."

"It wouldn't have mattered. The documents were fake. If you had released them, it would have made you look like a bigger fool. I'm glad you didn't. That was your one saving grace. It told me you still cared enough to be protective of me."

"But Katrina showed me the original documents. I know your signature. She couldn't have possibly forged that."

"That was the only thing real about them."

"How do you know that?"

"I gave them to her. She was acting under my instructions."

"You're telling me that you set the whole thing up? You wanted Katrina to blackmail me? If that's true, it would mean…."

"Yes, I wanted you to cheat on me."

"Why?"

"It gave me an excuse to steal your money."

In the moment that I lay in stunned silence, she rose and left the room. I assumed she was simply stepping away to use the bathroom, but after a minute or so had elapsed without her return, I jumped out of bed to follow her. I found nothing more than the faint trail of her perfume.

After fruitlessly searching the houses, I returned to bed and tried to sleep again and, surprisingly, I did so. Several hours later I awoke and, stepping outside, found the place alive with people once more.

Workers were running systems checks, adjusting monitors and otherwise keeping themselves busy. Giancarlo commanded the center of attention, making observations, calling out instructions, directing people through their various tasks. I told him about Kerry.

"Are you sure it was her?"

"The whole place is under surveillance. At least one of the cameras must have spotted her."

"Bambi would have shown her how to get around them." He dialed his cell phone and waited impatiently for the call to be picked up on the other end. Getting voicemail, he said, "Call me as soon as you get this message." He looked at me, explaining: "Bambi hasn't checked in since last night. Did Kerry ask you about the conference?"

"No. In fact, we talked about everything *but* the conference."

"Good. Its best you didn't."

"What would have been the problem if we did? I assume she and Bambi are working on it on the other end, too."

"What makes you assume that?"

"You! That's what you implied last night."

He regarded me for a moment. "I did, didn't I?"

"Is she or isn't she being coached on her end? Never mind. NTK."

At that moment, a male assistant approached us with a small, weathered old man in tow. The old man was glancing around nervously, dodging busy workers and, generally, trying not to get himself knocked over.

"You're wearing an outdated security badge," Giancarlo absently informed the assistant.

Even before he had finished the sentence, everyone was in motion. The assistant was shrinking back, the old man was charging at me, Giancarlo was lunging forward to intercept. He caught the old man and wrestled him to the ground, simultaneously shouting for security. The old man shrieked in terror and struggled to break free. A pair of burly security officers rushed over and reached out for Giancarlo, but he frantically directed them to his assistant, wanting to subdue the old man himself. The assistant offered no resistance as they grabbed his arms to detain him.

Shocked at Giancarlo's behavior, I leaped into the fray to separate him, but he kicked me away violently. "Run!" he cried.

The old man proved surprisingly difficult to pin down, considering Giancarlo's strength. The reason soon became apparent as his wig fell off to reveal a much younger man. Eventually tiring out, however, he sprawled on the floor, panting heavily.

"What's gotten into you?" I exclaimed, pulling Giancarlo away after he, too, paused for breath.

"Don't touch him!" he said, too tired to resist me.

"It's in my pocket," the man addressed me, pleadingly. "My left jacket pocket."

"No!" cried Giancarlo, scrambling to prevent me from following through on the request.

He was too late. I pulled out an envelope, which Giancarlo then tried vainly to tear from my hand.

"Open it," the man encouraged.

I did so, discovering an official looking document inside.

"He's a sheriff," Giancarlo declared. "You've just been served."

I dropped the paper fearfully, as if suddenly finding it crawling with maggots. Giancarlo stood up, dusted himself off, and studied the assistant who had escorted the sheriff into the room.

"Don't I pay you enough?" he asked.

"I'm an intern. You don't pay me at all."

Giancarlo reluctantly agreed.

"He's a mole," said the stranger, triumphantly. "We know every detail of your plans for the press conference. Mr. Wallinsky sends his regards."

I picked up the document gingerly. "It's an Order of Protection. I'm not allowed within a hundred yards of Kerry, effective immediately. Is this order legal?"

"Yes."

"That means we can't hold a joint press conference, at least not together in the same room. But that would defeat the whole purpose, wouldn't it, since we have to be physically next to each other."

"Looks like it, doesn't it?"

"What do we do now?"

Giancarlo turned to the security officers. "Get them out of here," he commanded. He waited until the door closed behind the two men.

"Don't worry," he said. "We suspected we were being watched. All the rehearsals were for his benefit. We needed to keep Fabio distracted."

"Distracted from what?"

"From our real plan."

"So we're *not* holding a joint press conference?"

"Of course, we are. Never change horses in the middle of the road."

"Good advice, if you own horses. But I suppose you mean that we shouldn't change our plans? We go on with the press conference?"

"Precisely. Fabio doesn't want this press conference to succeed. Let him think he's got me backed into a corner. We must be on the right track."

"But didn't he agree to it? Why would he want to sabotage it?"

"The conference wasn't his idea. It was Kerry's."

He considered the document, frowned, and ran a wet finger across it. "Inkjet printer," he said, displaying the smudge. "It's a fake."

"What does he gain by serving us with phony paper?"

"What does he gain?" he repeated. "Assume, for a moment, that we cancel it. If we do, he'll accuse us of backing out because we had something to hide. If we then try to defend the cancellation by showing everyone the supposed Order of Protection, he would prove it was a fake and accuse us of trying to perpetrate a scam. My agency would suffer a catastrophic blow to its credibility. I might as well hand him all my clients on a silver platter, then."

He bit his lip pensively, took a deep breath, shook his finger at me, and exhaled. "No. He knows I wouldn't change horses. Cancelling a press conference at the last minute is one of the worse sins you can commit in public relations, next to giving the same scoop to two reporters and telling them it's an exclusive. He'll expect me to hold the press conference as scheduled, but make up an excuse to explain Kerry's absence. That's when he hopes to strike the fatal blow."

He looked at his watch and dialed his phone again, then hung up in frustration.

"Are you still trying to reach Bambi?"

He nodded.

"Should we be worried?"

"Always be worried."

He led me to a small control room, tucked out of sight from the rest of the houses. Several assistants watched surveillance videos of every part of the premises, including the exterior. I was startled by what I saw on the monitors facing the front of the house. Thousands of people packed the streets as far as the eyes could see, with banks of satellite news vans spanning the block like tanks preparing for battle.

"More than ten thousand people are outside the house, with probably a hundred million more on TV," he said. "All the major TV and cable networks are there. Traffic is backed up for ten blocks around. This is the Big One."

"You'd think they were all coming to watch a hanging."

"They just might be. The question is, whose? By the way, I've got to tell you, whatever happens today, it's been a great ride. Who would have thought a year ago that you and I would be together again, standing on the precipice of greatness?"

"'Standing on a precipice' is not generally considered a positive thing."

"It's the only place to be. Our names will be immortalized in the annals of history. I'm glad I haven't been drinking today, 'cause I'd start pumping out the tears right about now. We play this right and we'll both hit the big time with more explosive power than ten shooting stars combined..."

"Shooting stars don't explode. They usually burn up in the atmosphere. I think you mean something like ten supernovas."

"You've got to start drinking again. You're much funnier after a couple of doubles. Give me a hug."

We hastily dispensed with the ritual as the female assistant discreetly looked away.

"Hey," said Giancarlo, studying the monitors with the crowds outside more closely. "Isn't that your picture by the Bermuda Lighthouse on all those spectator signs? Yes, that's a screen grab from the Jumbletron image, and it's in full color. That's definitely a picture of your ass. Can't tell from the monitors what they wrote on those signs, however."

"Does my ass need a caption?"

"The reporters are arriving," an assistant announced. A partition had been lowered to the press room, so that our activities were shielded from them.

Giancarlo handed me his cell phone. "Send me word the moment you hear from Bambi. Meanwhile, stay in the room until I call you. Timing is everything. You'll reveal yourself to the audience when I give you the password. It's 'butterfly.' Got it?"

"We need a password?"

"Come on, repeat it."

"Okay, 'butterfly.'"

"Good. Don't forget it. No matter what you see or hear from the press room, don't – under any circumstances – come out until you hear the password. Everything's about proper timing."

"You're the boss."

"Oh, and another major sponsor's come on board," he said. "Chase Manhattan Bank is kicking in three million for us to slap their slogan on the podium – you know: *Chase: The Right Relationship is Everything.*' All right, it's show time."

I followed him on one of the monitors as he headed out. Closed circuit cameras captured every corner of the room. Withing a quarter of an hour, the place was standing room only. Giancarlo appeared and reporters excitedly sprang into the aisles and crowded around the stage (security guards prevented them from leaping on it). Thousands of flickering camera flashes bathed the room in an almost white light. Giancarlo extended his arms like Jesus Christ at the Mount of Olives, as if about to benevolently multiply the loaves of bread and fishes for the masses, and serenely proceeded to answer their diverse and disjointed, rapidly fired questions.

The assistant raised the volume on the monitor, allowing us to hear him clearly. The questions went on for nearly an hour. Most were simply variations of the same basic theme, and Giancarlo was more than happy to answer them again, patiently. "What finally led to the reconciliation?" "Is Kerry returning the money?" "If Cain isn't the child's father, who is?" "Are Cain and Kerry in the building?" "Can we talk to them now?"

Finally, he requested a moment of silence. They acquiesced like petulant children being told they must stop talking because it was time for bed. Amid the low muttering of impatience from the audience, he began his introduction. For the next ten minutes, he recounted the tumultuous history of my relationship with Kerry and, surprisingly, he got most of the events correct, though his interpretation of them could have been brought into question. The truth was more of an opinion than a statement of facts.

He paused, finally, and looked to the side of the stage ominously. Instantly, as if one massive animal, the reporters leaped to their feet and attempted to storm the stage again. Security barely managed to contain them. Several reporters who did make it past the front line of guards were caught by the second line and flung back into the crowd. The reporters moaned, bickered among themselves, and hurled insults at each other. One reporter complained to another that he had cut in front of the line (though there was none). Another cried in pain, having been accidently elbowed by a colleague. A female reporter accused a nearby male of fondling her breasts and, in general, being a pervert. Suddenly, gunshots rang through the room. The reporters dove to the ground in panic. Several people screamed; a few fainted under the weight of their colleagues, who had jumped on top of them as they threw themselves to the floor. The scene was reminiscent of the one at the museum in Turkey, except that the audience was bigger here. When no more shots rang out and no one appeared to be calling out in pain or claiming to be wounded, the reporters slowly got back to their feet – only, this time, they were quiet, looking warily around the room to see if there was a shooter anywhere.

"Sorry," said Giancarlo, "that must have been a technical glitch in the audio.

The audience groaned, convinced they had just been victims of a practical joke.

"We don't want to waste your valuable time," he continued. "We all know why you're here. There won't be any dancing girls or preshow commercials from our sponsors. We respect your positions as responsible members of the press. Frank!" He addressed one of the reporters in the audience. "I haven't forgotten our conversation. Casey is going to send you that press kit on my new clients after this."

"Can you stop stalling? How about bringing them out!" called a reporter.

"Of course!" said Giancarlo, as if wounded to the core by the suggestion. "She doesn't need an introduction. Come on out...."

He gestured to the side of the stage and waited expectantly. The room held its collective breath. The minutes dragged on. After it became clear that Kerry had missed her cue, another groan swept through the crowd. Giancarlo peered into the darkness of backstage. He introduced her again, and again the seconds ticked away without her appearance. This time, he signaled to the ushers in the room and they scattered away, presumably in search of an explanation.

"While we wait," he said, "I might as well introduce to you our second guest of the evening, Mr. Cain Kahn."

Everyone was again on their feet, pushing toward the stage, but more politely. They had learned their lesson and cautiously prepared for my entrance. I started for the door, when the assistant grabbed my shirtsleeve. "That's not your cue," she said.

"He just introduced me."

"He didn't say 'butterfly.'"

As reporters craned their necks for my appearance, the image on the giant screen in back of the stage, behind Giancarlo, suddenly flashed to the back of the press room to show a door opening. Into view sauntered a dwarfish looking man, very fat, thinning hair, yet moving with surprising fluidity. There was a sensual fascination about him, as if by sheer willpower alone he could make you believe that he was not the inferior human being before your eyes but actually a superior example of his own unique species.

The image on the monitor cut back to Giancarlo; his blank expression failed to disguise the look of pure hatred in his eyes. There was no doubt about it. The dwarfish man was the legendary Fabio Wallinsky.

For every evil in public relations of the past two decades, this was the man to check in with, according to Giancarlo. He masterminded the notorious Joe Camel cigarette ads, which subtly promoted to young people the coolness factor of smoking. He convinced the public that strip mining was an ecologically sound alternative to logging. He positioned canned milk as a status symbol to lactating mothers in Third World countries, subverting medical evidence that breast milk provided maternal antibodies that strengthen infants' immunization system. Giancarlo also accused him of being the driving force behind the inexplicable success of actor David Hasselhoff in Germany and musician Yanni practically everywhere else in the world. He even blamed Fabio for the popularity of disco back in the '70's.

Fabio paused midway up the aisle. He proudly and calmly surveyed the room, savoring the moment. Giancarlo, meanwhile, stood poised like a man on the precipice, knowing that the next few minutes could forever cement his legendary reputation – or destroy everything in his career that he had worked so hard to achieve.

"Where are your special guests?" Fabio demanded, though he too, surprisingly, did not seem any more confident that he had a better answer. It was, I realized, a battle of one-upmanship, with neither side revealing exactly what it was that they truly knew.

Everybody spun around to see where the question had come from. Many in the audience immediately recognized Fabio and let out a collective gasp. They comprehended the enormous significance of seeing the world's two greatest PR practitioners in the same room together, just feet apart. Giancarlo calmly disappeared back stage, eliciting murmurs from the crowd. They assumed he was going to get one of us. After what seemed like an eternity, he reappeared, but he was still alone. Fabio shrugged uneasily, completely baffled by the seemingly meaningless maneuver. Someone in the crowd made a mysterious comment, and it elicited an equally mysterious response. A smile crossed Giancarlo's face. Fabio caught it. And he trembled.

Giancarlo tapped the microphones several times. "Everyone, please remain in your seats for a moment. Mr. Wallinsky..." he began, and everyone held their breath. He reached for a bottle of water brought by an assistant. He twisted the cap off and poured himself a glass. He took a sip.

"Mr. Wallinsky," he repeated, and every eye shot to the place where Fabio, having advanced, meekly acknowledged that he was, indeed, the man being addressed. "You ask about my special guests? I would like to ask the same thing of you. Isn't Kerry, in fact, *your* client? She has been your client for many years. Isn't that so?"

Fabio nodded faintly and cautiously, as if ready to change the direction of his head at any moment, should it better serve his purpose.

"For the past year," Giancarlo pursued, "you have been waging an aggressive PR campaign on her behalf, have you not? Only, you've been doing it clandestinely, through a proxy agency that you set up as a front to hide your activities."

Fabio glanced around as another murmur swept the audience. Summoning up his courage, he waddled the rest of the way up the aisle, and stopped before the stage. His face was ashen with concern, as he didn't know where Giancarlo was going with his line of questions. Beads of sweat popped out from his forehead, but I had learned enough from Giancarlo to know that this physical reaction didn't mean he was panicking. His mind instead was working furiously, revising his strategy on the fly, and this made him an even more dangerous adversary.

"Yes, Ms. Daniels is my client," he said, cautiously. "But I beg to disagree with you. I never hid that fact from the world, intentionally. The world simply never cared to ask, and is that my fault?"

"Perhaps it is not," said Giancarlo, thoughtfully. "But since you now admit that she is your client, didn't the responsibility fall upon you to ensure that she made her press conference today?"

"Maybe…" he responded, warily.

"So, wouldn't it be more appropriate for me to ask *you* the question: Where is your client, Kerry Daniels? Where is she now?"

Fabio hesitated – and then smiled again. "Where's Ms. Daniels now?" he declared. "I have a strange feeling that you know the answer better than I do, Mr. Galilei."

"Why would I?" countered his rival. "Isn't it your job to keep track of your clients?"

Fabio was visibly agitated and shrunk back from the stage as if fearful of the light. "You know I don't know where she is, because you stole her from me," he hissed.

"I can't steal someone who comes to me willingly."

"All right, she's your client now," he admitted, irritably. "So, let's stop wasting everyone's time with these theatrics? Why don't you bring her out?"

"The fact is, as I have just learned, she has been delayed," said Giancarlo, "in traffic."

"Well," said Fabio, "as long as we are waiting for Ms. Daniels' arrival, I believe we can start with Mr. Cain Kahn, can we not? He's still your client, is he not?"

"That's always been public knowledge."

"Why did he not come out when you introduced him? I have it on good authority that he is actually somewhere nearby, awaiting your signal. Yet, you continue to toy with the media. Time is very precious to our press corps, and it would not serve our cause to trifle with it."

"Your information is correct. Mr. Kahn is somewhere nearby, but he is in hiding," said Giancarlo. "He is reluctant to enter the room out of fear for his life."

"Nonsense, the press doesn't bite…too hard," said Fabio. He was joined in expressing amusement at the joke by several members of the audience.

"There are other animals with a stronger bite," said Giancarlo, mysteriously.

It was obvious from Fabio's expression that the conversation was making him nervous. He resisted a retort, wary of falling into another possible trap.

"I'll be happy to call Mr. Kahn now, if you'll guarantee his safety," continued Giancarlo.

"Why would I…" began Fabio, and then quickly went silent again.

Cain watched all this on the monitor. He wasn't sure himself what was going on. Giancarlo was clearly stalling, but for what? Giancarlo's cell phone buzzed in my hand. "All system's go," said a voice.

"Bambi? Where have you been?"

"Cain?"

"Giancarlo's in the middle of the press conference right now. He gave me his phone in case you called. He's been very worried about you."

"I got all his messages. I just literally had no time to call him back. Did you expose the mole?"

"As a matter of fact, we did."

"Good. I've been getting everyone into place since yesterday. I must have traveled 200 miles and made a hundred phone calls, all under the tightest veil of secrecy. The only project I've ever tackled that was more complex involved a famous Arab sheik. He's a patient of mine now. At that time, he must have had an entourage of 40 people, and everyone had to be accommodated without raising suspicions. The slightest leak could have plunged his country into a bloody civil war."

"Bambi, can you tell me the short version, for now?"

"Of course. Let Giancarlo know everything's in place and to hang tight. Things are about to explode."

I gave Bambi's message to the assistant, who immediately relayed it to a colleague on the phone. In the press room, meanwhile, Giancarlo and Fabio continued to square off. Shortly, an assistant rushed over to Giancarlo and huddled with him on stage. Giancarlo scanned the audience idly as they spoke. Presently, he patted his assistant on the shoulder and sent him away. He regarded the audience once more, took a deep breath, raked back his hair, returned to the podium, and beckoned to someone at the back of the room.

At that moment, a single policeman burst in and made his way up the aisle. Giancarlo beckoned again and, suddenly, more than 20 additional policemen poured in. They fanned out along the back wall as the lead police officer, now having reached the stage and turning to the audience, whipped out his badge and raised it high into the air.

"I am Officer Malloy. Everyone please stay in your seats. Mr. Galilei, is the suspect in the room?"

Giancarlo pointed to the middle of the room, and every head rapidly rotated to the designated spot. Instantly, a policeman threw himself into the audience and, as if from the impact of a meteor, people flew out in all directions. When the confusion cleared, the officer was holding on tightly to a strangely animated, impeccably dressed, elderly man with a long, white beard. A pit bull couldn't have shown more determination to tear itself away.

As the policeman ripped off the elderly man's fake beard, I recognized him from that night in Bermuda, when I had spied on Kerry as she danced around the bonfire. He had been among the participants. Seeing him on the screen, however, I realized that I also knew him from somewhere else; yet, I couldn't immediately place him. He put up a valiant, if futile, fight, but soon relented as other officers joined in and completely overpowered him. He relaxed his body, smiled derisively, and surrendered with a flourish. Unimpressed with the dramatic gesture, an officer snapped handcuffs on his wrists.

Fabio let out a scream, seeing the strange developments, and hurled his body into the crowd, lunging for the elderly man with surprising energy. He didn't get far, however, as a wall of policemen quickly formed in front of him to bar his progress. Undaunted, Fabio wrestled a microphone from a reporter and started to speak, but he was barely audible. The microphone was attached to a miniature tape recorder, which could not amplify his voice.

"I demand to know what's going on, here!" he attempted to shout above the din.

Giancarlo bowed as the police dragged the elderly man to the back of the press room, where he quieted down. Giancarlo then pointed stage left.

"Our special guest," he said, "needs no introduction."

Kerry appeared, but it was not the glamorous Kerry that had graced the cover of thousands of tabloids around the world. She was dressed very plainly, in a pale gray, one-piece skirt and leather loafers. Her face sported the barest hint of make-up. But if her intention had been to tone down her stunning beauty, she accomplished the exact opposite. She looked more beautiful than ever before. A gasp, rising from the audience, confirmed my assessment. Reporters, frozen in place from the shock, spontaneously launched into wild applause. Even the generally irritable and cynical Fabio stood in awe, as if he had never seen his client before; as if, like the rest of the world, he was being introduced to Kerry Daniels for the very first time.

She walked across the stage toward the podium. Her hair floated about her face as if tossing in the waves of a tropical ocean, forcing a sound that was like "ahhh!" from the audience. Her lips curled into just the slightest hint of sadness and, finally, she spoke.

"I would first like to categorically deny the unfounded rumors that I am pregnant. I have no idea how that could have ever been started." She gave the slightest glance toward a sheepish Giancarlo.

A low rumble of disappointment swept through the room. Several major supermarket tabloids ripped up their notes. Kerry raised her hand to calm the audience.

"I came here to return…to Mr. Kahn…the money that I…withdrew…from his account more than a year ago," she announced. The room erupted into deafening applause. She raised her hand to quiet people down, and when they did, she continued.

"There were good reasons for my actions, which I was not in a position to reveal before, but I can now."

She pointed to the back of the room, where the police had now been joined by members of the FBI, CIA and SWAT teams – so indicated by the large letters emblazoned on the back of their jackets. Their elderly prisoner stared back defiantly at her. The veins on his forehead throbbed violently; his hands were tightly clenched into fists, his mouth quivering with hatred.

"That man…" began Kerry.

"No!" the man shouted, his body coiling like a caged tiger, ready to spring from its cage.

"That man," she continued," is disgraced financier Gerald Bledsoe, the man responsible for one of Wall Street's most notorious scandals. If you'll recall, several years ago, he made an ill-timed trade on the TraXEN Telecom account that cost him hundreds of millions of dollars. Seeking to recoup the losses before being discovered, he raided his company's pension to fund a series of wildly speculative trades in derivatives. It resulted in the bankruptcy of several major financial institutions which momentarily crippled the world financial markets, forcing the SEC to halt trading for the day."

"Impossible. He's dead!" exclaimed a writer for the *Wall Street Journal*.

"It *is* him!" asserted a writer for *The New York Times*, who could not disguise his animosity for his rival at the competing newspaper. For that reason, he instinctively blurted out the complete opposite of whatever any member of the *Journal* said at any news conferences, regardless of what it was that they said.

The audience gasped. The elderly gentleman squirmed, endeavoring to break free again, but being held fast in the grips of zealous law enforcement officials, he failed.

"For many years," continued Kerry, "he was my mentor; then, he was my confidant and, finally, he became my jailor."

One half of the split-screen image zoomed in on her youthful face, the other half held fast to a close-up of the craggy and weathered face of Bledsoe. The rapid-fire bursts of camera flashes reached a fevered pitch. Numerous photographers jostled their way through the aisle to position themselves for a better picture of Bledsoe.

"Traitor!" shouted Bledsoe. "Bitch!"

He snarled at the circling photographers as law officers swatted them back with their clubs.

"If you will indulge me for a moment," said Kerry, "I will explain everything to you…."

Fabio raced toward the podium, but an alert police officer flung himself in his path. Being somewhat fat, however, the policeman fell short of his target, letting Fabio wheeze by. "I would just like to explain…" Fabio began, trying to be heard above the pandemonium.

But before he could proceed, a second police officer finally reached him, shoved him to the side, against the wall, and pinned him there.

"I will have to escort you out of the building if you do not allow the lady to continue," said the police officer.

A visibly distraught Fabio stared at Kerry, who simply shrugged. He trudged off to the back of the room, livid with rage.

Kerry raised her hand to calm the audience again and, when they finally did so, she continued. "Most of you believe that you know the story well," she said. "But I'm here today to tell you the real story behind the headlines. This is the story of one man's relentless pursuit of vengeance and his willingness to abuse the sacred trust of the people closest to him in order to destroy the lives of those he felt had wronged him."

"Lies! Lies!" Bledsoe shouted from the back. "I will crush you like a bug!"

A wave of breathy, shocked reactions followed; then quickly subsided as Kerry signaled a continuation of her story. "If you'll recall, as the government closed in on him, Mr. Bledsoe had a highly publicize meltdown on Fox News in which he railed against everyone he believed responsible for his disgrace and inadvertently admitted to his crime,. The next day, an armed swat team descended on his residency and led him away in handcuffs."

"It was unnecessary! They did it to humiliate me!" he cried.

"He posted bail and, the following week, he went sailing on his private yacht in clear violation of the terms of his house arrest. Two days later, the Coast Guard discovered the boat floating in the middle of the Atlantic Ocean, just off the North Virginia coast. His two crew members lay below deck, unconscious. Mr. Bledsoe himself was nowhere to be found."

"Stop her! For the love of God!" begged Bledsoe, in vain.

"The crew recounted the story of violent winds that knocked out their communication equipment and massive waves that nearly capsized the boat and swept them overboard. The last they saw of Mr. Bledsoe, he was standing on the bow of the ship, looking quietly around him, even as the waves pounded the deck. They begged him to get to safety, but he refused."

"This is madness. She's lying!" exclaimed Bledsoe tearfully.

"At that moment, a huge wave roared onto the deck, knocked them off their feet and, fortunately, swept them down the stairs and into the cabins below. It knocked them both unconscious and, when they awoke, they discovered coast guard personnel were hovering over them, endeavoring to bring them back to consciousness.

"Bledsoe's body was never recovered and he was presumed dead at sea, washed overboard. But that was not the case. He had planned his disappearance all along and took advantage of the storm to make his escape. Unknown to his crew, another vessel had shadowed them into the open sea, waiting for the opportunity to secretly pick him up, and when the storm hit and the men were swept below, they did so."

"Lies! Lies! Lies!" barked an exhausted Bledsoe. By now, however, few treated his interruptions as anything more than background noise. Kerry had them mesmerized.

"The vessel took him to Bermuda, where he successfully hid himself to plot his revenge on those he believed to be responsible for his downfall. I turned out to be an unwitting victim and the prime vehicle for carrying out his scheme."

"You? A victim?" questions a stunned reporter. "Kerry Daniels? The Bombshell of the Bonds Market? The Siren of Securities? The Temptress of Trading? How could any man take advantage of you?"

He identified himself, needlessly, as a writer for the *New York Post* tabloid.

"Mr. Bledsoe is not simply another man," she said. "He is also my uncle."

The room erupted into chaos again. A thousand camera flashes detonated simultaneous, bathing the scene in blinding light. Several reporters ran out of the room, presumably to file the scoop, not considering that it was being broadcast live. Others started feverishly talking into their cell phones. When the room had quieted down again, she continued.

"I met my uncle – Mr. Gerald Bledsoe – during a business trip to Bermuda, where he was hiding out after faking his death."

"Did you know he was there?" questioned a reporter.

"No," she responded, pensively. "Although, thinking back, I realize that the trip had been suggested by a business associate, who wanted me to meet a potential client there. That lead never materialized, so perhaps I was set up. Mr. Bledsoe contacted me through an intermediary and we met at a secret location. My reaction was mixed, to say the least. I was happy to see him alive. He had opened many doors for me in the business world. More importantly, he was family. I have many fond memories of him from childhood, when he came to our family functions. But I was also mortified, knowing what he had done and why he was in hiding.

"To make a long story short, he shrewdly manipulated my conflicted emotions to convince me of his side of the story: that he was a wronged man; that certain people had conspired to ruin him. After weeks of relentless persuasion and brainwashing, he convinced me to help him orchestrate his revenge."

Heads turned in unison toward the back of the room and the perpetrator of this dastardly deed. He seemed to shrink into himself, as if trying to make himself smaller and less visible.

"The first opportunity came with Harold Bollinger, famous hedge fund manager, who had given Mr. Bledsoe the stock tip on TraXEN. He had heard a rumor that the company, struggling financially, was about to announce that it had finally secured an investor to save it from bankruptcy. Mr. Bledsoe loaded up on TraXEN stocks in anticipation of the news that would send their value skyrocketing. As you know, the funding never materialized and TraXEN was forced into bankruptcy, making Mr. Bledsoe's shares practically worthless."

"Yes, yes…" murmured some of the business reporters, reminded of the fateful day.

"The resulting setback led a panicked Mr. Bledsoe to start 'borrowing' from his company's pension to buy highly risky derivatives in an effort to quickly recoup his losses. Each trade led him to bigger losses and more 'borrowing' to try to recoup them. By the time auditors discovered the illegal transactions and alerted the SEC, his company had lost more than $7.2 billion.

"I carried on a secret affair with Bollinger and finally persuaded him to leave his family for me. On the night he came to my apartment with his divorce papers, I shut the door in his face and told him that I never wanted to see him again. The following day he discovered that he had been completely wiped out financially. His accounts had been hacked and all his money stolen. Worse, much of his assets, including his real estate and stock options, had been transferred to his ex-wife."

"I remember Harry," said a reporter. "Poor man! I heard from someone that he now lives on a farm somewhere in upstate New York, raising chickens and making goat cheese."

Kerry nodded. "Then there was Mr. John Lin, Sr. officer at TraXEN."

"What was the poor man's sin?" asked a reporter.

"Lin confirmed the rumors in confidence to Mr. Bledsoe. Mr. Bledsoe was convinced that Lin had intentionally misled him. In truth, the sudden departure of a major TraXEN client had spooked the investor, who withdrew its offer at the last minute."

"I used to see Lin at Nobu during lunch," said a reporter. "I overheard him talking about you, one day. He was madly in love with you. Who wouldn't have been?"

"I manipulated him too," she confessed. "And, as you know, he and his money suffered the same fate as Bollinger's."

"Incredible!" uttered another reporter, and murmurs of agreement followed.

"Other men came to similar ends. You know all their stories," said Kerry. "My uncle worked behind the seen to coordinate the hacking and to plant fake documents that brought their denials into question. He bribed those who tried to help them or, failing that, blackmailed them with secrets about their pasts and compromising photos that I had helped set up.

"By the time Mr. Kahn entered the picture, I was already a harden professional, an expert at destroying men's lives, all for a man who cared for nothing more than to crush his perceived foes and reclaim his wealth."

She paused. Her audience fell into an equally pensive mood, holding their collective breath until she resumed her tale.

"I confess, now, Mr. Kahn was just another target to me, at first; another one of the many men whom my uncle blamed for his downfall. Mr. Kahn doesn't know my uncle personally. He was just unlucky enough to have been the one who placed his order for TraXEN stocks. In his distorted mind, my uncle believed that Mr. Kahn knew that the company was about to lose the investor and could have warned him against the trade. He was convinced Mr. Kahn was jealous of his success and wanted to see him ruined.

"But what neither Bledsoe nor I could ever have anticipated was…that I would fall in love with Mr. Kahn. In the guise of taking the initiative, I convinced my uncle to let me coordinate the computer hacking and document dump. This allowed me to keep track of everything – including Mr. Kahn's money – so that I could return them at the appropriate time. I then intentionally broke into one of Kahn's accounts from my own computer to leave an electronic trail back to me. This permanently sabotaged my uncle's plans for revenge. I knew, as blind with rage as he was, he would not want any harm to come to me.

"It was fortunate – or perhaps unfortunate, depending on how you want to look at it – that our situation became a national scandal. With Mr. Kahn under the glare of the media spotlight, my uncle was forced to employ a more circuitous route to ruining him. That's when he hired the PR firm of Wallinsky Worldwide, which set out methodically to destroy his reputation while sparing mine. To avoid discovery, I played along with the decision until I could find a permanent way out of the dilemma."

She concluded, "All the details are in a special report that I have prepared, and which is being distributed to you right now."

The audience eagerly grabbed up the reports, chattering excitedly about the latest twists in the Kerry Daniels/Cain Kahn saga. They flipped rapidly through the pages, uttering shock or surprise or astonishment, as the case may be, depending on where they opened to. Soon, however, the room fell silent again. Some, puzzled by the sudden hush, looked around in confusion; then slowly turned toward the stage, where they finally discovered the source of the phenomenon.

Kerry had closed her eyes, visibly choked with emotions. A single tear trailed down her cheek. A tight close-up of her face, overwhelming her slender figure on the giant screen behind her, drove home the extraordinary significance of the moment. The violent whirling of cameras and frenetic popping of flashes created a powerful, strobe-like effect upon the scene that left the members of the media dazed and, for the first time anyone could remember, speechless.

I too looked on in wonderment. It all made sense to me now – my sudden inability to find work after Kerry left me and, later, Dan Cameron firing me. I now appreciated the risk Dan took to bring me onboard and the pressure he endured to keep me. Then, Bledsoe must have finally uncovered his modeling scandal and threatened to expose him, forcing him to fire me. But money speaks louder than shame! Following the debacle of the PipeStation IPO and subsequent hit to Capital Partners' credibility, Dan must have considered my return worth the risk of Bledsoe's wrath.

Kerry's actions would also explain the inability to find evidence of John Denver's purchase of PipeStation stocks with her money. She had simply made up the story. She provided me with many clues throughout all our interactions in the past year and I could have caught on to them simply by doing one thing: trusting her. That was her greatest frustration with me. And my greatest failure.

Kerry raised her hand again to silence the room, though she didn't need to. Like children after a severe scolding from their parents, the reporters all seemed contrite, remorseful for their past lewd and malicious coverage of her many affairs. No doubt, the sexism in their coverage will subsequently be taken up again in "The View" TV program, where the chatty women will point out that, if she had been a man, the media would have lauded all her past conquests as evidence of her shrewd business acumen.

"I know that I will never be able to give them back the lives I destroyed," she said of her victims. "But I hope that, through my confession, I can begin the process of restoring their reputations, their careers, and maybe even their personal relationships."

Another chaotic scene ensued as Kerry's former victims – many who had not been seen for many years – walked tentatively unto the stage and surrounded her. A mighty roar reached us from the streets as the crowd, watching it all on their monitors, went wild with excitement.

"Not butterfly yet," the assistant shouted in my ear, endeavoring to be heard above the din.

Bledsoe gave out a scream of protest. This time, he twisted his body around so violently that the startled police officers lost their grips on him and he fell to the floor, flapping like a fish out of water. Quickly recovering, he leaped to his feet and started blindly toward the stage. Then, reconsidering, he spun around toward an unguarded exit. A policeman lunged for him, but just missed him as he cleared the door.

The room erupted into panic and confusion again as police whistles pierced the air and the entire army of blue and gray uniforms streamed out after Bledsoe. Realizing that Bledsoe was the key to the success of the press conference and his escape would put Giancarlo's entire plan in jeopardy, I ran after him. I reached the front door just in time to see him plunge into the crowd. Recognizing him, the crowd started to boo, though they parted in fear and awe of him. The paparazzi instantly gave chase, knocking innocent bystanders out of their paths as if they were bowling pins. TV networks swung their cameras toward the commotion; reporters leaped from their vans in pursuit.

A tremendous roar went up from the crowd on the farther edge, as they realized that the drama on the giant outdoor monitors was actually unfolding live before their eyes. Bledsoe stopped abruptly and looked around in confusion, wondering what had happened to incite the crowd into such frenzy. He caught sight of the reporters barreling down on him and resumed his run, fearing for his life. Unfortunately, that moment's hesitation allowed the crowd to close in around him and, soon, to freeze him solidly in place and prevent his further progress.

The paparazzi consequently caught up with him, and reporters, with years of experience in regions of conflict, expertly sliced through the crowd until they reached their quarry.

I struggled through the swarm of swirling, bobbing humanity and made it to the fringes of reporters that now closed in on Bledsoe. He spun helplessly about, looking for daylight, but found every avenue blocked. Yet, after an initial look of panic, a mysterious smile crept across his face, and that smile soon became a full-blown grin.

He grabbed a hand that was extended to him and shook it vigorously; and then he shook another one. Reporters shouted questions. He responded excitedly, giving two thumbs up. I clawed desperately through the crowd to get to him and, upon doing so, discovered why he was so jubilant. He wasn't being harassed by the media. He was being propositioned. A Fox News president offered him a job as an on-air host with his own show. A talent scout from ICM promised him representation. A Hollywood producer declared he had a movie in him. Someone else suggested he could make millions in speaking fees.

"Hold him for the police!" I demanded.

The reporters stared at me as if I was babbling nonsense. When the police finally arrived, they snapped handcuffs on him and, as they led him away, he beamed victoriously and thanked everyone profusely. He was once again on top of the world.

I remembered about the press conference and quickly returned to the press room, where everything had come to a grinding halt as Bledsoe's drama unfolded on-screen. With Bledsoe finally led away in a police car, reporters began streaming back into the room. Kerry, a bit distracted, concluded her speech, but the mood in the room was now a listless one. Reporters' attentions were divided between Kerry's confession and the recent excitement of Bledsoe's notorious escapade outside. Fabio was practically dancing in the aisle. His nemesis' plans were in tatters, while Bledsoe, who was still his client, like the mythical phoenix, had risen from the ashes to perhaps a bigger success than he could have ever imagined.

Kerry stopped mid-sentence upon seeing me. "Cain," she began, and I simultaneously uttered, "Kerry..."

You might as well have announced a cure for cancer and the end to all wars, because the entire room suddenly erupted into thunderous applause. Reporters, realizing I was in the room and the significance of Kerry's reaction, high-fived each other, pumped their fists in the air, leaped from their seats and rushed at me like a pack of teenage girls after their favorite member of a boy band. Cameras snapped away furiously as I inched up the aisle and, finally, reached her.

"Kiss her, kiss her!" they urged me.

We stared at each other for what seemed like an eternity and, finally, we both looked away embarrassed, almost in shame. It felt as if we had both been stripped of all the ill-will and misunderstanding and stood on the stage naked before the world.

I was the first one to make a move, bringing my lips close to her cheek. I hovered there for an infinite moment and finally made contact. She turned at that moment to look at me. Tears welled up in her eyes, streamed down her face, and stained her cheeks as she tried, in vain, to wipe them away.

"You tried to tell me many times," I said to her.

"Yes, many times, but you were such an ass-"

I touched her lips in affectionate rebuke. We were live on TV, sharing the most intimate moment of our lives with a global audience of a billion people. At the moment our lips finally touched, pandemonium erupted around us again, with a sound like the thunder of a jet plane at take-off. But the noise wasn't coming just from the room: it was also coming from the massive crowds outside, which were transfixed upon the drama unfolding on the screens before them. Electrical circuits overloaded as the video raced around the world. The lights flickered in the room as back-up generators sprung to life to handle the overload. But they were hardly needed, as the frenetic popping of camera flashes generated enough illumination to rival Vegas.

Epilogue

"I want you to have it, to prove my sincerity," I said.

"No, thanks. That's how this whole thing started," replied Kerry, tearing up the strip of paper with my passwords. "And we're keeping separate bank accounts, too!"

We were standing next to the Gibbs Hill Lighthouse, looking out at the shimmering landscape of Bermuda. The ocean beyond was calm and iridescent in the afternoon sun. Nearby, Troy and his wife, Nancy, nodded approvingly as Kerry and I, along with Bambi and her fiancé, took our vows in a double wedding. Giancarlo stood next to the Wesleys, beaming at us like a proud father. Bambi was already contemplating her future role as a mother, thanks to my assistance. Her new wife also beamed with the glow of motherhood; *also* thanks to me, though Kerry had insisted on lending a hand with her.

Meanwhile, Fabio's triumph was short-lived, as the true extent of Bledsoe's criminal actions soon came to light. The public backlash was swift, and Fabio's complicity lost him countless clients and tens of millions in fees. True to his word, Giancarlo took him on as a client and began the long road toward rebuilding his reputation.

Bledsoe avoided 20 years in a maximum-security prison with a plea deal that involved complete restitution of all the money he stole, plus interest at the prevailing rate. In return, he received a ten-year sentence in a minimum-security prison, the possibility of serving just four years on appeal, and the expectations of being released in eight months for good behavior. A movie of his life was in the works at HBO, in which Michael Douglas had signed on to play the leading role. As part of the plea deal, Bledsoe also signed away all future profits from his life story to various nonprofit agencies serving battered men.

The world was right by me again, with Kerry in my arms. It was a brilliant day in one of the most beautiful places on earth. And this time, I had kept my pants on.

The End